JUST ONE LOOK.
THAT'S ALL IT TOOK . . .

A girl, one of the dancers from the chorus, busy
snapping her skirt and buttoning her blouse. Her
hands flowed from move to move, supple, smooth,
practiced, but I had a hard time watching because of her face. To me, it was a wonder. Who
knows how these things happen? Maybe the lighting was just right. Maybe I simply caught her
good side. But for some reason the line of her
lips, the angle of her eyes, reached into my head
and locked with every fantasy of woman I ever
had. It was my first look at Ramona Wolfe, and
for a moment, haloed as she was against the sunlight, she had me so dazzled I wasn't sure I had
really seen her at all.

THOSE LIPS, THOSE EYES

———— ◆·▶ ————

David Shaber

A DELL BOOK

Published by
Dell Publishing Co., Inc.
1 Dag Hammarskjold Plaza
New York, New York 10017

ISBN: 0-440-18493-2

Printed in the United States of America
First printing—August 1980

For Bertie
Take a bow, kid

1

Some day
you will seek me and find me
Some day
Of the days that shall be

Sure-lee
You will come and remind me
Of a dream that is calling
For you and for me . . .

—*The Vagabond King*

The truth? Before that Sunday morning I don't think
I had thought about any of it for ten minutes in the
last fifteen years. Make that twenty years. Oh, the no-
tion to call him may have crossed my mind when I
first came to New York, I won't deny that. Maybe
some night in those early idiot years when I was trying to get across the perilous no-man's-land between
lights-out and sleep, some night tucked up there in
that cruddy hall bedroom on West Seventy-third
Street dreaming of great triumphs to come; when one
of the grace notes to that triumph would be picking
up the phone and dialing his number. And then I
probably thought of it only because the words I
would use made me smile there in the dark. "Remember me?" I was going to say. "I play the drum." But
in the end I never did call, never even looked up his
number, and if it weren't for that item in the *Times* I
wouldn't be talking about him now. Which isn't sur-
prising, considering the way I ended up.

The thing is, I write movies.

Not a fate worse than death, maybe, but you couldn't exactly call it the highroad to creative immortality, either. If I sound a little jaundiced, it's probably because the whole idea of authorship in films is something of a lost cause, anyway. Movies, after all, did move before they talked. And if you write them the thing you have to face is that most people don't know who you are. Ask your average educated American who wrote *A Streetcar Named Desire* and he (or she) will tell you Tennessee Williams, ask him who wrote *Saturday Night Fever* and he will probably say John Travolta. Especially if he (or she) is my wife.

"*Casablanca.*"

"Here we go again. I hate it when you start this."

"Come on, coward. Who wrote *Casablanca?*"

Pained pause.

"Ben Hecht?"

"That's the only screenwriter you know. If I asked you *The Birth of a Nation,* you'd say Ben Hecht."

"Don't get snide. I'm trying, aren't I?"

"I'm not being snide. Howard Koch and the Epsteins, and it was merely brilliant. Okay, *Gone With the Wind.*"

"I know that one. Margaret Mitchell."

"She wrote the *novel.* Sidney Howard wrote the screenplay. Come on, Bertie, you've been to see the thing a dozen times. Don't you read the credits?"

"I do, but I forget."

"*All About Eve.*"

"You're going to hate me. All I can think of is Bette Davis."

"See? Story of my life. Nobody knows who I am."

"*I* know who you are," said Bertie stoutly. A friend of mine claims that Bertie reminds him of porcelain. It's probably the ash-blond hair (and not out of a bottle, either, thank you) and the fine tracery of her features. She also has green eyes, is breathtakingly level-headed, and absolutely wise. So you have to forgive her for things like Bette Davis. "Your children know who you are, too," she said. "Honey, everyone in this house absolutely knows who you are. Doesn't that help? A little?"

It does, of course, and all of that is wonderful. But it doesn't do much for all those childish fantasies you never quite grow out of, the giddy fanfares of revenge you sang yourself to sleep with during those early years in the wilderness; all those people you were going to get even with for not knowing you were alive, who were going to repent the foolish mistake they had made. Mary Lou Busby, say, opening the morning paper back in Cleveland and pausing in awe at the sight of your name. (*Did you see what Artie did? He got the Nobel Prize. Maybe I should've gone to the senior prom with him, after all.*) Or Marlene Goldhammer sitting up in amazement as she watches *The Tonight Show. (Wait a minute, isn't that Artie Shoemaker? Maybe I'll call him the next time we're in New York for the Orthodontists' Convention, if he's still in the phone book.*) (He is, Marlene. And waiting.)

No, that you don't get from screenwriting. For such glories you have to turn to something like the theatre, a place where the word still counts—which was the dream that brought me to New York in the first place. All that has pretty much faded now, of course, the movie work has pulled me away; though I do try to see at least some of what's around each season. I tell myself it's for the good of my soul. Whatever the reason, I still keep in touch from time to time, like an old lover waving wistfully to his first sweetheart who is receding across a growing gulf of screen credits and the seductions of a fat first-draft price, promising to come back and marry her some day.

And on that Sunday, unexpectedly, someone on the other shore waved back.

Bertie was propped up in bed that morning with her second cup of coffee and the *Times* Drama Section on her lap while the kids, poor little New York hothouse waifs that they are, were pitching a tent in the wilderness of the dining room. I was lying beside her really only half-listening, staring hypnotically at *Sesame Street*.

"How about *Elephant Man?*"

"If we can get in," I said doubtfully.

"There's always *Chorus Line*."

"Again? I don't know, isn't there something else with a little meat to it, a little weight?"

"Well," she said, running her eye down the page, "how about this revival of *Long Day's Journey?* That meaty enough?"

"Who's in it?"

"Nobody, really. Lang, Fred Alexander, Crystal—"

"*Who?*" I turned my head.

Bertie checked the paper again. "Somebody named Harry Crystal. Why?"

"Nothing. Let's try *Elephant Man*." But for some time after that I didn't move.

Jesus Christ. Harry Crystal.

At the mention of that name a shadow floated to

the front of my mind and resolved itself into a daisy
chain of half-forgotten faces and names I hadn't said
to myself in years. Oh, he wasn't the only one. There
were others I could think of from that first season of
stock at the Kempton Hills Theatre, that innocent
cycle of days back in Ohio almost twenty (my God,
was it *twenty*?) years ago. Cooky Finn and Fuldauer
and Ramona, Ramona the Queen of the Nile. But
when I closed my eyes and visualized that time, like a
saint in all those tinted religious pictures the guy
with the halo and the light of God around him was
Harry Crystal.

Shall I tell you what that summer meant to me? Of
what sweet revenges planned, what fantasies concoct-
ed to shrivel the souls of Marlene Goldhammer,
Mary Lou Busby, and the other stone-hearted, ice-
cream-faced madonnas who haunted my dreams?
Shall I recount for you the secret discoveries made,
the theories verified, and how it first came to me as a
miracle that certain people could bear the lives they
led? It was the summer before I dropped my middle
name and was still known to the world at large as Arthur Leroy Shoemaker, the last summer when I was
taller than my kid brother and the first when I was
taller than my father, a summer under the arching
shadow of Harry Crystal. For in those days Harry
wasn't just another actor in a summer stock company,
but the man who was taller than us all.

2

━━━━━━━◆▶━━━━━━━

My desert is waiting
Dear, come there with me
I'm yearning to teach you
Love's sweet melo-dee . . .

—*The Desert Song*

If you were an Ohio fly on the wall, you wouldn't
know where you were.

The central thing was the mirror but the mirror
told you nothing. Just a reflection, harsh and unfor-
giving, of a small bare room in glaring light. There
was a long stillness and that was full of nothing, too.
A distant voice, an occasional far-off car, and through
the high-up window the softness of the sun sliding
toward dusk in the summer of 1960. Nothing but the
pregnant silence waiting for fate to make its entrance.
Then there was a sound, something between a sigh
and a groan, the rasp that people make when they
come back from the dead. And the face of a man
loomed unsteadily up in the glass.

It happened to be a remarkable face. Antic, singu-
lar, with an insinuating curve to the eyebrow, a sen-
sual fullness to the lip, an expressive mouth, an
aquiline nose that would have made Barrymore
green. All in all, a face extravagant with life—though

14 DAVID SHABER

at the moment it didn't look like anything much except death-warmed-over. The eyelids drooped, the skin was ashen, the sexy mouth was slack. About what you'd expect from an all-time, major-league—make that Olympic—hangover.

The man looked at himself and groan-sighed again. It was all he could do to move. His fingers rose slowly to his face and shakily pressed his forehead. Then the hands came away again, revealing two strange, startling orange blotches left on the skin.

And that was when you knew.

That was when you did the double take and saw that the mirror was attached to a cluttered table and saw the small tubes scattered among the clutter and all at once realized what the blotches were. Greasepaint. The room was a theatrical dressing room; the man was an actor. His name—O destiny!—was Harry Crystal. The fabled Harry Crystal.

As his fingers began to work the makeup across his forehead, on the suburban street up the hill outside something was beginning to assemble. First one car dropped out of the flow of traffic to park at the curb, then another, then two more. In no time there was a steady stream pulling over, mostly modest sedans, hump-trunk Plymouths and toothy Buicks; and if the cars didn't tell you what you were up against, the bumper stickers did. *See Mammoth Cave Kentucky, America Get Your Heart in It or Your Ass Out, Souvenir of Chillicothe Ohio, Visit Mackinac Island, I like Ike.*

Doors opened and closed as the people got out. They could have been a crowd going to church. But the place where they parked wasn't outside a church. It looked in fact like the edge of a small suburban park, just some grass and shrubs falling away into a landscaped ravine. Through the trees you could see tennis courts and a baseball diamond marked out below. But then if you looked a little further along the street you saw the small ticket booth and the sign, *Kempton Hills Theatre,* and an asphalt walk leading down the hill. *Now Playing,* said the sign, *The Red Mill by Victor Herbert; Next Week The Desert Song.*

In murmuring clots of twos and threes and fours the people drifted down the walk and collected at the bottom, waiting politely for the auditorium gates to open. Bland midwestern faces fresh from their suppers of cottage ham and creamed potatoes and lima beans and Jell-O, real food, for this is Bob Taft country and fantasy is something Democrats indulge in. Handkerchiefs flapped daintily at throats in the muggy twilight above the shuffle of spectator pumps and brown-and-white wing-tip shoes, the limp linen and flannel of an Ohio summer. Suburban Cleveland in 1960. If it wasn't the sticks it would do until you got to the Ozarks.

Back down in the dressing room Crystal had spread the makeup across his entire face now, covering the pasty skin with bright, unreal Max Factor health, but he was still plenty rocky. He picked up the liner-pencil; it slipped through his trembling fingers. He stopped, rummaged through the clutter on the table, came up with a crushed pack of Camels. He stuck one in his mouth, looked for matches, found a box, tried to take one out—then saw that it wasn't matches but an empty box of Trojan condoms (the folks up the hill would have *loved* that) —threw the box away, and rummaged again. At last he came up with a light, held it to the crumbling fag end, and took a long life-preserving drag. Then with the cigarette hanging from his mouth and using one hand to steady the other he managed to get the pencil to his eyebrows.

One wobbly stroke. Then another.

Puff of smoke. Now the other eye.

Another puff. He flexed one brow, then the other. Mephistopheles emerging from the fog. Coming from the nether regions, but coming. Coming. Almost imperceptibly his shoulders straightened. He hitched himself closer to the mirror. And continued.

You could literally see it happening. As he went on applying the makeup you could see the life flowing back into him. With every line of the pencil, every dab of rouge, the muscles grew firmer, the eyes brighter, the chin jutted more bravely. When the face was finished he reached steadily (well, almost steadily) for his costume, slipped into the false shirtfront, drew on the loud-checked trousers, even gave the suspenders a tentative snap. "Half hour," called the stage manager from the corridor. Harry snapped the button at the back of the high celluloid collar on the first try, then deftly clipped on the bow tie. Almost there.

Outside, the audience was filing in, starting to fill the seats of the large open-air amphitheatre under the Ohio sky. There were the first scraping strains of the musicians tuning up in the pit. By the time the five-minute call came Harry was really flowing, each new movement beginning before the previous one had ended. Into the jacket of the garish 1910 suit, buttoning the jacket, and before the button was through the hole snapping his cuffs and before the second cuff reaching for the talcum to powder down his makeup. Then he paused as he spotted the small slip of paper that had been hidden under the puff.

He turned the paper over.

There were three words scrawled on it in a female hand. *I love you.*

Harry didn't even blink. With one hand he tucked the paper into his vest pocket, with the other he went right on with the puff and powder, then stepped back to check himself in the mirror. He was humming. "Places," came the voice. "Places, please." Harry picked up his 1910 derby, flipped it expertly back along his outstretched arm. As it fell precisely into place on his head, he grabbed his cane and did a time step to the door.

Watch out, World.

Two hours later he was right in the thick of it, on stage under the lights, the cock alive and crowing. For this was indeed Harry Crystal, the fabled Harry Crystal, sailing through his ten o'clock number. And if that fly were still around he would have been as dazzled as the rest of the Ohio cottage-ham-eaters, swaying happily to the corny old words:

> *You cannot see*
> *In gay Paree*
> *In London or in Cork*
> *The girls you'll meet*
> *On an-y street*
> *In old-New-York.*

What could you say about Harry? That lightning played about his head, sparks flashed from his eyes? That he was the essence of all baritone song-and-

dance men, of gallantry, of the Dawn Patrol? He
could have been a bum, a rake, a hustler. Or a god in
disguise. One thing for sure—he was going over big in
Ohio.

Every pair of audience eyes hung on the lilt, was
riveted to the hinge of his movements, the skipping
feet that seemed barely to graze the stage. Even the
stage crew and those members of the company who
were not in the number had drifted down to the
wings to watch him. That was the picture you saw
backstage; the shifting shadows, the clumps of figures
lined up along the edges of the scenery, their faces
staring whitely out at the stage. And the only face
that really had no business being there was mine.

Had I not just enrolled in the summer session at
Western Reserve? Did I not toddle dutifully down to
the campus that very morning and sign up for a ballbreaking course in comparative anatomy, the same
ballbreaking course that I had already failed once before? Was I not the very model of a modern pre-med
general, slogging through chemistry courses I hated,
physics courses I could not understand, and biology
courses I had to take twice in order to pound rare
items about circulatory systems and vestigial gill slits
into my reluctant skull?

I had, I did, I was. A captive of the grind to get
into medical school because I was terrified of the
nothingness I would face if I didn't. I secretly had another itch and was waiting only for destiny to scratch
it. But I had already resigned myself to six weeks
spent in the Biology Building heat, the special swelter
that melts your undershorts and resolidifies them on
the seat of the laboratory chair, binding the two of
you together more surely than any pair of cuddly

THOSE LIPS, THOSE EYES

chromosomes. Some summer. It seemed no divine
power could deliver me. And then, just before noon
that same day, I had bumped into the hand of God in
the form of Danny D'Angeli at the soda fountain in
Wechsler's Drug Store.

On the way home from registration I had stopped
off at Wechsler's to drown my sorrows in a cherry
phosphate—when D'Angeli appeared behind me. He
taught wood shop at my old high school and during
the summer picked up a few extra dollars for his
family as the scene designer and technical director of
the Kempton Hills Theatre. Stocky and thick-lipped,
D'Angeli was a fretful soul who wore gray chino work
shirts and goggled owlishly at you through thick-
lensed glasses. He also had a strangely formal manner
of speaking, somewhere between Shakespeare and
W. C. Fields. He thumped me on the back in Wechsler's
and said it was lucky we had bumped into each other
(what he actually said was This is indeed a fortuitous
meeting; you have to know D'Angeli) because he had
been looking for me.

"Not me, I didn't do it," I said promptly.

"Ah," said D'Angeli, dilating his nostrils. "Ah, I
wouldn't be too sure." Then he cocked his porky
head pontifically. "Let me pose a basic question," he
said. "How would you like to handle the prop crew at
Kempton Hills this season?"

There was a wild silence before I said, "This summer? You mean this summer?"

"We are barely into the first show and my propman
has had a greeting from Uncle Sam. The draft board
is calling."

"Well, there was this one other thing I was sort of

planning to do. At school. I have to check this one other thing."

"Then check, do check. Why don't you think it over and drop down to the theatre tonight?" The gleam came and went in D'Angeli's eye. "I think," he said, "that you have the necessary sagacity, capacity, perspicacity, and rapacity for the job." Then we nodded soberly, shook hands, and I went home to think over what needed no thinking. D'Angeli had to shout after me to tell me the salary was four hundred for the season.

And how glad he would be to have a college man.

So that night there I was with the others in the wings, watching Harry do his stuff. And was it ever stuff. There was something going on out on stage that I didn't quite understand, like a telegram with certain key words missing. But the verbs were there, I'll tell you, and as I watched I was busy filling in the blanks. Harry was working in front of a chorus line of girls who were dressed in 1910 Dutch costumes right off the rental house rack. But never mind; to me they looked glorious. One of them, in fact, had her melting eyes glued right on Harry. As he turned his back to the audience in the dance now I saw him half-slip a folded piece of paper out of his pocket as though to show her he had found it, then wink. The blonde flushed right through her makeup and puckered her lips in the promise of a kiss (and more) as Harry whirled away again. She may have thought the pucker went unseen, but I caught it. Oh boy, did I catch it.

My eyes were big enough to swallow the whole stage, anyway. I was just past twenty, eager and above all ripe. It must've stood out all over me like a rash;

my entire face was lighted with the kind of innocence
that yearns for guilt. No wonder I caught Harry's
next little move, too. He was still dancing in and out
among the girls in their Dutch costumes, and his gaze
had now shifted to the other end of the line and a
brunette whose bust would break every dike on the
Zuyder Zee. As Harry passed her I saw him, without
so much as a break in his step, slip the paper out of
his pocket and into her hand. The brunette didn't
break step, either, simply palmed the note. Still moving, a few beats later she covertly opened the folded
slip and looked at it. Still with that plastic Dutch
smile on her face her eyes widened, darted to Harry—
who went right on dancing. All the butter in Ohio
wouldn't melt in his mouth.

Such is the stuff of genius.

It was a stroke of pure inspiration, exactly what I
would have liked to do with Marlene Goldhammer
and Mary Lou Busby (except of course I couldn't
soft-shoe and neither of them had ever sent me a note
saying anything other than *What's tomorrow's English assignment*). But even in my most Byronic fantasies, where all maneuvers unwind like silk and gold
from the spool of perfect moves, I had never imag-
ined anything quite like that, and my lips parted in
admiration—which was when I felt a tug on my arm
I turned to see the owlish face of Danny D'Angeli
motioning me to follow him.

"Okay, Shoemaker," said D'Angeli as we walked
through the bustle and pleasant confusion backstage,
"whaddya say—you ready to shake on it?"

One of the girls was doing a quick-change in the
wings nearby, her bra gleaming at me through the
gloom as though it were made of phosphorus. I was

having trouble trying not to look and look at the same time. "There's just that one thing," I said finally.

"What thing?"

"That schedule thing I have to check. But I'll let you know tomorrow." What was I talking about? Comparative anatomy was comparative anatomy, three hours a day in class *plus* the studying after that. But I couldn't quite let go, not yet.

"Well, I hope we're gonna get together," said D'Angeli. "When I go home tonight I want to get in bed, pull the covers up under my chinny-chin-chin, and close my eyes, secure in the knowledge that I have my new propman."

There was a burst of music from the stage. I turned to look back. Through an angle in the wings I could see Harry on the stage taking his bow at the end of the number. On one side of him was the blonde who had written the note, her eyes melting with affection. On the other side stood the chesty brunette who thought the note was a promise to her. With Harry in the middle, bowing like the little boy who had stuck in his thumb. And was about to pull out two plums. As I turned back to D'Angeli my eyes swept across the backstage corner where the chorus girl had been changing her blouse. The corner was empty, but the melody lingered on.

I stuck out my hand. "Mr. D'Angeli, who knows?" I said. "Maybe we'll both have pleasant dreams."

When I reached the street at the top of the asphalt walk I looked at my watch and broke into a trot. Jesus, ten thirty. Cinderella was long overdue getting home from the ball. And at the end of the long line of parked cars there it was, the pumpkin. A battered

Chevy pickup truck with the faded painted words on the door, *Barney Shoemaker Non-ferrous Metals.* I vaulted into the seat, risked hernia tugging off the emergency brake as usual, cranked up the ancient motor. Then lifted my foot from the gas pedal and listened. From far off down the hill the sound of applause still floated faintly on the night air. Did I dare, I wondered. Did I actually dare?

Then I fought the old Chevy into gear and rattled off.

The pickup almost knew its own way. Along Taylor to Cedar, then up Jackson to Farland to Brockway, across to Silsby, and gently, gently, holding my breath because it made the truck sound quieter, into the driveway, right up through the backyard and into the garage. I sat and let the noise settle, then opened and closed the truck door as softly as I could. It wasn't yet eleven o'clock, but the houses loomed like quiet mounds in the dark. People went to bed early on Silsby. It was a neighborhood of small, middle-class homes from another generation, built in the twenties when the word bungalow was hot stuff, frame and mock-Tudor stucco; the kind of houses that have real basements with coal furnaces, screened-in back porches, and sometimes a front porch, too, and the garages all separate little boxes marching along the backyards in a row. I crept out of the garage and stood for a second, looking warily at the dark house. Not a light showed. I went quietly to the side door and let myself in. Enemy territory.

Like a blind man trying to sense the barriers ahead of him I groped my way into the kitchen, felt along the wall for the refrigerator, and pulled the handle.

Using that pale shaft of light I got a glass from the
cupboard, poured myself some milk, and took two
brownies from under the wax paper on the counter.
Then with one brownie stuffed into my mouth and
balancing the other with the milk, I padded softly up
the dark stairs.

Though I didn't know it, Harry and I were already
brothers of a sort. For at right about the same time
his hand was holding something to drink, too, though
in his case it was a bottle of beer. His other hand was
around the waist of the luscious blonde as they left
the theatre. Truth be told, Harry had a pretty good
head start in the dressing room and was already two-
and-a-half sheets to the wind. As they started up the
path he took a swig of the beer. Then he made a face
and looked at the bottle, his lip curling in Prome-
thean scorn.

"Three-point-two beer," said Harry disdainfully.
Then, louder, "Where else but Cleveland would they
ask you to drink three-two beer?"

"Shhh, Harry," said the blonde, looking apprehensively at the quiet houses, the quiet street up ahead of
them. The postperformance traffic jam was over, the
audience was gone; the only thing left was one lone
police car waiting to see that everything was quiet before moving on.

"This isn't a town, it's a large open grave," said
Harry, louder still.

The blonde had spotted the cop. "Har-ree, come
on," she said, low. But Harry was not to be denied.

In a flamboyant gesture he flung his arm out and
declaimed to the quiet houses along the street. "A
grave, I tell you," he boomed. "We are playing a ten-

week season in the graveyard!" He nodded genially to the astonished policeman, who had seen Harry two nights before in *The Red Mill* and was probably trying to decide whether to give him a summons or ask for his autograph. The policeman thought Harry was terrific. Harry bowed low. "Give my regards to Yorick," he said with dignity. "I knew him well." Then with an elaborate finger to his lips, he said, "Shhh. The peasants are asleep." And rambled on down the street with the blonde.

Back among the peasants I stood in the darkened upstairs hall, listening to the heavy silence and sleep-breathing from my parents' open doorway. Then I slipped into the other bedroom, closed the door silently behind me, groped my way to one of the twin beds in the dark, and sat. I was just beginning to undress—when the reedy voice of my kid brother Sanford broke in softly from the other bed in the dark.

"Boy . . . your ass is gonna be in such a sling." The voice was low so as not to be overheard in the other bedroom. There was a pause before it went on ominously, "You took the job, didn't you?"

I kept my own voice low to match. "Not exactly," I said.

"Bullshit."

A small bed lamp snapped on—and there he was. Sanford, my thirteen-year-old brother, staring at me accusingly from the other bed. Sanford wasn't all there yet, but he was about to be. You could see the growth ready to come out all over him, the Adam's apple, the shoulder blades, all the projections waiting to be filled in and rounded off. He was like cartilage waiting for bone with that deceptive softness of thirteen, a spring coiling itself for the jump to six feet. He was wearing my old summer pajamas with bunnies on them, which I was glad to see looked pretty ridiculous. Because I knew my days with Sanford were numbered. He had the edge on sense and I had the edge on age. But he was gaining. In the meantime, a state of genial scorn existed between the two of us, and I probably felt nothing for him—except undying affection.

"Artie, are you bananas?" said Sanford matter-of-factly. "You're starting school this week—*tomorrow*, in fact. How're you gonna have time?"

"Big deal. It's just a summer make-up course."

"Yeah," said Sanford, boring in. "And if you flunk that anatomy thing *again*, you know what happens, don't you? Good-bye pre-med, hello U.S. Army."

This kid would've done great with the gestapo. But I was ready for him. Or so I thought. "Look," I said, "the course meets early, at the crack of goddam dawn, so that's no problem. And I can easily knock off the homework at night after the show, or something." I solemnly held my hand to my heart. "Sanf, I promise. The first hint of a conflict with school, and I'll quit the job. I mean, it's only the prop crew, anyway."

"The *what*?"

"It's just running props," I said lightly in my best David Niven tone. But I was careful not to meet his eye. "You build a little furniture, crud together some odds and ends, and borrow the rest."

Sanford sat bolt upright with an incredulous look on his face. He was so stunned he almost forgot to lower his voice. "Artie, who're you kidding? You can't build shit. You're scared pissless of the table saw, you don't know how to hold a hammer, you don't even know which end of the nail goes in."

"I got a fifty-percent chance," I said gallantly. But I knew he had me.

"I don't like the odds," said Sanford.

He should know. Sanford merely happened to be a mechanical genius; and our house was like a local branch of the Smithsonian, full of his monuments. Not all of them a hundred percent in the way they actually worked, maybe, or ticked, or hummed, but each undoubtedly inspired. There was the timer he had built, for instance, because he liked to fall asleep with the radio on and needed something to turn it off afterward. So he took the guts out of an old alarm clock, stuck them in an old wooden Philadelphia Cream Cheese box, and added his own switch and from an Eskimo Pie stick. You threw the switch and started the clock, which was set to a half hour or so, and at the end of the time it shut off the radio. Never mind that the wooden box turned out to be an echo chamber and when you threw the switch the ticking not only kept you awake, it almost drowned out the sound of the radio—the idea worked. As did his collapsible desk which hung against the wall and became a bulletin board when you folded it, and the cocktail table that was a thicket of tooled legs because he thought it was fun to run the lathe. Sanford also built model airplanes that actually flew, developed and enlarged his own pictures, and in general was possessed of that mysterious sense which eluded me, the occult understanding of How Things Worked. He was wrong about me, of course; I did know how to hold a hammer. But in another way he was right.

Sanford's problem was that he had a low tolerance to disaster, and he knew when he saw one coming.

"Well, I'm moving out," he said now, his voice flat. He nodded toward the other bedroom beyond the wall. "I don't want to be around to see the blood when they find out."

"I'm not afraid of them," I started bravely—then broke off. Was that a sound from the next room?

"*Shhh,*" hissed Sanford, and dove for the lamp. Darkness again. There was a brief moment of silence while we both strained to listen. After another tense second or two, Sanford's voice came hoarsely through the dark.

"*What's so great about a crummy theatre, anyway?*"

The answer was at that moment about twenty blocks away. Harry Crystal, creeping silently up the night stairs of a local rooming house, one of the large old homes in the poorer section of the Heights where the widow in residence was hard-up enough to rent to the chorus gypsies from Kempton Hills—and then fought the losing battle to stay respectable. As Harry reached the second-floor landing he tiptoed to one of the doors and scratched softly. The door opened just wide enough for him; he slipped inside, already reaching to undo the buttons on his shirt.

And about the time that I was buttoning my pajamas, Harry was waiting for his breath to come back, lying on a girl in the widow's back bedroom. Not the luscious Blonde he had walked out of the theatre with, of course, but the alpine Brunette, who was now minus her Dutch braids—and everything else. Harry's nose was in the valley between those rosy-tipped mountains, his yodel spent. Finally he slid off her and rolled onto his back.

"You okay?" she said.

"How but fine, how but fine," said Harry. "Nirvana has claimed me." But his voice sounded odd.

The Brunette smiled good-naturedly. "Well," she said. "Slambam Thank You Ma'am at one in the morning. You really circulate, don't you, Harry?"

"Got to move, kid." Harry was staring into space. "Motion. Only thing that separates us from the dead." And he continued to stare upward as though he saw through that ceiling to the Ohio sky, as though some crack had opened in that sky to the universe beyond, and somewhere in it he read the letters of his own destiny.

Whatever he saw, twenty blocks away in my own bed in the dark I think I was looking at the same thing, staring at the emptiness, the space beyond the space that is the future. That was when Sanford's voice came for the last time from the dark across the room.

"Artie. You can't blame them," he said softly, sounding a lot older than thirteen. "If you're not gonna be a doctor, then what?" What, indeed. "They're just worried what's gonna happen to you." He sounded a little worried himself.

"Welcome to the club," I said. And continued to stare.

Biology 221B, comparative anatomy and the study of the vertebrates, was a legend in its own time. At Western Reserve it was the traditional flunk-out course, the moat which all pre-med students had to

cross before they entered the sacred castle of medical
school. The work was rough enough during the regular school year but in the summer session it was plain
murder, a one-hour lecture or recitation followed by
a two-hour lab every morning starting at the chipper
hour of eight A.M. Two hundred and thirty students
had signed up, and there was room for only one
hundred and twenty in embryology, the next pre-med
course up the line. So the biology department figured
to knock off half of them, and the chief knocker-offer
was Professor Clement Brown.

He was a clean-shaven man with flinty blue eyes
and wiry hair which was a perfect match for his wit.
You had an impression of neatness under the floppy
lab coat he wore, except for one blue thumbnail that
was permanently discolored with the gentian violet
he used to stain the slides of chick embryos for his
cherished course in embryology. Chick embryos were
Brown's passion; he filed them, stroked them, had
closets full of them. The rumor was he was building a
giant Frankenstein chicken out of chick embryos.
And feeding it our blood.

"Ah, Shoemaker," he murmured that next morning
as I filed past him into the bio lab, "back with us
once more. If at first you don't succeed, fail, fail
again." After we were all seated behind the rows of
lab tables he smiled pleasantly and said, "Gentlemen.
We won't be doing much today, just getting organized
and setting up our labors. For this course you will
need a dissecting kit, a laboratory manual, and a
textbook. Also a brain, f you happen to have one."
Then he paused and surveyed the anxious faces before him. "Now. Let me introduce you to your com-
panion for the summer."

On those words a graduate assistant with a smile like Torquemada started trundling a smallish garbage can down the aisles between the tables, handing out the goodies. With a thunk, a large rubbery-looking fish was dumped on the tray in front of me.

"Class chondrichthyes," said Brown, "subclass elasmobranchii—that's *two i's*—order selachii, genus squalus. Or as she is known to her friends, the dogfish."

The dogfish shark may be one of evolution's marvels and God's wonders but it is definitely not what you want to see gazing at you with its dead eye at eight o'clock on a summer morning, fresh from a bath of formaldehyde. I stared without enthusiasm at the specimen, which stared right back.

"Observe her carefully, gentlemen," Brown went on. "You will soon be sharing her most intimate secrets—and she will, I trust, never be far from your thoughts." She was plenty far from mine, I can tell you. I sneaked a look at my watch. He was droning on about lab procedures, grading and marking, and there was the organization of the lab and recitation sections yet to come. But I still had a good shot at getting away by 9:30. My God, there was just a possibility that I was right, that the thing at the theatre would work out, after all. Brown was going on again now about the wonderful romance we were all going to have with those hunks of walleyed rubber lying before us. "In fact," he said with that flinty glint in his eye, "here is your first love note. For tomorrow—"

There was a general stir as people reached for their notebooks. I opened mine, pencil poised.

"—Please read the first four chapters in the lab manual."

I winced, but wrote it down. A lot more than I had figured, but I could still make it. There was going to be an evening of heavy reading after the performance tonight. I sighed and closed the notebook.

"Also pages 1–112 in the text."

I just looked at him, stunned.

"There will also be," said Brown with immense pleasure, "a spot quiz covering the material on Thursday." A massive groan went up from the class. I was having trouble catching my breath. Brown sounded apologetic. "I'm sorry to start so slowly," he said. "Perhaps we can pick up speed in a day or so."

I sat there still numb, waiting for the news to reach my extremities. In one stroke he had severed my heart from my body and my summer from the land of dreams. Well, that was the end of Kempton Hills Theatre. *Requiescat in formaldehyde.*

The other set of wheels in the Shoemaker family (not counting the bicycle Sanford inherited from me and on which he promptly rigged his own gearshift) was a semi-rusted-out blue Pontiac sedan, which was available to me on suitable red-letter occasions such as my first day in summer school. And the atmosphere inside the Pontiac was thick with despair when I pulled up on the street outside the theatre about eleven o'clock that morning. I turned off the motor and just sat, unwilling to reach for the door. I riffled the pages of the notebook, then reread the homework assignment once more. And sighed.

Finally I got out of the car and started down the asphalt walk.

Maybe it was because I knew I was about to say good-bye. But the theatre looked especially alluring, more than ever a world apart, and going along the ramp was like a trip through the looking glass. First, down the hill from the street, the tall shrubs and trees gradually shutting out the humdrum houses of Cleveland Heights as I went. Then through the gate, a turn to the right—and I came in at the side of the empty amphitheatre. I looked one way. Rows and rows of benches stretching up the hill in the sun and behind them, a rehearsal area. The other way; on the stage was the quaint little cartoon Dutch village that was the setting for *The Red Mill*, tucked incongruously under the Ohio maple trees. From somewhere behind the scenery there came the sound of hammering, muffled voices, the whine of a table saw.

I walked down the aisle of the empty auditorium, over the bridge across the orchestra pit with its shrouded piano in the late morning sun, then right up to the cartoon houses. The first two had doors that were painted on, but the third had a door that actually worked. I turned the knob, opened it, and stepped through.

Into another world.

Scattered here and there in the backstage area, the crew was at work building the scenery for the next show. With their bare backs burned black in the sun and their hammers tucked into their belts like ancient flintlocks, they could have been a band of Barbary pirates. No one so much as cocked an eye to look at me; they seemed lost in their work and each other, chuckling among themselves. No doubt over who had just walked the plank. From somewhere further backstage a voice shouted, "Cooky. . . . Anybody see Cooky?" For some reason that got another chuckle. And a leer.

The place was full of secret signs. Including the backs of the scenery, for instance. On the rear of every flat that comprised the quaint Dutch houses there was painted the words *Spratt Eats It* in large letters. And while I was looking at the words, as if on cue from another direction came a querulous voice. "No, no, no. *On* the line, dear."

I turned to look. In a rehearsal area under the trees at the far side of the stage a small man was staring with waspish scorn at an actress who had stopped in confusion. It must have been Spratt himself, and he spoke with elaborate sarcasm. "You move *on* the line. That means, *while* you are speaking the words. Is that too much to ask?" The fuddled actress mumbled something; the other actors looked as though they wished they were somewhere else. But Spratt was relentless. "You do understand the mother tongue, don't you, dear?" It was like pulling the legs off a fly that already had no wings. That kind of cruelty always made me nervous. I hated it but I could never manage to interrupt and be a hero, and I was turning away in embarrassment—when something else a short distance away caught my eye.

A solitary figure framed by the trees.

It was Harry, his face standing out nobly against the leaves. The line of the jaw seemed etched, the curving brows and piercing eyes as compelling as a hypnotist's stare. But his movements were oddly preoccupied. He was wearing some faded pants from an old Panama suit, a polo shirt and, believe it or not, a cape. It was of course part of the costume he was supposed to wear for the role of the Red Shadow in *The Desert Song*, the next production. But at eleven o'clock on a summer morning in Cleveland a cape is the kind of thing that does catch your eye.

Completely absorbed, he adjusted the cloth on his shoulder, trying to get the folds to hang right. I was about to move on, looking for D'Angeli—when Harry made an experimental flourish.

I paused to look.

Not so good. The cape caught against his shoulder and bunched up, which left him looking like a road-show Quasimodo. Harry rearranged the folds and tried again. A little better, but not great. Patiently he rearranged it once more. Now. Now he was getting it, getting, literally, the hang of it. And then he really started going to town. He flung the cape out in a brave gesture, *There, men, there lies the foe;* he drew it around him to face the enemy, *What wouldst thou have with me;* he shrugged it behind him to be free for action, *Good King of Cats, nothing but one of your nine lives withall.* He whirled it about him in an imaginary wind, he strode, he wheeled, he spun. Then he cut the air with a final Douglas Fairbanks twirl—just as the stage manager called from rehearsal, "Hey, Crystal, your entrance."

Harry turned to leave, then paused, aware at last that someone was watching. Solemnly, best leg forward, he made an elaborate Restoration bow to me. And winked. Then he flung the cape over his shoulder, turned toward the rehearsal, and took his entrance line in a ringing voice: "Hassi! I want your promise. The sign of the head and heart!" And with the cape flowing behind him like his own exclamation point, he was gone.

I was simply rooted. If you were Artie Shoemaker

it was the kind of image that could stick with you
for life.

"Hey, you—Boy!" came the loud voice behind me.

Startled, I turned the other way. An ancient man
in a faded Panama hat and ill-fitting false teeth was
I had heard someone call him Mr. Henry, and he
shuffling across the stage toward me. The night before
may just have been old enough to have been around
Ohio when the pioneers first came through the Cumberland Gap and settled the place. "Whatcha think
you're doin' there, boy?" he went on. "I don't wanna
be botherin' with you people around here."

One or two of the pirate crew lifted their heads to
look.

Flustered, I said, "Uh, I've gotta see Mr.
D'Angeli—"

"Who? Who? What for?" asked the old man
crabbily.

"See, I was supposed to work here. That is, he offered me a job, I mean," I floundered on. "But I
hadda check this thing. I mean, something came up,
or rather didn't *clear* up, and I can't take it. The job,
I mean—"

"Don't tell me your troubles, boy," Mr. Henry cut
me off. "I'm only the watchman, and that's trouble
enough. You wait here." He indicated a spot just outside the double doors that opened into the dressing
room building. "And don't bother nothing."

"Thanks—" I started, but the old man had already
turned his back and was shuffling off.

So there I stood, feeling like a dork. I nodded
weakly at the buccaneers from the crew who were still
staring blankly, the way a cow will when it lifts its
head to look at you in a field. Then I glanced toward

the paint frame where two more of the crew, their arms vividly smeared with pigment, were mixing paint. One of them went stolidly right on mixing but the other smiled, his teeth suddenly showing white through a screen of spatters on his face. I started to smile back, but he returned to his mixing. And in that awkward moment a voice called again from somewhere in the nooks and crannies behind the scenery, "Goddammit, Cooky—where the hell are you?"

Maybe that was it. Then again maybe it was a trick of shadow or the whisper of a breeze that brushed the hairs on the back of my neck. But some instinct, some half-sensed flicker of light behind me made me turn and look through the crack in the dressing room building doors. It was the move that sealed my fate.

Through the crack I saw a long corridor with dressing rooms opening off it, and another entrance to the corridor open to the trees at the far end. And while I watched, a husky crew member stuck his head out from one of the dressing rooms, checking to be sure the coast was clear. Why was I so sure it was Cooky Finn? His coarse black hair fell across his eyes, there was a go-to-hell jut to his lip, his face was straight out of the Dead-End Kids. Perfect casting for the resident stud. He stepped into the corridor tucking in his shirt with broad, careless strokes, jamming his hands inside his crusty jeans. Then with a nod he signaled back toward the dressing room. And someone else stepped out after him.

A girl, one of the dancers from the chorus, busy snapping her skirt and buttoning her blouse. Her hands flowed from move to move, supple, smooth, practiced, but I had a hard time watching all that because of her face. Her face. To me it was a wonder.

Who knows how these things happen? Maybe the lighting was just right, maybe I simply caught her good side. But for some reason the line of her lips, the angle of her eyes, reached into my head and locked in sync with every fantasy, every sleeping and waking dream of woman I ever had. It was my first look at Ramona Wolfe, and for a moment, haloed as she was against the sunlight at the other end of the corridor, she had me so dazzled I wasn't sure I had really seen her at all.

But she was there, all right. Because Cooky stuck his finger into the gap in her blouse where she had misbuttoned it. And twirled the finger. "Am I gonna have to teach you how to put it *back* on, too?" he said with a leer. (I soon learned that Cooky did a lot of leering; it was his idea of a subtle approach.) In reply, with one deft movement the girl reached down and zipped up his fly.

"Teach me what, Cooky?" she said with a cool grin. "Teach me what?"

It was a flash of such dizzy intimacy that I could not move. Like the moment when you are sitting in the burlesque house and the first zipper goes, that first electric glimpse of bare flesh which runs straight from the zipper right through every nerve ending down into your groin, zocko, and nails you there. And nailed I was, watching the two of them. After another measuring look at each other they separated, Cooky going out the far end of the corridor and the girl heading right for me.

I pulled hastily back from the doors—just as they banged open and the girl strolled nonchalantly past me without so much as a look back, heading for rehearsal. She was eating a Baby Ruth. Snack time. And it was only eleven o'clock in the morning. Jesus. I watched the soft globes of her rear move away.

"Okay, Shoemaker," said D'Angeli, walking up briskly. "About the job. What's it gonna be, heads or tails?"

I turned to look at him, my eyes still dilated from the images in the corridor.

You guess what I said.

I was upstairs washing my hands when the pickup truck rattled into the backyard before supper that evening. As my father banged the screen door behind him I heard my mother say to him, "Thank heaven you're home." And then, pregnant with meaning, "I want to talk to you." I ran a comb through my hair, turned off the water, and started down the stairs. About halfway down I could hear them right around the corner in the living room below. I paused on the landing out of sight and held my breath to listen.

"Your son came home today with a job," my mother said.

"Which son?"

"The big one."

"Job?" echoed my father cautiously.

My mother replied, "At some theatre," as if to say The report came from the hospital, it's leukemia.

"Theatre?" said my father.

"Theatre."

"Theatre . . ." he repeated hollowly. Then after a moment, inquiring about the patient, "Where is he?"

"Upstairs, washing his hands."

"So," he sighed. "That acting business."

"Worse."

"Worse than acting?"

"It's something in the backstage, a stagehand something. I don't know."

"They're going to pay Arthur *money* to work with the stage crew?"

There was a silence. Now, I thought, now he'll ask how much. But instead he said, "So when does this marvelous job begin?"

"It began. Today."

"What about school?"

"What *about* school," she said. "That's what I'd like to know."

Again a pause. (Now? I thought. Now?)

"Well. It's only for the summer."

"Only for the summer?" said my mother in a pained voice. "Only for the summer?"

There was a final silence.

Then my father said, "He's always gotten fired. Maybe he'll get fired."

I turned and went back upstairs and flushed the toilet so they wouldn't know I had been listening. As I watched the water gurgle in a little whirlpool down the bowl, it didn't occur to me that I might be watching a symbol of my fate. But it should have.

3

Did you call for soldiers true
For gallant fighting
Men of France?
We are here to answer you
So let the bugle blow
Ad-vance!

—*The Desert Song*

And the next morning after class there I was standing with Danny D'Angeli in front of my new domain, trying to look like someone who was born with a hammer in his hand instead of a dogfish. My first day on the job. Frankly, the odds were with the fish.

About as wide as a generous one-car garage and maybe a few feet longer, the prop house stood off in one corner of the backstage area tucked between the scene dock (the storage shed for old flats) and the dressing room building. A separate little ivy-covered brick house three stories high with a gabled roof shaded by backstage elms. Except for the anachronistic folding garage door fitted into one end-wall, it was as cozy and quaint as the witch's gingerbread cottage in the enchanted forest. And all of it was filled with things I didn't know how to make.

Along one wall on the ground floor were sinks and a workbench; on the opposite side were racks of deep shelves running right up to the ceiling; at the rear an

enclosed stairway led to the upper floors. All the
shelves and the workbench, too, were stacked with
tin-can tankards, mugs, shields, wine glasses painted
red to look like wine, homemade lanterns painted to
look lighted, and plywood sabres. Practically all of
the space in the middle of the room was taken up by
the prop table that was rolled out onto the backstage
area during the show, a ponderous monster on thun-
derous casters, theoretically mobile but in reality a
ballbuster. On the table were all the hand props
(technically, anything an actor uses or carries which
is not part of his costume), spread out like the refuse
of some cockeyed scavenger hunt: bedraggled fans,
threadbare reticules, hammerless wooden pistols,
lensless lorgnettes, muslin sacks of booty clotted with
paint and clacky with plywood pieces of eight, a quill
pen topped with a wavering two-foot feather guaran-
teed to kill the people. Also a scroll which, when delivered on stage at the crucial point in the second act,
will be unrolled to reveal the message *Fibby Geyer
sucks* or something equally calculated to give the actor fits (though what it will give Fibby Geyer—the
overweight character actor who plays all the gover-
nors, uncles, and Hungarian counts—will simply be
another story to tell in another bar in another
season).

On the floor around the prop table stood the rest
of the furniture and accessories for *The Red Mill*—
homemade Dutch tables, plastic tulips, garden
benches with beaverboard profiles spattered to look
like stone. Nothing was what it pretended to be;
stone was made of wood, muslin passed for velvet,
cardboard for steel, all of it bound together with pig-

ment, glue, and grit. And the upper levels of the little house were filled with mysteries of their own.

"Okay," D'Angeli was saying briskly. "So you got your standard trunks, your pirate chests, goblets, and banquet dishes on the third floor."

I nodded sagaciously. "Right," I said.

"Then your gilded furniture, sofas, Tudor stools, benches, your weapons and flags, your mandolins and assorted musical instruments, that's the second."

"Right," sagaciously again.

"And your prop table, your current show, your paints and tools on the first, right here."

"Right here," I echoed.

"You oughta have a work sheet on the next show—"

"Got it," I said, tapping my pocket. The picture of competence.

He took the list. "Okay, so for *Desert Song*, whadda we need. For the two Moorish settees, there's a coupla Victorian couches up there you can profile with beaverboard. Then we'll want three or four Nubian slave fans. There's some poles you can use on the overhead rack on the third floor. You know the kind of fans I mean. Slender poles with a spray of airy ostrich feathers at the end." His stubby fingers fluttered in an imitation of the softness and delicacy he saw in his mind's eye. "Waved by creatures of fearsome desert sexuality to cool the harem gazontoids at the end of a long day's cootch. Do you apprehend my meaning, Shoemaker?"

"Ostrich feathers?" I said. "I don't think I saw any ostrich feathers. What floor are they on?"

"The third floor at Higbee's Department Store," said D'Angeli with a tinge of disappointment, "right next to the mink stoles. I don't mean *real* ostrich feathers, Arthur. This isn't Hollywood. We have a budget of maybe a dollar and a half. We'll use a fan of painted beaverboard. But while you're cutting it, I want you to *think* of ostrich feathers, I want the *quality* of ostrich feathers." He checked the list again. "Plus a coupla Moorish stools, your basic throne, that's about it. Remember, everything needs to flow, to curve back on itself, lotsa S-curves. When one of those girls sits on a stool I want it to measure her gazontoid." His nostrils dilated.

"No problem," I said blithely.

He checked the list one last time. "The only real construction job is gonna be that Moorish chaise longue for the harem scene."

With just the barest hesitation I said again, "No problem."

D'Angeli looked at me a moment, then decided to hope for the best. He handed me the list. "May Allah be with you," he said, and left.

I turned, marched briskly into the prop house—then stopped cold. For a second I just stood there, looking uncertainly from the list to the workbench and back again. Where did you start? I picked up a hammer. Start with something that needed a hammer. The Nubian slave fans. That was it. You got a pole, you cut an outline out of beaverboard, you painted it to look like feathers, you nailed it to the pole. Easy. I looked around. There was the beaverboard. There was the paint. The poles were upstairs. Hit it, Shoemaker.

Except when I got to the third floor and looked on the overhead rack there weren't any poles. Just some mop handles and broomsticks and one longish rectan-

gular wooden post. Then the brainstorm hit me. If I
cut the post lengthwise it would make four Nubian
slave poles, and I would only be using one piece of
lumber. How about that. I was getting the hang of it
already. So I slipped into the main tool shop,
snitched a hand saw when nobody was looking (anything but use the table saw, that snarling demon),
then ran back to the prop house. And I was on the
third floor happily hand sawing the post when
D'Angeli stuck his head up through the stairwell and
saw me.

Years of teaching at the high school—plus the need
to go *on* teaching at the high school—had taught
D'Angeli to curb his tongue. But the same years of
suffering with fumble-thumbed students had built a
volcano of woe that nearly strangled him three times
a day. So he had developed a vocabulary of personal
coded profanity which served to vent the anguish he
felt and at the same time kept him from being hauled
up before the principal for swearing like a ruptured
cockney sailor. Oddly enough, much of the language
had a Byzantine flavor. He said Constantinople instead of Shit, for instance, and instead of Son of a
bitch he liked to say Twenty-nine drachmas—though
the number fluctuated according to the pain he felt.

"Seventy-five drachmas," he screamed when he saw
me grinding away. "What're you doing? What're you
doing?"

"Making the Nubian slave poles." What was he so
excited about?

"That's a beautiful piece of four-by-four," he
wailed. "That is a twenty-dollar piece of virginal lumber you are raping. And that is a crosscut not a ripsaw, and why do it by hand? For that aching matter,

why do it at all? I said to use the poles on the overhead rack," he cried, stabbing his finger in the air.

"Those are broom handles," I said faintly, quailing before his fury.

"If you put a fan on them they will become, as if by magic, slave poles. We get very few Nubians in the audience here in Cleveland Heights, I doubt that anyone will notice the difference. Look," he said wearily, "why don't you drop that for now and get started on the chaise longue." He took another look at the gashed four-by-four. "Constantinople," he sighed, and turned for the stairs.

"Right, no problem," I said briskly to his disappearing back.

A chaise longue. How did you build a chaise longue? Better still, what *was* a chaise longue? I was like a man going down for the third time for the second time that morning. When I was sure D'Angeli had gone I ran downstairs, fiddled with a pencil and a piece of paper, grabbed a tape measure, ran back up again, and did some measuring against an old gilt Victorian settee. It could be sort of like that, only with no back and tilted up at one end. I drew feverishly, and when the drawing was done I looked at it with a sinking heart. Twenty-seven pieces of wood of varying lengths. There was no longer any escaping it. My moment of truth with the table saw had come.

Resolutely I grabbed the hammer, tucked it in my belt like a six-gun, and sallied forth. To the pile of scrap lumber behind the main work table out on the stage. Let's see. I picked a piece of lumber from the pile and examined it judiciously, checking from the corner of my eye to see if anyone was watching. I had not, of course, the foggiest idea of what I was doing.

Finally I picked up what felt like a reasonable arm-load and wobbled off toward the machine shop.

When I came in, Cooky was zapping away with a ratchet screwdriver while an older crew member named Roy Bliss, fair-haired and soft-skinned with a face that was always suspiciously clean, was sorting plywood keystones, the things that make the corners of the scenery rigid. I paused to watch Mister Resident Stud with his screwdriver. Zap-zap-zap, crisp and care-less, biceps bulging. I had no desire to be Cooky, but that zap-zap was the second of his talents I would have been happy to call my own. Now he stood up. "What time is it?" he asked Bliss.

"Ten thirty. Why?" Cooky started out the door. "Wait a minute," said Bliss, "we gotta keystone those new flats. Where you going?"

"Administration Building. Check my mail."

"Oh, I'll just bet," said Bliss archly. "Give her a special delivery for me."

"Up your mudshoot," said Cooky indifferently, "with a rotary screwdriver." And sauntered out.

Meanwhile, a third crew member, a midwestern twanger named Loomis, had come in to trim the ends of some one-by-three on the table saw. The saw hummed like a fiend when it ran, and as you moved the wood into it, whined fiercely as though offended, angered; with one last snap-bite-snarl of indignation as the blade bit through the final piece when you moved the wood out at the end. But Loomis was an old hand. With a cigarette dangling from his mouth he reached under the table and snapped on the saw, then whipped through three cuts, holding the wood with one hand, and snapped it off again.

My turn.

I set the wood down, careful not to look at any of the others. Then I put the first piece on the saw table and lined up the pencil mark with the blade. Leaning as far back from those menacing notched teeth as I could, I groped under the table for the switch, flicked it—then flinched as the motor roared on and the monster sprang to life. With my teeth clenched against the noise, holding the first piece of wood with both hands, I moved it into the blade.

Almost immediately there was a terrifying whine as the thing snarled at me, and the wood began to buck threateningly in my hands. Trying to control the jumping lumber, I pressed down more tightly, which only made the monster kick back even harder. Then everything started going too fast and in slow motion at the same time. I told myself to let go but couldn't, somehow. All I could do was watch one hand lurch helplessly toward the howling blade—when Loomis stepped in, reached quickly under the table, and cut the power off. "Jesus," he said to me mildly, "you wanna be left with the bloody stump?"

"Thanks," I said weakly.

He looked more closely at my ashen face. "You okay, Shoemaker?"

"Hundred percent. No problem." If I could just make it out of the shop without throwing up.

"When you use both hands like that you squeeze the cut edges together against the blade, sorta like steppin' on the brakes and the accelerator at the same time." He reached under again and took out a metal pusherlike affair, which he slid into a groove in the table. "Use the guide and she won't bind."

"Oh—yeah. I knew I forgot something," I said lightly, and reached under to turn the demon on again. Behind my back I could feel Loomis and Bliss look at each other and roll their eyes.

But I got through it somehow, carted the odds and ends back to the prop house, and started whaling away with the hammer. A couple of hours later I had gotten through about two pounds of nails and only half the framework, but I reckoned I was holding my own. My carpentry wasn't too great, I guess. Every time I connected something it wobbled, so I added another strut or brace and then *that* wobbled, too. By now it was an insane hodgepodge of wobbly braces and improvised struts and went every which way. Frankly, I was beginning to get a slight sinking feeling about the design, too. But I kept telling myself that when I got finished it would look more like a chaise and less like a sort of badly built dogsled. And I was pounding away with a mouthful of nails in front of the prop house when I heard the faintest footstep, and I looked over to where the enclosed stairs to the second floor came down to a little vestibule in the rear.

What did my blinking eyes behold but Cooky in the vestibule, tucking in his shirt but a little too cool for me, Watson, and then jiggling around to get his underwear to sit right inside his pants. And who followed him down the stairs but that same dancer, Ramona, who had been sent down from rehearsal for a costume fitting but that wasn't the costume she was supposed to have fitted, twisting her dance skirt around so the zipper would be in the back where it belonged and not in front where Cooky had left it. And I bent over the chaise sucking those nails, afraid even to swallow for fear they'd hear the gulp. There was something almost odd about the way they didn't

look at each other, just stood there tucking like mad.
And then they stepped through the back door and
were gone in different directions, without a good-bye
to each other, without touching, so matter-of-fact, like
two people who happened to be riding on the same
streetcar. They didn't have anything particular in
common, this just happened to be their stop, that's
all.

My God, the streetcar had been running right over
my head, too. As I raised my head involuntarily to
look at the ceiling I forgot the nails in my mouth and
nearly gagged. And while I was coughing I turned to
find Sanford perched on his bicycle behind me, staring at the eccentric wooden skeleton at my feet.

"What's that?" he asked quizzically.

That's what I really needed, my kid brother hanging around. "Beat it, Sanford," I said. "What're you
doing here?"

"Mother sent me. With some hard-boiled eggs for
your lunch."

"Some what?"

"She says you need the energy."

I looked around to see if anyone had heard. "Don't
be ridiculous," I said. "Nobody here eats hard-boiled
eggs."

"So be a pacesetter, start a trend," Sanford said.
"Be the first stagehand in history to eat a hard-boiled
egg. Come on, Artie, what *is* that thing?" he asked
again. "It looks like a dogsled."

"None of your business. Just some furniture for the
next show."

"Yeah, what's the show, *Nanook of the North*?"

"This happens to be a chaise longue," I said with
dignity. "Or it will be, as soon as I get it covered."

"Artie," Sanford started, more seriously now, trying not to laugh. "Artie, you can't put furniture together with *nails*. When they lift it the whole thing will come apart. You have to drill holes, use wood screws, brace it with glue wedges—"

"I know what I'm doing," I said doggedly. "Theatrical construction is different. It doesn't have to hold together for life."

"How about ten minutes?" said Sanford. "All that thing needs is someone to stand behind it and yell *Mush*."

"*Beat it*, Sanford."

"All right," he said, shaking his head as he turned his bike around. "But when they walk away with the top, don't come to me." And he rode off.

That crack about the glue wedges worried me, I admit. After Sanford was safely out of sight I took a critical look at the frame, and just for good measure put five or six more nails in each brace. I was hammering in the last of them when D'Angeli came around the corner from the light tower—and stopped flat. Behind the thick glasses his eyes goggled even wider than usual.

"Sixteen Egyptian dromedaries!" he cried, which was roughly the equivalent of Jesus Christ Almighty, "Shoemaker, what the hell are you doing? What do you call that?"

"Getting there, getting there," I said bravely.

"Jesus, and I thought you were a college man," said D'Angeli. He looked a little shaken. "Well, never mind, you'll have to let that go for now. You got that list of hand props? Spratt wants some of them up at rehearsal so the actors can futz around."

"Right," I said, pulling the list from my pocket. "No problem."

About to go, D'Angeli paused to give the chaise a last uneasy look. Then he said, "I wish you'd stop saying that," and left.

I ran into the prop house with the list in my hand and the knell of doom in my ears. There was no mistaking that look on D'Angeli's face. My days were numbered. Here I was, the slave poles a rape, the chaise longue a dogsled, and now not a single hand prop ready. I looked at the list; it swam before my eyes. How many times can you go down for the third time? I could feel tension rising in me like a flood. My eyes ran frantically around the room while I muttered, "I am not going to panic, I am *not* going to panic." I forced myself to stand still. I took a deep breath. Then I turned and tore up the stairs to the second floor.

The main rehearsal area was all the way up the hill behind the auditorium on a stretch of open lawn that was bordered by trees and low stone walls. The actors, night creatures all, looked out of place in the bright afternoon sun, holding their scripts to their heads for sunshades, making their entrances from behind bushes. They were rehearsing *The Desert Song,* and that didn't help, either. The exaggerated Arab gestures, the salaaming, and the head-to-hearting seemed a touch of midsummer madness, recess at the loony bin, under the Ohio trees. For that matter, I could have passed for one of the inmates myself.

I came up the hill clanking like a junkman under a load of daggers, mugs, wine bottles, tambourines—whatever I could scrounge from the upper floors that even vaguely fit the list. While I crept around the edge like a thief, Spratt was busy withering that same vapid soprano, who stood helplessly, her hair up in curlers for the performance that night. The poor girl wasn't too pretty in the first place. And with the curlers tucked under a bandanna above her high forehead she looked like a half-bald department store mannequin waiting for someone to bring the right wig. All Spratt had for her, however, was a crown of thorns.

"No, dear—gracefully, *gracefully*. This girl is supposed to be beautiful, her every movement should be like a poem. Can you grasp that?"

"I . . . I think so," said the soprano haltingly.

"I realize we all have to work with the equipment God gave us, which in your case makes it difficult. But try to remember you're supposed to be beautiful." Then with an airy gesture of his wrist, "Think beautiful . . . beautiful."

"Honest, Sherman, I'm trying," said the girl earnestly.

"Yes, dear, you certainly are. *Very* trying." One of the chorus boys sniggered, and you could see Spratt positively puff up with pleasure. "Maybe your Betty Boop pin curls are too tight, they're giving you a Betty Boop brain," he said. The soprano lowered her eyes; her lip started to tremble. "Now," said Spratt, "concentrate. *Concentrate*. Should I spell that for you—?"

And that was when the load of props spilled from my arms all over the table. Tambourines chinking, daggers clattering, wine bottles going *clunk*. Spratt turned to look at me from an Olympian height. Dead silence.

"I hope we're not disturbing you," he said acidly.

"Sorry," I said. "You asked for the props—"

"Thank you, Gunga Din," said Spratt. The chorus boy sniggered again. The actors shifted their feet in sympathy. (Could I be wrong, or did the glint in Harry's eyes harden a moment before he went on batting them at his new brunette playmate?) In a red haze of mortification I crept away.

And headed for haven with the eight or nine members of the stage crew who were sprawled on the ground far over at one side, their backs against a low stone wall. Grimy and unwashed from the morning's work they sat like unwanted dinner guests out in the scullery, a hardy and defiant band eating ice cream. "Catch," said Loomis as I came over—and tossed me a half quart of cherry ripple with a plywood chip stuck in it. "Don't pay any attention to him," he added. "He saw a Clifton Webb movie and never got over it. Drop your ass on the grass, relax." I grinned gratefully and took my first chipful of cherry ripple. At last. For a few minutes I could forget about being fired.

Break-time for the crew each day was called Munjah, an Ohio corruption of the Italian *mangiare*; which meant running several quarts of Sealtest through the band saw and divvying them up, half a quart per man. Then you took your half a quart and a plywood chip to use as a spoon and went up the hill to the rehearsal area and sat at the side and sneered at the actors. In addition to Loomis and Cooky and the fastidious Bliss (the only one who washed his hands) there was Westervelt, a handsome (you had to give him that) oafish baboon from prep schools and the social register, whose brain no doubt

suffered the ill-effects of inbreeding. His blood was
blue, but his mind was the consistency of Cream of
Wheat. Next to him was Emil Hlavacek, the speckled
stork who worked at the paint frame. Hlavacek was
so angular it looked as though a wire coat hanger ran
through his shoulders. Over six three in height, he
shambled along like a shy midget, but when it came
to pigment he had magic in his hands. The last one
against the wall was a ratchet-voiced refugee from
The Bronx named Moe Shenker, who had a suspiciously fancy vocabulary (he and Bliss were our senior statesmen) and worked on the scenery each day
while wearing battered wing-tip shoes and an old pair
of pegged pants. Hostility fermented naturally in
him, like wine; but then, of course, he was from New
York. As I sat among them, the whole rogue's gallery
was gazing fixedly off to one side of the rehearsal.
Their voices were low.

"Eight points," said Westervelt, staring.

"Bullshit," said Loomis.

"Come on, Loomis. That ass alone is worth at least
five."

What they were looking at was the group of
dancers across the rehearsal area, working out while
they waited for their entrance. The girls wore a
mixed wardrobe of sun gear and old rehearsal clothes,
leotards, halters, tank tops, tights, mostly covered all
the way up to keep the sweat in. But oddly enough
the effect was only to make them seem more naked.
You could sense their thighs, their nipples, the very
nub of their skin right through the fabric. The crew
was certainly doing plenty of sensing; their gaze never
wavered. And if you had a camera that would be the
picture you snapped. The beautiful girls flexing and

the grimy young men watching while they sprawled on the grass, spooning in their sawdusty ice cream with plywood chips, everything lazy but their eyes.

"I give you three for the ass," said Shenker, entering the discussion. "The boobs, maybe four."

Westervelt retorted, "Oh, yeah?" Then pointedly, "Well, it *felt* like *a lot more* last night, I can tell you."

"What do you say, Shoemaker?" asked Bliss, turning to me. "You're an objective observer."

As the sheer vastness of the possibilities hit me my eyes twitched from one girl to another. This one doing a *plié,* that one in the dance stockings stretching her legs, the redhead named Ginger, small-boned and fine, her nipples showing hard through her leotard.

"Well," said Westervelt impatiently, "what's the verdict?"

"Just a minute," I said. "I'm adding."

The others laughed. Score one for ol' deadeye Artie. At the far end of the rehearsal area now, two ten-year-old boys flashed into view, pedaling fiercely on their bicycles. Right behind them came Mr. Henry hurrying stiffly, arms flapping like some arthritic scarecrow. "G'wan, git," he croaked, "git!"

"Atta boy, Mr. Henry, go get 'em," shouted Cooky.

"Way to go," echoed Westervelt. "You tell 'em, Mr. Henry."

There was a general smile, the smile and chuckle that manly hunters reserve for an old half-blind hound of whom they are all fond. I was beginning to catch on. Once you got past Mr. Henry's bark there was nothing but more bark. It really was unfair. He griped at everybody and all they did was yawn back. But kids, now. That was his meat.

"Scare 'em out of ten years' growth," grinned Loomis.

"You're damned straight—" Cooky started, then broke off scowling at something moving in the rehearsal across the way.

It was Harry Crystal, of course. Entering from behind a tree, he strode across the grass with the special actor's walk which drew every eye, that ripple-step to a hidden drum, that flow pah-pah-pah-pah which always ended on the beat. *Pah.* We all watched; you just had to. As now when he swung to a commanding position near a lilac bush, raised an imaginary goblet—and suddenly you saw a lonely desert outpost in the Sahara and a gallant figure in the uniform of the Foreign Legion. I did, anyway.

"Gentlemen!" cried Harry, with the goblet of air at a flamboyant angle and that voice, that voice ringing under the Ohio sun. "I give you a toast to one of the glories of France—Margot Bonvalet!"

The pin-curled soprano actually glowed. Hushed silence. No one blinked or breathed. A golden moment of pure theatre.

"Fucking actors," muttered Cooky.

"Blight on the earth," agreed Bliss.

"Damn straight," nodded Loomis.

"Here's to the *Uber-marionette* and Gordon Craig," said Shenker.

"Who?" said Westervelt, baffled. "Nobody told me we hadda build puppets." I found out later that during the winters Shenker was a speech major at Syracuse, which qualified him as the resident intellectual. But Cooky wasn't listening, still scowling balefully at Harry.

"Fucking Crystal," he said. "Thinks he's God's gift. Him and his hotshit New York phone calls."

"Now, now, Cook," soothed Bliss. "You can always console yourself with Ramona." Sweet Consolation, speak to me. There she was with the others, wearing tights and a halter that halted nothing, her hair tied carelessly out of the way with a kerchief that hung down her back. At every movement of her head you got the accent-flip of that kerchief—not that it mattered. For me she had already become the undisputed queen among the dancers, some kind of radiant goddess. Whatever she had on, I always saw her through a film of heavenly flowing chiffon.

"I hear she blows," said Shenker with a sly grin.

"Yeah," added Hlavacek. "How many points for that, Cook?" There was a general chuckle. Cooky began to look more cheerful.

"The thing that gets me," he said, leering as usual, "is to remember the tomato. She always eats a tomato to get the taste out of her mouth. I'm trying to shift her to candy bars."

Another general laugh ran through the group—broken when Westervelt, who was sitting on the grass before me, suddenly ducked away. "Hey, Shoemaker, willya watch your lousy cherry ripple? You're melting all over me." For I was poised motionless, plywood chip halfway to my mouth, paralyzed by the thought of tomatoes squishing and Baby Ruths crunching right over my head that morning.

"State of shock, poor boy," said Bliss. "He didn't know the numbers went that high."

"Better go easy on him," Loomis said, taking pity. "If he keeps playing mumblety-peg with that table saw he may not be with us long, anyway."

It could have been on cue. For at the reminder that my future at the theatre hung by an inept, fraying thread, over at the rehearsal Fibby Geyer was just then saying, "I'm too scared." He was playing some kind of cockeyed reporter lost in the Sahara of 1925. "I was captured by the Red Shadow," he went on. "Here, you take the notes." As he handed the notepad and pencil to the horsey comedienne, Spratt interrupted loudly.

"Wait a minute. Props. *Props!*"

I jumped to my feet, dropped the ice cream, and rushed over. "Uh, here. I mean—yes?"

Spratt spoke ominously, pointing to the girl's hand. "What, pray tell, is *that*—if you don't mind my asking?"

I looked, and was honestly puzzled. It was the one item on the list that was easy. "The list said a pencil—" I started innocently.

That was all Spratt needed. "I ask for a pencil and you give me a pencil? I don't want a pencil, I want a *pencil*. What kind of a dummy are you?"

The entire rehearsal was frozen, staring. My stomach was about to take the train for Ashtabula. Stalking over to the other props on the rehearsal table, Spratt held up an empty Gallo wine bottle as though it were something that might infect him. "And what, pray tell, is this yummy little monstrosity?"

"It said . . . a wine jug," I answered apprehensively.

"It may interest you to know that *Desert Song* is set in the Moroccan desert. You think they have Gallo wine in Morocco?"

I didn't know if they had Gallo wine in Galilee, Galesburg, or Gallipoli, but I felt like ramming a gallon of it right up Spratt's nose. He was peering at me. "Where did you come from, what's your name?"

Name, rank, and serial number. Against the wall with him. "Shoemaker," I said palely. "Artie Shoemaker."

Spratt had all his wires out. "What are you, another of D'Angeli's brilliant discoveries, another Belasco from his high school drama club? Don't tell me, let me guess. I'll bet you played in his production of *Our Town*. The part of George—sweet but simple. *Very* simple." (Actually I had tried out for the part of Mr. Gibbs. And didn't get that. I ended up as Howie the Milkman.) Spratt turned with an elaborate sigh of weariness to the company. "Everybody take ten minutes. I suppose I'd better have a look at the rest of his gems." He started off, then turned back to me. "Well? Are you coming, Mr. Belasco?"

Off we went. There is a specified number of steps that lead up to the traditional gallows, I think. This walk may have been longer, but it was going to end in the same place. Down along the aisle, then past the box seats, up the steps, across the orchestra pit and through the set and the backstage area, Spratt marching ahead and me mutely behind until we reached the prop house, heading for what I knew would be the noose, the axe, and oblivion.

I wasn't disappointed. When we got inside, Spratt circled the rest of the jumble of hand props I had collected, like a vulture trying to decide what part of the carrion to tear apart first. It happened, appropriately enough, to be a dismal canvas prop chicken. Spratt picked it up with an expression of distaste.

"And this, I suppose, is your idea of exotic harem food. Pathetic." Next, he went on to a fencing foil that had a distinct warp. "I mean, would you just look at this? We need a sword for the Red Shadow, for the hero, someone dashing, larger than life—and you come up with this, this tin *toothpick*. What can he do with this? I mean, it's simply pathetic." He dropped the sword derisively. And then uttered the death sentence. "Look, where's D'Angeli? Does D'Angeli know what you're doing?" He was turning to go to the machine shop—when suddenly he stopped.

There was someone standing in the doorway.

Harry Crystal himself.

"Right on the money, Sperm," he said evenly. "Pathetic is the word."

Spratt paused, giving him the eye. "What do you want, Harry?"

Picking up the sword, Crystal continued, "I mean, there's nothing the Red Shadow can possibly do with this." But as Spratt started again for the door, Harry suddenly brought the sword to *en garde;* then flashed through a chain of lightning movements, thrust-parry-riposte-and-thrust-again, the steel whipping through the air *quirt-quirt-quirt-quirt* with a vicious sound—all of which somehow ended with him blocking Spratt's way again and the foil pointing right at the little man's throat. And on the pose came Harry's voice, lightly mocking, in a line from *The Desert Song.* "Men!" said Harry. "Do we fight?"

Spratt stopped short. "This happens to be none of your business. So don't get cute now, Crystal."

Harry was innocence itself. "Wouldn't dream of it, Sperm."

"The name," said Spratt stiffly, "is Sherman."

"That's right, Sperm," Harry said. "You tell 'em, Sperm."

For a second their eyes met. Suddenly Spratt turned and bolted for the rear door.

With a move right out of Errol Flynn in *Robin Hood*, Harry vaulted onto the prop table to cut Basil Rathbone off at the pass, then was down on the floor in front of the rear door, blocking Spratt's way once more. "Ha!" cried Harry, brandishing the foil. "Ha! Ho! Ha!"

"You really think you're clever, don't you?" said Spratt icily. But he looked a little oopsy around the gills.

"Just thought I'd back you up, Sperm." A close flick with the foil, and Spratt backed away, openly nervous now, his eyes on the naked steel point.

"Careful with that—"

"—Except I don't really think we need to bother D'Angeli with this, do you?" Another flick. "Do you?"

Spratt backed up yet another step. He was actually beginning to sweat a little. "This is ridiculous—" Yet another flick from Harry; Spratt was backed right against the wall now. "Crystal—"

"—*Do you, Sperm?*"

The foil was right at Spratt's throat. There was a pause. And the Adam's apple slid up and down past the point of the foil as Spratt swallowed.

"All right, Shoemaker," he said finally, his eyes on the point. "But you'd better have something decent by rehearsal this afternoon." Harry lowered the sword and bowed formally. Spratt edged toward the door. "I hope you enjoyed this infantile display—" he started, then broke off as Harry made a final lunge toward him. "Hah! Ho! Hah!" cried Harry.

Spratt fled.

Harry watched him disappear, then lowered the sword. "Putz," he said scornfully. Then he turned back toward the prop table. There was a pause while he surveyed the ragged odds and ends I had hastily grabbed from the upper floors. He shook his head. "This is really some sad-ass pile of shit you got here, Shoemaker."

"You're telling me," I agreed unhappily.

"Okay, coupla quick hints," said Harry, and proceeded to rattle them off like a tobacco auctioneer. "First, there's about thirty-five hundred seats in this barn—so everything has to be overblown, exaggerated, just to be *seen*. He wants a pencil, you get him one of those dime-store jobs a foot long, get him a club, get him a ball bat with a point on the end—anything, just so it's big."

"Roger," I said, laughing.

"Next, the food. Just remember that everything eaten on stage is bananas."

"Bananas?"

"Mashed potatoes are mashed bananas, scrambled eggs are bananas musheled around, steak is bananas patted together—"

"But steak is brown—"

"You leave bananas out, they *get* brown. Same with booze on stage, everything is something else. Scotch is tea, gin is water, champagne is ginger ale, ice cubes are glass. Soap all the mirrors so the reflected light from the spots doesn't blind the customers, leave a little water in all the ashtrays so cigarettes go out with one push, run one-inch plywood under all the sofa cushions. In fact, reinforce everything in sight with five-ply."

"One-by-three oughta hold," I said, trying to sound as though I knew something about *something*, anyway. But I couldn't sneak it past Harry.

"Get one thing straight, Shoemaker," he said bluntly. "An actor can destroy anything civilized man has ever made."

"But if they sit carefully—"

Harry snorted. "An actor is a piece of meat standing in front of thirty-five hundred people. Most of the time he's worried about whether or not his pecker is hanging out—and you want him to think of *furniture?*"

Which took me right back to the dogsled chaise, and my confidence abruptly evaporated. "They're gonna fire me, I know it," I said, discouraged. I could feel the gloom settling around my shoulders like an old familiar sweater that fit in all the accustomed places. "Boy . . . I stank up the place when I tried acting in high school, I'm no good backstage . . . I don't know what's left to try."

Harry said briskly, "By next week I want to see that plywood. Got it?"

"If I'm still here," I said moodily. I'll say this for my gloom. It has staying power.

"You'll be here," said Harry. "I got a feeling." Idly he picked up my anatomy textbooks from where I had left them on the worktable when I came in that morning. "These yours?"

I nodded. "My folks have this insane dream I'm going to be a doctor."

"See, Spratt isn't your problem," said Harry thoughtfully. He put the books down and his gaze swung to the neighboring suburban houses that bordered the theatre. "The real enemy is all around us, *that's* who you gotta watch out for." Then he looked back at me. "But I'm not worried. You'll survive. It's obvious you possess the prime qualification for the job."

"Yeah? What's that?" I said doubtfully.

Harry winked. "Hunger," he said.

My heart leaped up. Not that I believed him, of course. But if that was all it took, then I was home free. A thought suddenly hit me. "Listen, Harry," I said, "would you really have hurt Spratt with that foil?"

Harry shrugged. "You never know. Theatre people are crazy." He winked again. "Just remember—an actor killed Lincoln."

And he turned back to rejoin his fellow assassins under the trees.

4

Yet when I seek this beauty
Flower of youth's first dawning
I find a prosy work-a-day world
Stretching and yaw-awning

Love is locked up in cages
Kept for a poet's pages
Life and adventure
Don't seem to be
Paying attention
                to me . . .

—*The Desert Song*

Hunger was only part of it. There was also plenty of pity and fear, especially where my family was concerned. My pity for them, their fear for me; and a little of both that I felt for myself.

Take a for-instance: In the stall shower at home one afternoon the following week. It was just before supper, and there I was as usual, the one with the knobby knees and mysterious smile, full of what I wasn't telling, lost, long lost under the water, playing the three spouts like a virtuoso, one at my head, one at my belly button, one at the height of a dirty word. I mixed the streams expertly, first the lower, then added in the next, and finally all three, then back to the upper alone, weaving the spout back and forth across my chest, only my head above the spray: no break in that smile except to wince when my mother turned on the cold in the kitchen below to flower some radishes and my water went too hot, or to gasp at the cold when she used the hot to soak the skillet the cutlets were breaded in. Showers in our house were punctuated by muffled cries of "Who turned on the WATER? Do you HAVE to use the WATER now? I'm trying to take a SHOWER." But I endured in silence under the spell of the water, drifting with the current over the muggy line that divided the sweltering July afternoon from the evening. It was that windless, suspended hour when the only thing left of the day was the heat, when the sun hung at the side of the sky just above the garage tops and slid in across the backyard hedges and the backyards baked; the time when I crept home from the day's work at the Kempton Hills Theatre to give myself up as hostage to my family over supper. And the thing to keep your eye on was this: how fast I could escape their clutches and get back to the theatre.

For tonight's performance was the first time I was supposed to run the *Desert Song* props on my own. And all I wanted was to get out of the house (with luck, in the family car) and through the evening without disaster.

From the minute I'd walked in that afternoon, I'd taken one look at my mother rattling the afternoon paper like thunder and knew what was good for me. Without a word I slipped off my high-topped workshoes, propped them up with the others in the downstairs hall, and made a beeline for upstairs. In my room I wearily peeled off my T-shirt, my underwear tops (my mother did not recognize summer nor lower her guard against sudden frost until July 15), then my sagging socks, stepped out of my crusty blue jeans, balancing against the bedpost all the while, not even so much as breathing on the bedspread stretched like a drum. Then I scooped up my clothes, rolled them

into a soggy ball, and tiptoed swiftly across the upstairs hall, a naked spectre who made the five steps in
three, crammed the dirty evidence into the clothes
chute on one side, lifted a towel from the linen closet
on the other as I went. Once in the bathroom I
closed the door but did not lock it (unthinkable actually to fasten any door in the house, my mother could
hear the snapping of a bolt at forty paces—"What are
you locking, what strangers are you afraid of?"—and
in the summer nights we tossed on our damp sheets,
doors open to the hall, mingling snores and sighs and
sibilance of dreams fulfilled, Barney, Lillian, Sanford,
and I, the four of us sharing a common dormitory);
then I folded the towel on the antique-ivory toilet
seat, spread the bath mat to sop up the traces, and
stepped over the sill. In three minutes the only trace
of me in the house was the shadow on the shower
door that clicked shut behind me.

On the other side of that door I stood exposed to
the elements at last. And the elements were these: the
three spouts that climbed the green tile before me, at
my right shoulder the soap dish with its cake of
Sweetheart, dome light overhead, drain at my feet,
and in the center, myself, the naked ninth wonder of
the world, all edges and ridges and angles, a love song
to late adolescence. At the age of twenty the skin still
draped skimpily on me at the corners, I hung off my
skeleton, and when I drew in my hands to lather the
washcloth the shoulder blades emerged from my back
like wings. But I had been witness to such religious
mysteries as Ramona and Cooky tucking in their
clothes and sepulchres whited by tomatoes and Baby
Ruths, and the salt edge of perspiration in my mouth
was the taste of life. Real life at last.

Outside, across the steamy air of the bathroom and beyond the bathroom window out of my sight, the houses drew in for supper. Family sedans rested empty in the driveways, sprinklers hissed lazily, toy cars and tricycles stood abandoned on tree-lawns, and there was only the occasional straggler, wet bathing suit wrapped in a towel beneath his arm, his shadow marching home before him, studying the baseball card of Lou Boudreau or Jimmy Foxx while he ruined his appetite with bubble gum. In our own backyard the tomato plants along the side of the garage sagged against their stakes, the dusty leaves pulled down by the coarse green fruit. We picked them like that, a little green, and put them in bowls on the windowsills in the sun where they ripened off the vine. By July we couldn't give them away anymore; through friends and relatives we stretched long diarrhetic fingers into other neighborhoods, and beachheads of our tomatoes rested in other bowls ripening on other windowsills, could I but see them.

Here's what else I couldn't see while I was tucked away in the shower:

1. My mother below in the kitchen, Lillian the Lion-Hearted, her face arising like an avenging angel above the steam of the pressure cooker. Tall, smooth, not one bead of perspiration at the neatly waved hairline, squinting fearlessly through the sizzle and flashing fat on the stove as cool and astringent as dry ice; turning sharply from stove to sink, covering her rear, a woman who was in a state of siege with life, her red nails flashing like sword blades through the vegetables. Whose face did she see in the potatoes, whose heart was quartered with the tomatoes, whose limbs sectioned with the cucumber, whose remains

swept into the Disposall? As she laid the table like a line of battle and prepared to dare us with another menu, should I pretend not to understand?

2. My brother Sanford, Sanford Gable Shoemaker, named as part of the suburban Celtic Renaissance, my brother taking his tutored Latin lesson in the den with Dr. Fuldauer, who also taught at the high school. That strange, blunt-faced boy, my brother, his hairline beginning at the eyebrows, wrapped around his chair like a corkscrew, legs threaded through the rungs, toes of his Red Goose shoes gouging the carpet, hunched at the desk where he has been since five thirty. The same thing each day, Sanford summoned from wherever he had been to shamble in after Fuldauer, that strange man still in his dusty winter suit, lugging his briefcase (which somehow spoke of winter, too), resolutely genial with "How iss my scholar today? Zo. Please take up your *Caesar* to page—" and closing the door behind them. From then on behind that door they were two voices, one mumbled, patient, leading, and the other reedy and thin, Sanford tracing the words with a finger that bore witness to every place it had been, airplane glue, paint, bicycle grease, wrapping his mouth around the strange words, *Amo, Amas, Amat; Amamus, Amatis, Amant* Fuldauer would lean over his shoulder to underline the chance word with a hand-sharpened pencil, then sit back on the foam-rubber hassock and stare at the blank face of the television screen and the ivy overgrowing the Chinese statuary in the bookcase and occasionally at the backyard through the bowls of tomatoes on the windowsill.

3. In that yard the sigh of my father's rusty blue Pontiac sedan coasting past the house and into the

garage where it muttered for a moment, then died; my father taking the key from the ignition and leaning back; home. To sit motionless then in the shadows of the garage amid the arsenal of garden tools blunted in the battle with nature, clippers with dull blades, weeders bent and disabled, a fertilizer-spreader with one wheel off; maybe to make some last note on one of the seven thousand scraps of paper sticking like a bouquet of confetti from the old leather wallet bound with a rubber band, notations of secret treasures of backyard junk, the strange collection places where stranger languages were spoken, Hungarian, Polish, Czech, all consonants, and the Slovak Radio Hour on Sunday was the call of the wild. Finally to leave the car, pulling his legs out one at a time, then sliding off the seat and emerging from the garage, warily eyeing the grass, his mortal enemy, as he headed for the house. My father, his automatic pencils clipped in his pocket until the pocket sagged, no pencil anonymous: Bessemer Smelter, Woodland City Lumber, Buckeye Steel, all homage to Big Barney Shoemaker the Junkman. For though the sign over the one-room concrete blockhouse built around a safe and a lavatory down near the Pennsy R.R. tracks on Union Avenue said *Barney Shoemaker, Non-ferrous Metals,* to himself he was nothing so elegant. "Hello," he would holler over the phone, "this is Shoemaker the Junkman—who'm I talking to?" Still, at least it was his own junk. And so he proceeded in that rolling step in the late afternoon heat, heavy-footed but blue-eyed, something of the boy still there behind the moustache, wavy hair not yet so gray as it would be later, life in the hair and the firm nails with the clear half-moons, the outline of his underwear tops showing through the perforations of his air-breathe Arrow shirt. He paused to lift the leaves of a tomato plant carefully and take one or two of the less-green ones, then bent again for a weed he couldn't resist. And at last, loaded with leather wallet, pencils, suit jacket, tomato, and dead weed and finding two free fingers in which to clasp his clip-on bow tie delicately at the knot like some living thing, he continued toward the house where his wife waited.

But Mother, Father, Sanford, Fuldauer—all were lost on me, hermetically sealed away upstairs, advancing into the water, solemnly bumping and grinding to work my loins around the bottom two spouts, watching my navel give up its last bits of sawdust, and accompanying myself with a ringing chorus from the current production: *Ho!/ So we sing as we are riding/ Ho!/ It's the time you'd best be hiding low/ It means the Riffs are abroad*—I broke off at the sight of my big toe, large with anger, the nail discolored where I had whacked it but good when I missed a swing at the chaise. I bent over, flexed the toe experimentally. *Go!/ Before you've bitten the sword. . . .* And then on his way to the side door my father turned on the backyard sprinkler, and I blinked as my water died again.

Up through the tile in the sudden quiet, suspicious thumps. Was that the bang of the screen door? Then two clumps, which was him stepping out of his shoes, followed by the rhythm of his stride through the living room in his stocking feet to hang his jacket in the vestibule; at every step the ashtrays jumped respectfully on the coffee table, the windows rattled, the china trembled in the cupboards. Then I heard him

turn back to the kitchen and a second later it began;
his first questioning thunder, the answering lightning
from my mother. It began, the same as it had every
suppertime since I started to work at the theatre, me
upstairs in the shower and them below, circling each
other in the kitchen, my father taking a roll from the
table, chewing but never stopping, Mother after him
with the napkins, nipping a carrot stick maybe, now
over her shoulder to him washing his hands at the
sink, silence only when Sanford hit another tongue
twister and they cocked their heads toward the den;
then back to their own responsive reading, alto to
bass in counterpoint and harmony. If my mother was
the blade, my father was the handle of the axe; together they made a fine tool, and the edge did not
point to Sanford, either.

I smiled and shook my head and turned up the
water until the voices below faded. Children. They
were such children, and I was a child no longer. And
I stood for another second or two, making the hair on
my chest lie flat under the water like new grass in the
rain, savoring the last moments before I anointed
myself with Wildroot Cream Oil, parted my hair on
the left, and assumed my disguise as their son
through supper.

And if not their son, who was I then?

Well, for one thing I was now the big-eyed boy who
walked through the playgrounds next to the theatre
after work each afternoon, through those idiots playing basketball and the pink-and-white girls covertly
watching them from behind their Popsicles, two ten-
der tents in each summer blouse, milk chocolate
mounds, and I passing through them—not just a
dreamer with a sore toe but a dreamer who had seen

Ramona rebutton her blouse and dare Cooky to Teach-her-what. And what could they—or my poor parents—know about that? How could Barney and Lillian know about the life down at the theatre, know how pale it made everything else seem? No way I could tell them, they knew me not. What could I say to anyone who looked at me and still saw only the child I once was, an eater of hard-boiled eggs instead of someone who had joined (almost) the brotherhood of buccaneers? But I forgave them their ignorance. I forgave them, mothers, fathers, basketball players, and wiggly asses all, because there was no way to set them straight. And anyway, what fun would it be if there were?

And then just as I was smiling at my own generosity somebody down among the Forgiven did something to the water, and I jumped back scalded and came down funny on my sore toe, and lifted my foot with a great gasp.

What are we—Arabs, to fight over the water?

As soon as I could breathe again I balanced against the barre of the soap dish and peered down through the water at the woeful toe. Suddenly other wounds, long denied, confronted me. The welts left on my ankles by my high-top workshoes. The gob of glue and paint that had congealed in my armpit. The matched bruises on each shin and the three blisters on the palm of my right hand which merely healed and reblistered, perversely refusing to become calluses. At the sight of each wound I forgave a little less, not of my parents and the Popsicle girls, but of myself.

Why were my bones so soft? So unexpectedly near the surface? And then everything dented me, everything left its mark. I glared at myself helplessly, remembering Cooky's bulging biceps and looking at what I had to offer, baby bruises and muscles hanging like decoration, this lousy Benedict Arnold of a body, not one weathered edge to its name. All at once my new worldliness was gone down the drain with the afternoon's dirt; and trapped alone with myself there in the shower I was overcome with a sudden flood of misgivings.

What, show this body to a woman?

I didn't see how I could ever do it. Oh, I had had my share of adventures in parked cars and lights-out living rooms, all masked by the tactful blanket of darkness. But in broad daylight? Where you could see each other? How were you supposed to act? Did you just sit and smile as though nothing had happened and you were only out for a walk? Did you pretend you were sitting by a pool except you had forgotten your bathing suit? What? How could I stand or sit or lie or go through any of the acrobatics I had planned like that—wouldn't being naked get in the way? How could I take my clothes off in front of some chorus girl and not have her bust out laughing? Brotherhood of Buccaneers, indeed. All at once there yawned between Cooky and myself a gulf that would take more than half a quart of cherry ripple to bridge. How did you just go upstairs at eleven in the morning and whack away like that? You were supposed to *know* the way, that was the thing. But where did you find out? And how?

And the water dribbled off my back while I bent, nailed over that toe by the uncertainty of everything I didn't know.

Then I saw that the fingers clasping that foot were

shriveled and wrinkled like the hand of an old man from being under the water so long. I straightened up and stood, shining wetly in the gloom, holding off for just another moment before going out into the murky pebbled world beyond the shower door. I folded and refolded the washcloth, dreaming of the day when I would know what Cooky knew, when I would know the answers, staring at the shower wall as though I would find them written there. But there was nothing before me except the spouts and handles festooned with other Shoemaker washclothes, relics of other private worlds.

For how many others had stood hermetically sealed behind that glass and folded their clothes as I did? And caught up in those cloths, absorbed from the water, what dreams? I couldn't tell whose was whose, but they were all there. Who could name the dreams of Barney Shoemaker the Junkman, brooding and moody? And his wife—if I wrung out her cloth what fantasies would drip to the floor, caught up from another time? My mother bathed at secret, unknown hours; perhaps she perspired then as well, and who could say what secret reward seemed always to elude her grasp, what dim answers she sought on that wall. It's doubtful that Sanford bothered to use a cloth but he must have bothered to dream, too—as we all did in that damp repository of the unconfessed doubts and fancies of the Shoemakers. Well, I had no time to bother with them now. For there was the theatre and the performance to get through that night. And anyway, my dreams were different from theirs.

I turned the water off and added my damp cloth to the others. Then hobbling to favor my toe I emerged reluctantly from the shower into the bathroom at last.

And when somewhere behind me in the empty shower my washcloth seemed to sigh as it slid slowly off the spigot and hit the floor with a soft, soggy plop, I did not even turn to look back.

"Do you have to eat so fast?"
"I'm not eating fast."
"Put down your fork, chew a minute."
I'd come downstairs briefly dry and sweetsmelling once more, to find the questions hanging as always in the air like so many birds of prey, roosting on my father's shoulders, nesting in my mother's hair, poised to swoop down over me at the breakfast-nook table.

"You know what happens if you don't chew your food?"
"I'm chewing, I'm chewing—look at me."
"That's just how people constipate themselves, gulping like that."
"Dad, will you please? I'm not eating fast."
"All right, I don't care. You'll be the one drinking milk of magnesia, not me." And he gloomily salted himself a radish. "Running to get back to that theatre."
"Who's running?" I forced myself to reach casually for a carrot stick. "I have twenty minutes yet." But my eye was on the Pontiac, wagging its rusty tail at me from the garage, and while I chewed, my mind hatched plots to the rhythm of my jaws. Carrots, radishes, we sat for a moment deafened by the crunching thunder of the vegetables. Then my mother finished her celery and, with plastic tongs raised to dissect another stalk from the salad, could restrain her natural eloquence no longer.
"How can he have time to chew? He has to spend

two hours dancing a fandango in the shower. Any minute now he'll tell you he's late and has to have the car all of a sudden."

I said nothing. Bitter experience had taught me that the only way to get the car was not to ask for it.

"Look at him," said my mother. "Gobbling a beautiful supper in two bites."

"Running," said my father. "Like a fool, he's just running." He looked at my mother as he reached to spear his second breaded veal cutlet. But he said nothing. He never did.

For the theatre was not the only world of unspoken passwords. My parents were wordless before me, there was no telling what they really thought. But was I china, was I crystal? Would I break, or merely tingle if struck with the truth? Who could say—my parents wouldn't take the chance. In front of me there were nothing but looks and nods—a grammar for deaf mutes; an eyebrow is the verb, a glance the predicate, the paragraphs indented with a shrug. And through these dinners we lived by implication; what we were talking about was never what we were talking about.

As when without looking at me now my mother said, "He's not wearing those pants. What pants is he wearing?"

"Mother, this happens to be what I work in," I said. "It's my job."

"I don't know how he can be seen like that. Filthy torn blue jeans full of paint. At least let him put on a decent pair of slacks."

"You want me to wear a tuxedo to change the scenery?"

"Change the scenery. Some job," said my father

darkly. "Buncha swell fools they must have down there."

My mother shrugged at him, daintily picking up her cutlet bone. "People will think he's crazy. What will people think?" My mother had the unerring habit of first answering her questions, then asking them. "It's bad enough the way he limps around from that job, he thinks I don't notice. I just don't know how he can let people see him like that."

She should see Cooky. "It doesn't make any difference what I wear."

"Sure, some job," said my father.

"I get paid, don't I?"

"Sure, sure," he said, wringing off half a roll like the neck of a chicken. "Some swell job."

"What's wrong with it?"

"What's wrong with it?" he echoed, and looked at my mother again. This time their eyes held each other a moment. A look ripe with meaning. Then he nodded slightly, as though something had been confirmed and not constipation, either; no, some other profound suspicion about this serpent's tooth that sat at their table and bore their name.

A look, a nod, and nothing more.

What could it be about the theatre that they were so afraid to mention in front of me?

Oh, I would hear them while I was upstairs, I heard the nightly ritual parades, discussing, wondering, accusing; I knew they were unhappy enough, all right. But never really knew *why*. As far back as my first brush with the high school dramatic society, of course, they had been worried that I would get sucked into show business and starve to death, and at first I thought it was part of that same old moan. At least I'm getting a salary now, I thought; they'll get used to it. But as the first days at Kempton Hills passed and my paychecks didn't seem to ease their heartburn, I began to realize they were not going to get over what was really bothering them. No, nor name it, either.

Because it was not quite what I had thought. Gradually I began to sense there was something else about the theatre, some bogeyman that went beyond money, a premonition of some more basic doom to come. I could only put it down to some nameless fear for my very life; that all my days from now to the very end would be spent in some spiritual vacant lot, weedy and wasted, that I was slipping into a twilight world forever. And they would not even trust that fear to words in front of me, because saying the words would put it in the air and invite it to be so.

So they talked about it by talking about something else. And each night I came downstairs after my shower to those same looks, those same vague arguments in which I never quite knew what was at stake, except somehow that it was my entire future. If I tried to pin it down more closely the only things I could put my finger on were constipation, a pair of decent slacks, and dancing a fandango in the shower. In some way it was all the same thing to my mother's inscrutable logic. And finally what throwing away my life came down to was whether I would leave the house five minutes earlier or later, and whether I would be walking or riding when I did.

"How are you getting to canasta club?" I said then to my mother innocently.

"I don't know why it is," she said sweetly to my father, putting down her cutlet bone to wipe the lipstick and flecks of breading from her fingers, "but the meat closest to the bone is always the sweetest."

"Lovely," said my father, pretty busy himself. "Sweet as sugar."

We ate for a moment further in silence before I tried again. "I mean, you are playing cards tonight, aren't you?"

She looked at my plate. "Don't tell me you're finished."

"No, I was just wondering where your club is tonight."

"Look at that," she said, shaking her head. "Beautiful cutlets, he hardly took a bite."

"Running," said my father. "Sure, what do you think?"

"It's these beans," I began, giving up for a minute.

"What's wrong with them?" said my mother, her eyes narrowing.

"I told you, you gave me too many lima beans, that's all. If I finish my meat, maybe I won't finish my beans."

"Oh, is that so? You'll eat what's on your plate."

"I ate my potatoes, didn't I?"

"Don't make me any bargains. You're not leaving the table until you wipe your plate clean."

"I just said," I replied with dignity, "that *maybe* I wouldn't quite finish the lima beans, that's all."

"And maybe you quite will," said my mother promptly.

"My God," I shouted, "I'm twenty years old, and I can't even make up my mind about my own lima beans! My God!"

"I don't care how old you are, Mister Big-Shot-on-the-Stage-Crew. There's nothing wrong with those beans. You don't get any sleep because you're such a Mister Big-Shot-on-the-Stage-Crew while you're trying to go to school, and you've got to do something to keep up your resistance. In two minutes you'll come down with something."

"In July?"

"Summer colds are the worst of all," she said imperturbably. "I've seen the way you perspire."

"Of course, I perspire. You make me wear underwear tops all summer."

"Sure, what do you care? You're not the one who has to nurse you when you're sick. Running up and down those stairs with a lunch tray—try it sometime."

"But I'm not sick!"

"That's right, change the subject."

(What subject? Where were we?) "Mother—"

"And don't plan on taking the car tonight, either."

"The car? Did I say anything about the car?"

"Yes, well, just don't plan on using it, because you're not."

"Who said anything about the car?" I said plaintively, turning to my father.

"You heard your mother," he said.

Inscrutable? Inscrutable.

And then fresh from another siege with Sanford, Dr. Fuldauer appeared in the dining room doorway, which was not exactly what I needed at the moment. To tell the truth, I had never gotten used to seeing him in our house in the first place. It was a long way from when he was my homeroom teacher and taught eleventh grade Latin back in high school. Even then I never noticed him much. About all I remembered now were those mornings when we boys waited restlessly at (dis)attention during the Pledge of Alle-

glance at assembly, giggling and punching and
playing Two-for-flinching while he stood alongside us
muttering distractedly, "Shhh, shhh, boys . . . you
should be ashamed in front of the principal." So we
would hang our heads, weaving slightly, faces averted
from each other because the slightest glance would
bring paroxysms. And it was at such times that I
might tear my gaze from the back of Marlene Goldhammer—succulent, marvelous Marlene, who was delivered to school each day like a just-ripe piece of
holiday fruit, pink and glossy, a stone at the core perhaps but soft at the edges and gift-wrapped, and who
if the fates at assembly had smiled might be standing
directly ahead of me in the next row—might, as I
said, tear my eyes from her and glance perfunctorily
at Fuldauer before passing on to the one to whom I
was about to shift my affections (also unwanted),
Mary Lou Busby. Mary Lou with the straight hair
and freckled skin of the true Anglo-Saxon exotic, as
carelessly thrown together, as improvised as Marlene
was premeditated, and who offered the promise of dis-
covering America—a promise which Dr. Fuldauer
looked as though he could have used himself.

For the truth also was he seemed a little out of
place at the high school, too. Dr. Julius Fuldauer, a
portly little gray-haired refugee with chubby fingers
and of all rare things, a goatee. The way he showed
up every day in the same dark blue suit and vest, every
buttonhole buttoned, he looked more like a little boy
than a Ph.D., and even then I had questions about
him.

For example, did he ever wash his hair? Did he
ever come completely apart as I did when my mother
used to wash mine at the kitchen sink and poured the

measuring cup of warm rinse water over my head, and the water ran down inside my undershirt leaving me with the dissolved uneasy feeling of wetting my bed? No, everything on Dr. Fuldauer had grown together. At night he unzipped a concealed zipper, pants, shirt, coat, and vest all come off in one piece and he slipped into—what? I certainly couldn't imagine him in pajamas. By day he was put together and maintained, though somewhat flaked over. He seemed a little dusty in general, as though he washed with his mind on other things.

My mind was on other things then, too. And after staring at Princess Busby for a few yearning moments my eye would pass blindly over Fuldauer again, returning back along the row to my first love, La Goldhammer, perhaps to try and catch the heady outlines of her brassiere strap under the cherry-red cashmere sweater she wore, perhaps to marvel at the way each amber hair so precisely followed the other across the back of her neck, maybe even scrunching my nose forward for a breath of her White Shoulders perfume which, as I remember, was the general odor of the eleventh grade girls that year. And what chance had Dr. Fuldauer stood against that kind of competition?

About as much as he stood now, wandering into the kitchen while my mind was on desperate matters, wandering as though he had forgotten the way out, blinking in confusion to find us there at the table. The same Dr. Fuldauer still wearing that same blue suit, vest and all, July or no July, tugging at the straps of his shapeless ragbag of a briefcase, puffing through his goatee. Even the Gilroys' dog next door was sheared in the summer heat, but not Fuldauer.

His hands were swallowed in the shirt cuffs that rode far out of his jacket, sticking to his palms and wrists, and now he peeled the limp handkerchief from the neckband of his shirt where he had tucked it like a bib to absorb the perspiration.

"Excuse me," he said, "I didn't know you are at the supper table—"

"No, no," gulped my father hastily. "Come in, Doctor Fuldauer, come in."

"I am just now on my way out," said Fuldauer, trying to wad the handkerchief into his breast pocket and looking for some place to deposit that impossible briefcase. "It iss a shame to disturb you . . ." All of his sentences had a habit of hanging in the air unfinished, not quite definite, no meaning but what it could not be changed. The tense of his verbs was Maybe; the tone of his voice, In Case. In conversation he left no walls to put his back against but only bridges to retreat over. And the suspended sentence, the throat-clearing hum, were both a part of the general atmosphere he brought into the room with him—musty, close, and clammy, the smell of wet wool on a summer's day, the feel of all things clinging, a worn brown breath of misfortune. It always twitched my nose, but it didn't faze my parents. And whenever Fuldauer's path crossed theirs they always felt obliged to welcome him to America.

Still, it is an uncertain welcome at that, because no one knows exactly what it should be. Usually when the lesson was over Fuldauer picked up his briefcase and wandered out the side door. Occasionally he called good-bye and my mother yelled a startled good-bye in return, almost as though she had forgotten he was in the house. Sometimes she tried to get

me to say something also, and when I made a face she
always said, "Quiet! You don't know what he's been
through." If I did happen to bump into him in the
house he would nod gravely and say, "Arthur," and I
would nod back and say, "Doctor Fuldauer," but usually he was gone before I got home. It was just as
well. To me Fuldauer was only a winter high school
teacher from a few years ago; and standing there in
our kitchen in that blue suit in July he was not only
out of place, he was out of season. Altogether then,
his status was vague, ranking above the paperboy or
the man who came to pick up the dry cleaning, but
not so high as the canasta club or other regular company. And so now I was distant and my mother was
formal and my father was boisterous, because none of
us knew exactly what to do with him.

"Sit down, Doctor Fuldauer," my father boomed
now. "Have a cup of coffee, a little dessert with us."

"No, no, please don't trouble. Go ahead with your
supper, I am just on my way out . . ." But he
made no move to go. Finally he set the briefcase
down in the middle of the kitchen floor, then said to
no one in particular, "But it was a little longer
tonight, the lesson. And perhaps the telephone, one
call, if you don't mind . . ."

"Here, please, help yourself, help yourself," said my
father, waving wildly at the phone on the breakfast-
nook wall. "Make all the calls you want"—an offer
none the less magnanimous for the fact that the
phone was unlimited.

"You sure you won't change your mind?" said my
mother. "Not even a cup of coffee, maybe? Feel free,
because the one thing we don't stand on in this house
is ceremony. Isn't that right, Barney?"

"Absolutely, absolutely."

"No, please, thank you," said Fuldauer. "My wife has something marvelous waiting for me at home, something tasty, you know . . ." He nodded gravely to me. "Arthur . . ."

"Doctor Fuldauer," I nodded gravely back.

Now he was squeezing around the table to reach the phone, muttering as he bumped the back of each chair in turn, "Excuse me . . . excuse me . . . please keep eating, keep eating, I am sorry, keep eating . . ." By the time he reached the phone he was awash with perspiration and embarrassment, and pinned against the wall he murmured apologetically once more, "The lesson, it is just we finished a little late tonight . . ."

"By the way, how is our Latin student," asked my father, not wanting to seem impolite.

"Oh, Sanford," said Dr. Fuldauer, and cleared his throat. "Well, I tell you, Mr. Shoemaker, Sanford is absolutely a bright boy, yes, absolutely. But a boy who is in love with moving parts."

"I'll give him moving parts," said my mother grimly.

"Tutorials now are always difficult," the little man went on, almost apologetic. "Latin is a matter of application—which goes out of season in the summer. Conjugations, declensions, the beauties of Caesar, Virgil, and the month of July—these do not harmonize. The young people have other things on their minds at this time of the year."

"He wasn't such a quiz-kid in your class last winter, either," my father muttered. "Yessir, two quiz-kids we got here, I'm gonna put them on the radio."

"But he is going to pass, isn't he?" my mother broke in anxiously.

"Mrs. Shoemaker, I assure you—"

"Lillian, don't shift into high," said my father. "He'll pass. I'll make him pass." Followed by a grim look from my mother and a belligerent look from my father in reply, all of which ended up, as usual, with my father agreeing to drill a little extra with Sanford after supper. And meanwhile Fuldauer was saying Please keep eating and Don't let me intrude, and my mother was saying That's all right, some of us are eating and some of us are picking at our food hoping it will go away by itself, with a dark look at me.

"Tell me, Doctor Fuldauer," she said finally, "do you have children?"

"Oh, yes, my Naomi. Arthur, you know my Naomi . . ."

It was a second before I remembered that skinny sparrow I used to see in the high school corridors, walking always in her own shadow. "Oh. Naomi. Sure."

"Well, you were lucky," said my mother. "Just don't have sons, take my word."

"Quiz-kids," my father muttered again. "One of them gets a D in Latin because he can't keep his hands off a screwdriver, and this one"—with a hunch of his shoulder in my direction—"fails his comparative anatomy in *college*, but all he can think of is running back to some theatre every night."

"A theatre—?" said Fuldauer.

"Yes, what do you think of a grown boy who wants to do nothing but play with scenery?" said my mother.

Fuldauer took off his glasses. "Where, a theatre?"

"At Superior and Lee Road, in Kempton Hills Park somewhere, I don't know." If my mother didn't approve of something the geography suddenly became vague, she wiped it off the maps.

"In the park? Movies?"

"No, no," I said. "The stage. Actors."

"Yes, the real thing," my mother said bitterly. "Only fools allowed."

"You're in high, Lillian," said my father quietly. "Better throw in the clutch."

"A regular theatre. Imagine that." Fuldauer seemed struck by something. "But how do you get there?"

"It depends," I said. "If you drive, there's a parking lot up in back—"

"*If* you drive," my mother said.

"—But tonight I'm walking, so I'll just take the bus and walk down the hill."

"So you will take the number thirty-two bus together with me," said, Fuldauer. (Terrific. Lima beans, no car, and now a bus ride with Fuldauer.)

"Believe me, with each one it's something," my mother was saying, but Fuldauer wasn't listening.

"A theatre . . ." He put his glasses back on, turned finally to the phone, and shook his head as he dialed the number. "Well, here it's a different world—" There was an audible squawk from the other end of the line. "Hello? Hello?" he said. "Hello, Mama? *Hier ist Julius. Ja, Mutter, Julius. Ich will mit Frieda sprechen, bitte.*" He was practically shouting. "*Mit Frieda, Mutter.*" He smiled uneasily at us. "My wife's mother iss an old lady, and her hearing—Hello, Frieda? *Ach, Naomi, nein, nein. Deine Mutter, Mutter, bitte—ach, endlich, Frieda. Ich bin beim* Shoemaker *jetzt.* Yes, still. *Ja, ja. Ich weiss. Ich weiss.*" He pulled a crusty pocket watch from his vest. "*Ja, ja. Ich weiss die Zeit. Halb sechs.*" He put the watch away, still smiling apologetically at my father.

My father smiled back, but it was an effort. He could not hear German spoken without wincing. The closest he has ever been to Europe, actually, was the eastern shore of Lake Pymatuning, Pennsylvania, on a fishing trip; but he ran a turret-lathe on the night shift at Warner and Swasey during the war and kept the scrapyard going at the same time, and it was damned hard work. The war, of course, has been over for years, but let Harry Truman and Eisenhower and the Coca-Cola Company do business if they want to; my father did not propose to forgive or forget so easily. More than just principle, it was a personal matter, like a neighbor he would not speak to. Even though he would have given his soul for an economical car he wouldn't spit on the best part of a Volkswagen. "They can keep their thirty-two Nazi miles to a Nazi gallon. I couldn't touch the wheel, my flesh would crawl." When it came to the Germans he gave no quarter. He loved dogs, but the Gilroys next door had a German shepherd, and he wanted no part of him, either. So although Fuldauer was a refugee and not exactly Hitler, still it was that language, and in his house and over his own telephone. And he found it hard to smile, that's all.

Maybe that was why, when under cover of Fuldauer bellowing embarrassedly over the phone my mother formed with her lips the words, "You should offer to drive him," my father said aloud, "What?" But he had heard her perfectly well, and with his own lips then he said silently, "Sanford. Am I going

to practice with Sanford after supper, or aren't I?"
And my mother just looked murder, and he said,
again loud, "Lillian, what do you want from me?"

"*Frieda, was willst du von mir?*" On the phone Fuldauer was having troubles of his own. "*Ja, ja. Ich
komme. Bitte, Frieda. Ich komme schnell.*" Finally he
hung up. As he began to struggle out around the
table again he smiled feebly and said, "So, we drill a
little with Sanford, and I see him Wednesday—"

"Just a minute, Doctor Fuldauer," said my mother
with a last look at my father. "How far do you have
to go?"

"Just to Altamont Road, but please don't trouble. I
will take the number thirty-two bus and make a trans-
fer at Taylor Road." He retrieved his briefcase from
the middle of the kitchen floor, and then I pushed
back from the table and got to my feet.

"And where do you think you're going?" asked my
mother.

"Mother, if I'm going to walk, I have to leave. It
takes twenty minutes."

"You're not walking anywhere. The theatre will
have to wait, you're driving Doctor Fuldauer home
first." She turned to the little man. "Here, Doctor,
take some tomatoes with you when you go."

"Please, we have still from the last time—"

"Then have more. Just a few in your hand—here."

"If I take Doctor Fuldauer," I said, holding my
breath, "I won't have time to bring the car back."

"Then keep the car, Mister Backstage," said my
father in exasperation and flung me the keys. "*Keep
the car.*"

"Oh, no," said Fuldauer. "I couldn't impose—"

"Don't worry. It's no trouble," my mother said, and

looked at me with complete understanding. "Is it, Arthur?" Before I could answer, she wheeled to the window. "Sanford! Put down that airplane and get in here. Your father's waiting to drill you. Sanford, did you hear me?"

And there was Fuldauer waiting for me, and the car keys in my hand. Well. Who knows from whence cometh my salvation next?

Smooth as silk. Sanford droning away again at irregular verbs in the den, Arthur and Dr. Julius F. backing out of the driveway in the trusty rusty Pontiac. Then next to me in the car Fuldauer spoke suddenly. "So. Tonight as it happens I am not after all taking the number thirty-two bus, and you are not walking. It appears, Arthur, that we serve each other." I glanced quickly at him. But he was staring straight ahead, the briefcase cradled on his lap and on top of that the tomatoes. "So tonight I will go home to dinner and you will go on to . . . the evening." His face took on a lost, pensive look. "Imagine," he said. "A regular theatre. It is an opportunity, Arthur. You should appreciate."

"Yes, sir, I'm trying to."

Abruptly my eyes were drawn to his vest peeking from behind the tomatoes. It was misbuttoned. For one wild minute I was tempted to stick my finger into the gap and twirl it. I looked at him again; he was still sitting that way, eyes straight ahead, humming. Or clearing his throat. And I turned away so he couldn't see my smile, because it was so preposterous what some people didn't know in this world.

We sat in silence the rest of the way, Fuldauer with his thoughts and I with mine. Turning into Altamont

at last, the scenery abruptly changed. No more bun-
galows, no more mock Tudor, nothing in sight but
batteries of two-family frame houses. One family up,
one down, a cavernous porch above and a scrawny
square of grass below, the concrete drives cracked and
canted crazily, and in the backyards the garage doors
yawed open because the garages had settled and were
no longer quite true. The houses were in good repair
actually, nothing that a little paint and the Fountain
of Youth wouldn't fix, but tired now, tired from all
the two families, up and down, that have tracked
through them on their way to greener pastures.

I pulled over at the address Fuldauer gave me, a
house like the rest. On the second-floor porch, only
her head and neck showing above the railing, an old
lady with white white hair rocked slowly back and
forth. Next to her like a graven image stood a tall
blond woman, staring down. Fuldauer nodded to me
as he got out; I nodded back. On the sidewalk he
looked up to the porch, cradled the tomatoes and
briefcase in one arm, and lifted the other in greeting.
The only response was the old lady groping a waxen
hand up to tuck in a wisp of white hair while she
continued to rock, and without moving the blond
woman said very distinctly to her, I could hear it,
"More tomatoes."

Fuldauer bent to me at the car window for a last
word. With a small cryptic sigh he said, "You are for-
tunate, Arthur. Some of us have only the comforts of
Virgil. But you have the mysteries of art. Remember."

I pulled quickly away again, away from him heading up the walk with the tomatoes in his arms and
the briefcase banging against his legs, away from the

two women on the dark porch and the darker rooms beyond. And headed for the theatre.

He could have the mysteries of art. I just wanted to keep the job.

5

---◆--→

Give me some men
Who are stout-hearted men
And will fight for the right
They adore

Start me with ten
Who are stout-hearted men
And I'll soon show you
Ten thousand more ore . . .

—*The New Moon*

He's always gotten fired. Maybe he'll get fired.

I think it started when I was twelve. For the first time that spring there had been ominous hints in the roll call of honorable sons that was ticked off nightly across the dinner table.

From my father:

"What do you think of that Chester Dempsey? Without anybody saying a word to him he went and fixed himself up a job selling refreshments at the ball games. Without anybody saying a word, mind you. I don't know, I guess some fathers are born lucky."

Silence while I bowed low over the gravy lake in my mashed potatoes to contemplate lucky fathers who don't have to say a word, and their unlucky sons.

And from my mother:

"I don't know what to do with that Hilda Green anymore. Her Alan brings home twenty-four dollars a week from that stock-boy job at Franklin Simon, and the first thing he did was to open his own bank account." And then in time to each spoonful of peas (which she knew I hated) dumped on my plate, "Twenty. Four. Dollars. A week. He can't wait to leave for work each morning, and Hilda's so stuck-up she hasn't got two words for anybody."

"He hates it," I mumbled at the peas.

"What?"

"Al hates it. Al says he hates that crummy job."

"For twenty-four dollars a week he can afford to hate it," said my mother, and added another spoonful for emphasis.

What difference did it make if I knew that Al left for work an hour-and-a-half early because his mother was terrified they would dock him if he was late, and that he put his money in the bank only because she would have crucified him if he didn't? Or if I knew what Chester Dempsey really had to say about lugging beer and hot dogs around the bleachers in the sun where they stick the little kids and just let them catch you looking at the game for one second even, or that Gary Himmelfarb had to be seduced into working in his father's hardware store with the promise of a new first baseman's mitt and a Louisville Slugger bat? At the end of each hint there was still the same unspoken question. And you, mister, what are you bringing home, what bank accounts do I notice you opening, mister? Plus the pointed report on my day from Lillian to Barney: "While other people work His Highness went riding on his bicycle, he took the air today." By the first of May the other fellows had all been shanghaied; the Saturday streets were empty, and I pedaled around under my own personal cloud of guilt.

It drove me finally to offer myself that spring to the

little, one-clerk, no-meat-counter, neighborhood A & P
on Taylor Road, vestige of a simpler time, where for
forty cents an hour I dodged the rheumy eye of the
clerk, a shriveled vestige of something herself, click-
ing teeth and sour old lady smell, struggling against
the encroaching supermarkets with her personalized
service, neighborhood know-how, and me, her good
right hand, God help her, stocking the shelves, misfig-
uring the produce, and spilling the coffee. (Me, who
dragged home at the end of one of those interminable
afternoons to hear my mother cooing innocently into
the phone, "Listen, kid, you could have bowled me
over, absolutely with a feather. Because without anybody saying a word Arthur went out and got himself
a job for forty cents an hour." I wondered if the
woman at the other end of the phone had a son.) It
didn't last, of course. Four weeks and even the shriveled Grandma Moses of a clerk couldn't take it, I was
out. And spent the rest of the summer cutting lawns.

  That was just the beginning. From then on the end
of the school year always hung heavily over me with
its need for a job. At one time or another in the sum-
mers following, until I was thrown out (usually a
matter of weeks, a month at the most) I sold colum-
nar pads and graduation greetings in a stationery
store beside older salesmen with broken wind and
families to support on their commissions; made de-
liveries for Polshek Quality Florist, where between
streetcar rides to funeral homes I listened to the
railing of the corsage man ("Look at this junk he
gives me to work with, that Polshek, junk, I could
pick prettier weeds in the backyard") ; or else sorted
delivery tickets down at my father's scrapyard, where
the truck drivers called me Little Shoemaker and it

was hard to tell which of us, my father or I, endured
more shame that the likes of me should have been in-
troduced as the boss's son among such men. Or had
that paper route (the three-week fiasco) or sold shoes
for that relative (one week), or, finally, learned every
crevice and stain on the lavatory wall at Hruby's
Fashions for Men, where Alex Hruby (who played
pinochle with my father) did me such a favor by hir-
ing me and teaching me to tie a Windsor knot on my
forefinger ("Now I think *this* is *very* smart, don't
you?") to dazzle the Croats and Serbs of Union Avenue. When I was losing the sale I was supposed to
call "Counter, please," for Mr. Hruby's wife Melba,
cruising up and down behind the showcases like a
dreadnought, to sail in and save the deal. Because of
pinochle politics it was awkward for the Hrubys to
fire me outright, but I did spend a lot of time in the
stockroom.

Or maybe that stretch at Hruby's was during a
Christmas vacation instead of a summer, I didn't
remember for sure. But I did remember that just as I
hated the other jobs so, too, I hated that store; hated
bland Alex and salty Melba and all their worldly as-
signs down to their last pair of Jockey shorts. Because
Saturday nights after closing we had to straighten
stock and take inventory; and at about the time I
would have been leaving the house with the fellas—
nine of us jammed and howling in somebody's family
sedan, going nowhere except Out—down at Hruby's
we would still be stacking MacGregor sweaters and
counting Arrow shirts, and if I was bitter that sometimes I didn't get home until after eleven, that was
okay with my parents, too. There would be other Saturday nights, and it was too bad, but that's the way

things were sometimes, and the sooner I learned that the better.

"The better to what?"

"Never mind, just the better."

Because The Way Things Were Sometimes was the way things were supposed to be. Life, it so happened, *was* unfair. Life was not a thing where you could pick the flavors, and justice was not a law of nature. Life was bitter, unquote; and Alex Hruby didn't like it any better than I did. Nobody liked it, not Polshek nor his corsage man, not the shriveled lady at the A & P nor the drivers down at my father's scrapyard, not even my father himself (though if you asked me he seemed suspiciously to *like* not liking it), none of the bosses nor any of the help, nobody. The fact was we were stuck on this earth to pick our perilous way from pain to pain, to struggle through what we hated, to watch the clock, to be disappointed, to miss football games because of our paper routes and Fibber McGee because of our homework and yes, even to get home from work after eleven on Saturday nights, and the *last* thing you were supposed to do was like it. You were only supposed to recognize it for what it was, and that would somehow make it all bearable.

Not to me, Folks.

Despite the articles of faith they tried to teach I remained a conscientious objector. There had to be some kind of work I wanted to do, something you could love as much as the money it paid you. But what? In the war between us there seemed to be nothing that was not punishment or deprivation. And then like a star shell bursting over the muddy trenches there came the theatre, first in high school and now at Kempton Hills. The theatre. The prob-

lem was I didn't really know how to do any of it, only
how to love it. And the way the world went, it didn't
seem that would be enough.

The only hope was to find something in it you
could do *without* talent, then to get in so deep you
couldn't turn back. No wonder I felt that my first
night to run the show was like getting across some
kind of Rubicon.

After I got to the theatre and parked the car I was
in such a sweat to hit the prop house and start setting
up that I nearly blew right past Mr. Henry in his
chair at the backstage gate, theoretically sitting there
to check the passes everyone had been issued at the
start of the season and which no one had bothered to
use since the third day. But he was supposed to be
there and there he was, on his own wooden folding
chair which he carried across the stage each night, in
his galluses and Panama hat, one leg hung over the
other, pulling up the trouser leg to show the white
cotton sock flowering limply around the pale hairless
stem of his ankle. Sometimes he rolled a cigarette
from a pouch he carried (paper and tobacco fluttering together in his palsied hands) and smoked while
he waited. He seldom took the cigarette out of his
mouth and the smoke curled up, coiling around his
head, caught under the brim of the Panama. He was
smoking now, and there he sat, with his own cigarette
on his own chair in his own smoke. Self-reliant. Owed
us nothing. Eternal vigilance.

"Howza boy, Mr. Henry," I muttered, hurrying
through the gate.

Mr. Henry merely blinked. I was practically past
him when he said, "Too late now."

A stab in my vitals stopped me in my tracks. "Too late for what?" I instantly had the flash. The prop house had burned down.

"That door. I tol' ya to be watchin' it."

"The door to the prop house?"

He was still staring straight ahead through the brine of his watery eyes, pickled in his own solution. Then with two stiff fingers he forked the wet cigarette out of his mouth. "Left it open agen."

"I did?" Visions of the props ravaged, scattered to the four winds, the Rape of the Sabine Props, the Diaspora of the Props, the Props were in Babylonian Captivity. "I'll get right on it," I said, turning to run.

"Closed it for ya."

"You did?" I turned to thank him, but the cigarette was back in his mouth and he was staring again. Blessings on you, you salty old soda cracker, we are comrades to the death. More calmly now, I ambled on toward the prop house.

Let's face it. Running props was really nothing to be all that anxious about, anyway. You just set the furniture on stage before the audience came in, then trundled the monster prop table out of the prop house to its position backstage and plugged in the shaded tin-can lights so the actors could see to find their hand props in the dark. After that wherever there was a change of scenery you took the furniture from the previous scene off and put the furniture for the new scene on, then checked your list to make sure you hadn't forgotten anything. All you really had to do was have the new stuff lined up in the wings, watch for the scene-shift cues, then keep your ankles clear of the murderous pieces of scenery that rumbled every which way during a shift like runaway freight cars. What could be easier?

Since Kempton Hills was an open-air theatre and not enclosed there was no overhead storage, no place you could hoist anything out of sight as in a conventional theatre. That meant all the scenery had to roll on wheeled platforms called dollies. You built the scenery on these platforms and during the scene shifts you pulled them into place with towropes, which were basically lengths of clothesline, each knotted through a boat hook at one end. In between scene shifts you got to wear your towrope hooked around the waist of your crew coat, which had Kempton Hills Theatre written across the back, and paraded the whole getup as a uniform of glory, hopefully someplace where the audience could see. Strictly speaking, of course, the prop crew didn't need towropes since they didn't pull anything, but I wore one around my waist, anyway. For effect.

The Desert Song wasn't even a very complicated show. I had run through the changes in my mind a dozen times, and actually I was in pretty good shape. Everything was more or less ready. My clipboard, my lists, the giant pencil, an authentic wineskin. I had even managed to donkey through to the finish of that hapless chaise. Chippendale it wasn't, but as long as you remembered to pick it up by the sides and not by the top it was okay. Sort of. Whenever it wobbled or sagged anywhere I whacked in a few more nails at the offending spot and was begining to think it might even make it to the end of the run. What the hell, I had plenty of nails,

At first everything went tickety-boo. I got set up

easily before the show started, made the first change right on the dot. After the second scene had begun I checked my watch. Plenty of time. I could easily whip over to the refreshment stand halfway up the side of the auditorium (in my crew coat and towrope, of course) for an Eskimo Pie before the next change. Maybe Marlene or Mary Lou or somebody might be in the audience. Go ahead, Shoemaker, show the uniform, why not? A hidden door at the side of the stage-right light tower let you sneak out from backstage; I was through it and up the hill in a flash. And I had just started back down when I was brought up short by my first surprise of the night. Too bad it wasn't the last.

Not Marlene or Mary Lou, but there, standing with his back to me against the wall below the refreshment pavilion, was Dr. Fuldauer. At his side, a worried dark wart of a face, which I realized must be Naomi. She glanced apprehensively from side to side while Fuldauer stared straight ahead, his face shining in the reflected light from the stage. He still had his suit on, buttoned right up, vest and all. Naomi, in a wilted one-piece paper bag of a dress, plucked fitfully at his arm. "Poppa," she said. "*Shah*," said Fuldauer, brushing her away. "*Shah*." Under his suit his right shoulder twitched oddly, like a horse shrugging off flies. They did not see me standing behind them.

"But, Poppa, we didn't pay," said Naomi. "We just walked in."

"Only for a minute," said Fuldauer, not taking his eyes from the stage.

"But what if they ask us for a stub? You have to

have a stub," said Naomi, looking anxiously around her.

"*Shah,*" said Fuldauer. "*Shah.*" And now I could see the reason for the twitching shoulder. Down along the seam of his trousers his right hand was jerkily beating time.

Whatever they were doing, they certainly weren't the audience I was looking for. A little disappointed, I gave the two of them a wide berth, slipped back in through the light-tower door again and looked quickly around. No problem. Still lots of time before the shift. I smiled; everything was under control.

Dream on, Shoemaker.

It happened just before that next change in the first act, when the scene shifted from the Red Shadow's desert lair to the courtyard of the French general's house. The prop shift on the change was apple-pie, really. The whole desert lair was to roll off in one piece, props and all, including the tripod over the desert campfire, the celluloid fire itself, the twenty Riff wine cups, and a deck of Riff playing cards (painted with an inscription stolen from a pack of Fatima cigarettes; I was really proud of that one). All I had to do was bring the tambourines to the wings where the girls could pick them up on their entrance into the courtyard for the next scene; the other furniture—a table with some goblets and a champagne bottle—rode onto the stage with a scenery unit that was stored offstage left. So just before the cue to dim the lights I dropped off the tambourines, then dashed off into the stage-left wings to check the table. But as I got near the back of the unit I heard the voices of Cooky and Westervelt coming hoarsely from the other side, whispering and sniggering like teen-agers.

"Come on, come on, finish it already." That was Westervelt.

"You sure this is his, this is the one he uses?" from Cooky.

"Yeah, yeah I'm sure. C'mon, willya hurry up—"

I came around the corner. There was the taboret table with the goblets and champagne bottle on it, just as they were supposed to be. Cooky had his hand on the bottle.

"All right, you guys," I said. "Don't screw around with the props—"

Westervelt nudged Cooky, still sniggering like a fiend. "Hey, you hear that, Cook? Don't screw around with the props."

"Oh my doodness dwacious, naughty me," said Cooky, setting the bottle down. And the two of them started off.

"Come on, you guys," I said more sternly. But they continued to run, still laughing. They sure thought something was funny. I looked suspiciously after them, then bent over and sniffed the champagne bottle, certain they had filled it with something yummy like vinegar or ipecac. No, it was ginger ale, all right. And the glasses were in place. Everything looked okay. About to head back downstage, I absently wiped a damp spot from the taboret table with my fingers. Then froze, the blood congealing in my veins. The spot wasn't water or ginger ale. It was glue.

Something had been painted with glue.

I looked around frantically for someone to tell. There was the stage manager at his booth. His arm was raised, above to give the cue for the scene shift. "Hold it," I hissed at him in the loudest whisper I dared. But at that moment there was a burst of applause from out front, the spotlights dimmed, and he dropped his arm and called huskily, "Go!"

The crew promptly leaned against their towropes and heaved like slaves on the Mississippi. The unit began to move. I jumped back out of the way, and there it went, table, glasses, bottle, glue and all, heading right for the stage. As I watched helplessly, in the wings on the other side now I caught sight of Harry snapping the cuffs on his glorious uniform as an officer in the Foreign Legion, getting ready to make his entrance as soon as the lights came up again. Then I remembered what happened in the next scene, and that was when panic really set in.

I waved like a madman to get his attention, hissing, "Harry . . . *Harry*!"

No good, he didn't hear a word. Too busy jutting his chin for that super-mammary brunette.

I took a step toward him—but he was clear over on the other side. *"Har-ree!"* I tried again. No use, he didn't see me. My chest probably wasn't big enough.

The scenery was locking in place, the stage manager already hissing, "Clear! Clear stage!" The only thing to do was make a dash for it. The next instant I was out on the stage, running, and behind me the stage manager nearly had apoplexy. "Shoemaker, are you out of your tree? *Get your raggedy ass back here!*" I glanced up, saw the filaments in the spotlights start to glow, dove back for the wings, and just made it in time. Then turned to look at the lighted stage, sick at heart.

Too late. Too late. Oh, God, too late.

On the other side the unsuspecting Harry strode out from the wings. It was, frankly, a sensational entrance. He marched right up to the table in that same wonderful walk I had seen in rehearsal. Then he bowed formally to the circle of chorus girls including the vapid soprano, who smiled foggily, now with her hair down and minus her glasses. Next Harry clicked his heels and flashed his sabre to the other officers, each man holding his empty goblet. Finally Harry braced his shoulders over the bottle of champagne, ready at last. I wanted to close my eyes.

"Gentlemen," he announced in those clarion tones, "I give you a toast—" His hand came down in a graceful swoop, but stopped short as it gripped the bottle—which was, of course, glued fast to the table. Harry gripped more tightly and tried again. "A toast to—" Forget it. The bottle was like a rock.

The briefest flicker of surprise, followed by a flash of comprehension went across Harry's face. Cooky and Westervelt were standing next to me, grins splitting their faces while despair glazed mine.

On stage, still smiling through gritted teeth Harry tugged fiercely one more time. And with a great cracking sound the bottle came free, pulling a large ragged slice of the tabletop with it. A titter began to spread through the audience.

As though nothing had happened Harry poured champagne all round, then bowed deeply again to the girls. "I give you one of the glories of France," he started again, then paused dramatically, "Margot Bonvalet!" And there came the hand down in another graceful arc for the goblet, then stopped short again. Oh God, not the glass, too. Yes, the glass. It was glued as well.

The other actors on stage looked as though they were at a vintage alum-tasting, their lips gripped with that strange rigor which hits an actor when he is trying desperately to keep a straight face, not to break up, not to come, pardon the pun, unglued. In the wings Cooky and Westervelt were now guffawing outright.

Only Harry remained unfazed. With the slightest shake of his head as if to say children must play, he pulled harder on the goblet—and with a little click the stem snapped off neatly at the base. Still flashing the same unperturbed smile Harry lifted the glass in triumph. "Margot Bonvalet!" he said again, and drank his ginger ale as though it were Piper Heidsieck '98. The others hid their grins in their goblets, drank his ginger ale as though it were Piper-Heid-started to do the same, but, oops, at the same instant he realized the glass no longer had a base and would not stand. He brought the goblet back up to his chest. Clearly the disaster was to have no end. Harry would have to carry that goblet for the whole scene, the rest of the show, and probably all eternity. In the heavenly choir I would see him standing with that glass, looking for a way to put it down after his toast to the Betty Boop soprano with the pin curls and corrective astigmatism. But not Harry. Without an instant's hesitation he promptly raised the glass again and clicked his heels.

"Gentlemen," he said to the other astonished actors, "the Queen." And thus putting a monarch France never had on a throne that had been empty for a hundred and fifty years, with perfect aplomb he turned. And hurled his glass into the muslin fireplace. Solemnly, one after another, the other actors did the same. Harry's last triumphant look at Cooky in the wings said it all. Erin Go Bragh, Confusion to the French, Don't Tread on Me, and Up Your Mudshoot, Mr. Finn. With a rotary screwdriver.

As soon as the show was safely past that scene and some semblance of sanity had been restored, I slunk into the dressing room building, threading my way through the chatter in the corridor. Another legend had been born, everybody was still laughing over what had happened. Everybody, that is, but me. Go on, Shoemaker, I told myself, take it like a man. At least take it like a man.

I burst into Harry's dressing room without waiting to knock, ready to face the guns with no blindfold. He was at the start of a whirlwind costume change, tearing off his Legionnaire's tunic, about to throw himself into the mask and cape of the Red Shadow again for his next entrance. All in one breath I poured it out. "Honest it wasn't my fault except I should've been watching so go ahead say it."

"Say what?" He was peeling off his pants, head down. "Look, kid, I've kinda got a quick change here—"

"It *is* my fault, the glasses are props, it's my responsibility."

Harry glanced up as though he were really seeing me for the first time. "What, that?" he said shortly. "Forget it."

"You don't *mind?*"

"What's to mind?"

"That mess I got you in," I said miserably.

Harry shrugged. "Must have happened to some other guy. Me, I'm not really here. This Farmer Brown place doesn't count, nothing that happens here is real; anyway. I'm just waiting for Mickey Bellinger to get out here and catch me in the show, and I'm long gone."

"Who's . . . Mickey Bellinger?"

"My ticket outta here, baby," said Harry happily, "back to the land of the living. Mickey's the big gun in legit at MCA. As soon as I sign with him it's Goodbye Graveyard, Hello Shubert Alley." He was down to his shorts, moving quickly and efficiently. He looked as though he had been undressing and dressing in front of people all his life. "Back to the *real* theatre," he finished with emphasis, reaching for his next costume.

"You're leaving?" I said, with a twinge of disappointment and loss I could not help.

"Are you kidding?" Harry was tugging on the Red Shadow's pants and grabbing for the boots. "In New York they're doing *Bye Bye Birdie, Camelot,* Cole Porter, Frank Loesser, *real* shows—push," he held up a half-booted foot for me to shove the rest of the way, "—while I'm out here in the boondocks trying to breathe some life into Sigmund Fucking Romberg." Now I saw that the dressing room was littered with old copies of *Variety,* telegrams stuck in the mirror, programs, and on the table the ointments and balms of the trade, tubes, liner-pencil, all with that musky perfume, a sweetness beyond sugar. There were also three or four posters from New York shows thumbtacked to the wall, *West Side Story, Gypsy, Sweet Bird of Youth,* at theatres whose names read like an incantation, the Morosco, the Royale, the Music Box. *Broadway.* "Boy," Harry was saying as he slipped on the blouse, "the day I get back I'm gonna hit the Stage Deli, I'm gonna order me a Number Three—corned beef, tongue, Swiss, li'l Russian dressing—sit down right in the middle of Seventh Avenue and have a picnic."

"If I don't screw you up first," I said gloomily.

Harry looked at me. "Shoemaker, you worry too much," he said. "This is your first summer in stock. There's no season like the first season, you're gonna remember it all your life." He reached for cape. "You picked that dancer yet?"

"Which dancer?" I said, a little startled.

"Doesn't matter," said Harry matter-of-factly. "The best thing about dancers is the known fact that they *all* boff. Listen, it's 1960, this may be the last age in which screw is both a dirty word—and the Ultimate Glory." He stood, checked the folds critically in the mirror. "Get yourself some glory, Shoemaker—that's my advice." At the door now he winked, flung the cape behind him, and extended his hand. "Gentlemen—the Queen!"

And with a laugh he was gone.

After another moment I left the dressing room and headed back toward the prop table behind the scenery. As I came out the door of the dressing room building, in the wings downstage the little toy French soldiers with their rented kepis and cardboard puttees were getting ready to make their entrance. They were zapping the dancers beside them (whose harem brassieres were framed with feathers for some reason— D'Angeli must've done his ostrich number on the costume designer, too), the boys mimicking the sounds from the stage, pretending to do lip-sync with the girls' chorus out front.

Did you call for soldiers true

their voices trilled, and the chorus boys backstage mugged and grimaced, playing with their popguns, lining up. Still under the spell of Harry's words, I walked lazily through the dark shadows behind the scenery, feeling promising, potent, almost light-headed, as though I had been breathing pure oxygen. Take your time, Shoemaker, enjoy the stroll. One of the glory promenades of all time is walking backstage during a performance. Voices low, faces glowing in the darkness, it is like being in on the intimate secret of the world, the true behind-hand whisper of all of life. No King of England had a prospect so fair. You can have the gardens behind Buckingham Palace or the lawn at Windsor. I'll take backstage at Kempton Hills while the chorus is getting ready to enter and the strains of the orchestra drift to you over the scenery like your own personal serenade.

The redheaded dancer named Ginger walked by in the opposite direction, her red red lips and under-lined eyes floating luminously past me in the dark. Could it be true? Was one of those perfect Max Factor moons waiting for me, just for the taking?

I drifted around to the prop table, then moved on down toward the wings. As I passed the back door to the prop house from the corner of my eye I noticed Mr. Henry inside, about halfway up the stairs to the second floor. "Howza boy, Mr. Henry," I said absently.

Mr. Henry did not move. He seemed to be holding out his hand. "For. You," he said, but his speech was strangely blurred.

"Atta boy, Mr. Henry," I said. "You guard those props, now."

But Mr. Henry was not guarding anything. He stood rigid, eyes staring, a single glistening strand of saliva hanging from the corner of his mouth. Then to my staggered amazement, without a word, without a sound, slowly, so unbearably slowly, he fell.

And fell. And fell. Just toppled over like a tired tree, cartwheeling down the stairs in a great clatter and bumping and crumpling and ending motionless in a heap on the concrete at the bottom, sprawled half out of the doorway.

"Mr. Henry?" I said, amazed at the terror I heard in my voice. "*Mr. Henry?*"

On the stage meanwhile, there was that lumpen chorus in their rental costumes clumping inanely through that song about soldiers in Morocco.

> *Out we'll go to rout the foe*
> *For back at home*
> *There waits perchance*
> *A pretty charming light o' love*
> *An amourette we long to see ...*

they sang, while the girls jiggled their feathered breasts and waved their gazontoids and Mr. Henry lay against the cold cement.

In no time there was a circle of helpless people crowded and clucking around the old man. I knelt beside him, not knowing what to do. It seemed so cruel to have that face pressed so flatly, so bluntly against that cement, that grit. I wanted to help, but something went white inside me and I could not bring myself to touch him.

Suddenly Harry thrust his way in through the crowd wearing his full Red Shadow costume—the silken blouse, the Riff headdress, the red domino mask, the cape. Quickly he knelt beside the old man and gently turned him over. Mr. Henry's eyes were open; his mouth worked, but no sound came out.

"Hey, there, kid," said Harry gently, "what're you trying to pull, you trying to be cute?" Over his shoulder he barked low to the onlookers, "Don't stand on top of him, *let him breathe, for chrissake.*" Something in his tone made everyone back away respectfully. Turning back again, Harry swiftly whipped off his cape, draped it carefully over Mr. Henry. Then he took the old man's warty hand. Mr. Henry's mouth was still open, straining. "Take it easy, kid. Everything's gonna be strawberries and cream," murmured Harry. "Strawberries and cream." With a corner of the cape he gently wiped the spittle from the corner of the old man's lips.

At last Spratt elbowed into the circle. "Red Shadow, what're you doing, you've got an entrance coming up," he said nervously. Then to the others, "All right, let's go, let's go, nothing you can do here, the ambulance is on its way." The crowd started to drift off uncertainly. "Let's go, places for scene four."

Harry was still bent over Mr. Henry. At last the film seemed to lift a little from the old man's eyes. His stricken glance met Harry's. "I know, I know," said Harry. "But don't worry, we're not gonna let you get away with it."

"Harry, for God's sake, they're waiting," said Spratt. "We've got an audience—"

Harry rose reluctantly. He spoke to me in low

tones, looking down at the old man. "Keep him comfortable," he said, "as long as you can."

I nodded dumbly.

In a fever of anxiety Spratt said, "Red Shadow— *you're on.*"

Harry strode to the edge of the wings, hesitated for just an instant to adjust the angle of his headdress and straighten the mask. "What bullshit," he muttered. Then lifted his chin and set sail as the orchestra cue crashed out.

The time was deep twilight, that purple hour in an outdoor theatre when the spotlights first really begin to bite against the dark. The number was the big first act ballad, and the soprano was truly stirred. Never had Harry seemed so full of feeling for her. *Blue Heaven,* he sang, *And you and I,*

> *And sand kissing a moonlit sky*
> *A desert breeze whisp'ring a lullaby . . .*

The ambulance had arrived, not an ambulance really, just a police station wagon moving down the service road around behind the audience. I watched as they carefully lifted Mr. Henry onto the stretcher. From the old man's hand something fluttered to the ground. A feather? It was, from one of the dancer's costumes. I picked it up. He must have been bringing it to me when he collapsed. Preserving the props to the end. Eternal vigilance.

Out on the stage the soprano would have sworn there was moisture around the edges of Harry's eyes under the mask. *Only stars above you,* his voice throbbed, *To see I luvvvv you.* Of course, she was a little myopic and could not see that Harry's gaze went

past her and also past the shaken young man with the
feather, to the ambulance with the dying old man receding into the dark.

Later that night I sat in the basement at home with
Sanford. The furnace and the clothesline took up
most of the space, but on the other side of them Sanford had rigged his workshop. There was his
Shopsmith, his workbench, and a half-dozen demon
inventions in various stages of development and de-
cay. He was holding my anatomy text on his lap
while I struggled through what I needed to know for
the spot quiz the next morning. There should have
been another name for it, like the weekly verse of the
Executioner's Song. That would have been apt, considering what had just happened to Mr. Henry. We
had been fussing in the lab all week with the mass of
whitish cartilage known as the dogfish brain under
the skin over that rubbery head. Not exactly the same
as Mr. Henry's, of course. But death is death.

"Okay," said Sanford, "give me the ten cranial
nerves."

"Olfactory, optic, oculomotor, trochlear . . . uh,
trochlear . . ." There was a pause. My eyes had
drifted off.

"Artie, will you stop thinking about that old man?"

I snapped out of it, looking at him. "You want to
hear something awful? I wasn't."

Sanford sighed wearily. "Uh-oh. What's this gonna
be—more about the fabulous making-out down at the
theatre?"

"At least it's not the usual high school routine.
Mere necking." I tossed the next off lightly. "The
dancers all boff, you know."

"Bullshit."

"It's a known fact."

"Yeah? Then why're you sitting here with me?"

"It's just a question," I said airily, "of when I make my move."

My mother's voice broke in from upstairs. "Arthur! Are you two going to sit down there all night?"

"Through in a minute," I called back, then resumed. "Oculomotor, trochlear . . . uh, trochlear . . ."

"Artie . . ." Sanford's voice was low. "You really believe all that stuff? About the dancers, I mean?"

I smiled the smile of the man who has seen life.

"Trochlear," I said, smiling, "trigeminal, abducens, facial . . ."

6

Moonbeams shining soft above
Let me beg of you
Find the one I dearly love
Tell him I'll e'errr be true ...

—*The Red Mill*

And if you saw me heading for the theatre in the Pontiac three or four nights later you wouldn't have to be a genius to guess what was going on. My shirt was clean, my jeans were pressed, my hair was combed. Obviously this was the night. I was about to make my move.

Mouths and waists and hidden nipples and hips and calves dangled before my mind's eye while I tooled along Taylor Road, a rack of choice joints hanging across the windshield as though it were a butcher's showcase. This one from the dancer named Ginger, that from the singer named Dolores. It made a song in my head while I drove, *O Ginger and Dolores/They were ladies of the chorus,* and no wonder I smiled at each historic landmark that breezed by.

First, zipping past the corner of Bainbridge Road where Marlene the high school confection lived, and where tonight after whatever daring handholding in the movies, she and her basketball-dribbling, foot-

ball-punting, high-hurdling letterman would stand at
the darkened doorway burping politely from their
dudeburgers, kiss each other twice, pant three times
and call that Life (she's had her chance, they don't
come twice) . (Unless she begs me.)

And then, just at the upper edge of Kempton Hills
Park, Caruso's Coach House and Grill where some of
us who were past such adolescent games sat and
drank beer after the show, and let Marlene and those
other children chew on that with their Popsicles.
*(Did you see Artie Shoemaker leave that terrible
Caruso place last night? He was with this terribly attractive singer from the theatre named Dolores and
she just put her arm through his and gave him this
look, it was this terribly attractive girl named Dolores
or Ginger.)* Up ahead now there was the entrance to
the crew parking lot at the rear of the auditorium.
*(You know what I bet? What, Marlene, what? I bet
Artie Shoemaker goes all the way with those girls
from the theatre, that's what I bet; because he had
the car last night and when I happened to pass where
they were parked later on there was this terribly low
moan from the car, and then he got out with this terribly attractive girl from the theatre, the one named
Ginger or Dolores, and her blouse was unbuttoned, it
gives me gooseflesh to think of what they were doing;
then he stuck his finger right into her blouse and I
wish I knew what he said to make her laugh and look
at him like that.)* (So do I, Marlene, so do I.) And I
glided smoothly into the lot *(Have you seen the way
he drives)*, whipped neatly into a parking space
(What it is is, he has this style), then gunned the motor briskly one last time while I smiled again at the

empty seat next to me reserved for Dolores. Or Ginger.

Who knew what might happen on that seat in a few short hours? Maybe this was finally my night to sit alone with someone later in the dark parking lot under the tossing maples, watching myself carefully to see if I felt all the celebrated sensations at the sweet release of each fastening, buttons, zippers, hooks (*Oh Artie*) and the suddenness of bare flesh in the front seat of my father's Pontiac. (*You wouldn't know it to look at him, would you, Marlene? Would you know it to look at him?*) And as I got out, how tenderly I closed the door, because this was the night. This was definitely the night.

Probably nobody else would have known it to look at me, either, as I went down the hill through those midwestern faces, seven delicious flavors and all of them Jell-O. Like a package tied with twine in the middle and coming apart at both ends my cuffs kept falling down, my shirts billowed like sails at the back, my waist was bunched tight because I had no hips, no goddam hips at all. But the Pontiac was waiting up in the lot, and I stepped through the gate to the hidden tempo of rising hope.

Backstage I paused to look around. Everything was quiet in the idle hour before the show, with only the first scattered hints of the evening to come. Someone was mopping the stage on the other side of the scenery, the damp thwock of the mop on the cement, the rasp of the bucket being dragged after. From somewhere came a high, quick laugh, it sounded like one of the dressing rooms. And over near the door to the auditorium the young girls who were to usher that night were being instructed by the head usher,

Prudence Rendlesham, better known as Plenty Prudie
or Pussy Prudie, five eight and meaty but with a
heart-shaped face, truly a heart-shaped face and val-
entine lips to match, and all the little girls of fourteen, in their best-girl white, carefully neatened the
edges of the stacks of programs in their arms while
they listened. I stood there, inhaling it all.

Another laugh from the dressing room. A faint
scream.

I moved on.

Into the long corridor of the dressing room building, passing each door in turn. First the male dancers,
all titters and pouts and petulance, then the girls',
hoping to catch a glimpse of Ramona or at least a
candy wrapper. Next, Harry's dressing room where he
was stretching his whiskey voice, Ah-yah-YAH-yah-
yah-yah, then the other principals. After that it was
back to the peasants again, the busy home-cooking
hum of the female chorus, clubby and domestic, a
garden of hairpins and curlers; and finally the men's
chorus, Slavic ex-altar boys with thin, straw-straight
hair and thick southside accents and half a sense of
humor among them. I had almost made it to the crew
dressing room all the way at the end—when three feet
ahead of me Sherman Spratt stepped into the hall
from the men's chorus room on a wave of laughter,
mostly his own.

At the sight of me he stopped flat and smiled his
small-jointed smile. "Ah, Belasco," he said, "the very
man. Have you heard my marvelous new joke for the
fountain scene?" Spratt doubled as rewrite man on
the creaking operetta scripts, which consisted mainly
of changing three acts to two and spicing up the 1912
wheezes with wheezes of his own.

"The fountain scene?" I said.

But he was already gushing on. "You know, in *Marie* (Friml's *Rose-Marie* opened next week), where she sits on the fountain in the second act after the Mounties have left. Now picture this, see, it's divine. She's sitting on the edge of the fountain, see, and when he says 'The captain has discovered everything,' she reaches into the fountain and pulls out this kettle and takes a fish out of it and says—now get this—and says, 'Well. This is a pretty kettle of fish!' " And he looked at me, his mouth open, ready to laugh.

"A kettle?" I said.

"Yes, you know—a kettle."

"What kettle?" I said.

"A kettle. Any kettle, I don't care. We'll get this kettle. But can't you just see it? Isn't it marvelous?"

"Was there a kettle on the prop list? I don't think there was a kettle on the list."

"Well, get a kettle. Can't we get a kettle, for heaven's sake?"

"You want to officially add a kettle to the prop list?"

"That's the general idea, Belasco. What does it take, an act of God?"

"Look, Sherman, you're the one who always screams if we don't clear everything officially, and I was just—"

"All right, all right. I hereby officially and formally inscribe a kettle on the list. Okay?"

"What kind of a kettle?"

He looked at me blankly. "What kind of a kettle?"

"Well, a teakettle, a soup kettle, a kettle with a handle at each end, or a handle across the top—"

"Oh, *I* don't know. Any kettle, for heaven's sake."

"I mean, I've got a coupla old pots that I could—"

"No, not a pot. You can't say a pot of fish, how can you say a pot of fish? The whole point is the kettle, its nothing without the kettle. She has to take this fish out of it and say this is a pretty kettle of fish. It's nothing without the kettle, my God, can't you see that?"

"You want a fish, too?"

"Of course, I want a fish. The whole *point* is the fish. Can't you just make a simple fish out of canvas or something? My God, if you crew people are going to fight me over every little thing, every little cree-YATEive thing—I mean, God knows we have to do all we can to compensate for that designer of yours."

"Of mine?"

"Well, *I* certainly didn't hire him." (A pointed reminder that D'Angeli was a legacy from the City Summer Recreation Program.) "And as if that weren't enough there's this obstructive, this system-ATically obstructive attitude around here." He lowered his voice confidentially. "I mean, I think it's shocking, that terrible thing with poor Vinnie Krushar, don't you?"

"What terrible thing?" I knew perfectly well, of course.

"Oh, nothing, except that terrible Shenker person," and his lip curled, "that Shenker person kicked him."

"That's not what I heard. I heard Krushar got in the way of a shift."

"Oh, and poor Vinnie scraped his own knee, I suppose. Scraped the skin right *off*. I suppose you know what that can mean to a dancer's career, I suppose you know you can get blood poisoning from a wound like that. And now I ask for a simple kettle, and what happens? Well, never mind. I can see I'll have to discuss this with D'Angeli."

"Look, there's no need to make a federal case out of it," I said, beginning to feel a little uneasy.

"Oh, isn't there? I'll just speak to D'Angeli about the cooperation with the creative people around here, that's all." He was really winding himself up now. *"That's all."*

"—Something bothering you, Sherm?" said another voice suddenly. And Moe Shenker himself materialized behind Spratt.

Spratt froze. "Nothing I'd care to discuss with *you,* thank you very much."

"Okay, Sperm. Whatever you say, Sperm."

"I see you've been talking to the great Mister Crystal," Spratt said huffily.

"Me? Talk to an actor?" said Shenker. "Never the twain shall meet, Sperm."

"The name," said Spratt in a voice like ice, "is Sherman."

"Right, Sperm. Sorry, Sperm. Now was there something on your mind, Sperm?"

"Nothing I'd care to discuss, I said."

"Oh, go on, Sperm, tell me all about it." Shenker had started to grow a Fu Manchu moustache and was staring fixedly at Spratt with the beady eyes of a small Bronx mongoose. "What's his problem, Shoemaker?"

"It was something about another prop, for some gag," I said, feeling a lot better to have an ally.

"It happens to be concerned with the art of the theatre," Spratt said to him loftily, "so I wouldn't expect you to understand."

"That's right, I'm just a peasant, Sperm. Tell me all about the great art, Sperm."

"I suppose you think you're being pretty clever. Well, I'll have a word with D'Angeli, and we'll see how clever *he* thinks you are."

But you can't scare Shenker that way. "Yes, Sperm," he said, "you do that. You do that little thing. You go talk to D'Angeli and then maybe you can stop hocking us with these pathetic sad-ass ideas you call jokes." How I wished I had the guts to talk to Spratt like that. But Shenker wasn't through. "You understand, we'd love to listen, Sperm, but we're trying to do a show here."

"And just what, just *what* do you think I'm trying to do?" sputtered Spratt. You could see the red spread right out to the edges of his ears.

"I often wonder," said Shenker softly. "I often wonder."

I wished I'd thought of that one, too.

"Oh, my, that's witty," said Spratt, backing away, rocking his head from side to side. "That's priceless. I'm sure D'Angeli will appreciate that."

Shenker took a hefty hold on his own crotch, lifted it bluntly toward the little man. "How'd you like to appreciate about six inches of this, Sperm," he said. But Spratt had opened the door to the nearest dressing room and was already saying, "Oh, Teddy, have I told you my divine idea for the fountain scene?" as the door closed behind him.

"That chinless *schmeckle*," Shenker muttered as we moved on together along the corridor—interrupting himself to nod amiably at one of the passing dancers, "And how are you tonight, m'dear"—then looking after her with "Oh-my-yes" in his W. C. Fields imitation that sounded like Ohmyass. By then we had reached the door to the crew room, where each night we exchanged our street clothes for jeans and the gray shop coats with *Kempton Hills Theatre* in green script across the back. We entered on a breath of fetid air and socks gone to seed.

"Listen," Shenker announced to the room at large, "we ought to hold a court on that *schmeckle,* that Spratt. We ought to hold an inquisition."

"Yeah," said Hlavacek, peeling off his street socks to reveal feet heavily splotched with umber.

"You got it," said Westervelt, "an In-quee-zishun." He was folding his short sleeves into a cuff to let even more of his biceps show. "You know, Hlavacek," he said, glancing down at the stringy Slav next to him, "if you'd wear human shoes around the paint frame instead-a those fruity sandals, your feet wouldn't go home looking like dog poo."

"Feet gotta breathe," said Hlavacek stolidly.

"So do the rest of us," said Westervelt, and laughed, pleased with his once-a week joke. "How about that, Moe? How about those fruity sandals?"

But Shenker was restless, prowling among the lockers, slamming doors. "Boy, he really grabs my ass, that *schmeckle.* Listen, we gotta get mobilized on him." Moe was forever drawing up plots and coups and elaborately poetic schemes of revenge, he bore our bar sinister. "Whaddya say, Cook?"

Cooky was deep in his nightly toilette, cleaning his nails with a razor knife, the grime from each nail peeling off in a single gritty strip. Without looking up he grunted. "Gets in my way, I'll kick his nuts. I'll kick his nuts right over his head."

"You know it," said Shenker. "He don't watch himself in that scene-three shift, he's gonna be walking around on his ankles. All right then, let's get mobilized here. Look, Shoemaker, if he comes near you tonight—"

"Oh, I'll clobber him, don't worry," I said vaguely. Which was a rank lie, for which I would no doubt burn later, but my mind was on other matters (*Oh Artie*) more pressing. And while Shenker went on I grabbed my crew coat. "Hey, where you going?" he said, breaking off in the middle of something about Spratt's pants and the shower room urinal. "I just have to check something," I said, and headed out across the corridor toward the prop house. For tonight I had cunning plots of my own. This was my night to learn how buttons escaped their holes and zippers rode the rails (*Oh Artie what is it about you*), and everything would be all right as soon as I could get my hands on the inheritance that Mr. Henry left me.

As I walked in the prop-house door, back in the dimness behind the furniture something stirred, which turned out to be Joanne, the chubby prop apprentice, gimpies we called them. She was there fresh from high school to spend the summer learning about the theatre, but she had her eye on wider and wilder horizons, namely me. She had designs on my body, I could smell it. Now wrapped in a crew coat and huddled in a cruddy fraying old wicker chair she shifted her tail, her eyes brightened. "Oh, hi," she said sleepily (to tempt me?), but I was way ahead of her.

"Why don't you start with the chairs for the cafe scene?"

"The cafe scene, right."

"And then you can come back for the tables." The trick was to keep her busy. Dear Joanne: I am not interested but why don't you get a coat of paint on the prop house, the stage, and after that you can start on Euclid Avenue, which I am told runs to somewhere near Chicago. Wire if you need money. Yours truly.

And with her safely loaded down I was free to check what mattered. I lifted the lid of the tin dish that covered the canvas roast pheasant, dismal and brown with painted drumsticks, and there under the Pope's nose, right where I had stashed it, was the feather that had fallen from Mr. Henry's dying hand. I pulled it through my hand, felt the ripple of little tickles against the skin of my fingers, edges promising other edges, other tickles. Quickly I slipped it out of sight again on an upper shelf. Meanwhile Joanne was staggering back and forth under a mountain of tables and chairs. She thought to win me through diligence and efficiency, but I knew the Man Mountain Dean, the nonrigid dirigible which floated under her crew coat like an observation balloon in its hangar.

"Could we go over some things later?" she said. Busy-busy.

"Sure. Later."

And my mind was full of feathery, quivery things as I put my rear end against the prop table and backpedaled it thundering out of the prop house. Then running alongside to change direction at the same time (I was learning, I was learning), I trundled it like a mammoth baby buggy around the corner, scraped to a stop against a backstage tree, and plugged in the lights, then went to check on stage. The tables were set up, the chairs on their painted spike marks. A voice called "House open," and backing away I took one last look at everything just before the first of the audience wandered in. Coming back through the wings I passed Joanne still struggling under the last of the benches and nodded briskly to her.

"Something I wanna check. Hold the fort."

And I set sail for that feather in the prop house. On my way Prudie Rendlesham came briskly from the downstage light tower in her head-usher's shift, skating on the sides of her white ballet slippers all puffy and scuffy like large split marshmallows, heaved alongside, and gave me the hip. As I looked at her she arched one eyebrow, took my hand, and without a word led me around behind the prop house to the hidden angle where they park the pickup truck and scrub down the old scenery before repainting it. She promptly leaned back against the ivied wall, leaves scrunching down the back of her neck, and drew me against her white shift. Prudie rubbed against you whenever you talked; her material stuck to your material and you could feel her sliding around restlessly beneath it. She specialized in wearing things with one zipper, no buttons, jump suits, shifts, and smocks, demure but disposable.

"Good evening, sir," she said through unmoving lips, and gave something below her waist an experimental half-turn. "Can I show you to your seat?" Prudie was what my mother called well-spoken, but she was deliberately murmurous and ran her words together and affected what she thought was a sultry expression through half-lowered eyelids. Mostly she just looked sleepy.

"Something I can do for you, Prudie?"

"Mmmm. Funny boy."

"That's me. Well—" I started to turn.

"What's your hurry?"

"Nothing. I just gotta check something."

"Oh, pooh."

"Why, what's on your mind, little girl?"

"If you weren't always in such a hurry, you might find out. My goodness."

"Believe me, I'd love to, except you always catch me at the wrong time."

"I don't catch you at all, is my problem. Gracious!" She always accompanied the manipulations of her pelvis with little faintly scandalized puritan exclamations.

"I warn you, I'm going to take you up on that."

"If you don't," she said, "someone else will." And I felt her give an extra *utsch* down below. She was so frank it was hard to believe she meant it. But she did. I knew her back in high school, and she was famous for Meaning It. From the dressing room building then I could hear one of the chorus vocalizing, *Some day/ I will seek you and find you,* and Joanne's voice calling somewhere beyond the prop house, "Artie? Artie?"

Sure-ly

went the voice from the dressing room,

*You will come and remind me
Of a dream that is calling . . .*

But Joanne wasn't the dream, pudgy Joanne, over-ripe and rather like a very full hot-water bottle, with shifting hot air pockets. No, nor Prudie, either, whose

skin under those shifts and jumpers reminded you of
a sheared poodle, smooth but nubby, sort of, and
whose athletic kisses were rubbery, elastic but dry.
True, I had been having the usual predictable skir-
mishes with both of them in the few days since I had
joined the crew, here and there in every unlighted
corner in which I found myself with each. It made no
difference which one; there was no triumph in either.
There had always been that kind of girl back in high
school, even at college, the ones who couldn't make a
sorority because of their reputations. We cheerfully
called them pigs, and they proved nothing to Marlene
and the other milk-chocolate virgins, proved nothing
about the theatre or life—unless it was that you were
apt to find pigs everywhere. And if girls like Prudie
and Joanne only confirmed what girls like Marlene
and Mary Lou Busby thought about the theatre, anyway, just a collection of blackballs, how could they be
the dream?

No, I was beyond P. & J., I had enough of second-
stringers on high school hayrides; I was trading up.
Though the season was young my eye had already
been drawn to that brisk little redheaded dancer
named Ginger Treat (so help me), from the first
time I saw her walking away from me in tights that
were too small, a little vealy parenthesis of lean tushy
pinched out from each cheek, winking at me. Or as a
possible alternate there was Dolores Hrka, a Bohe-
mian contralto with long Shirley Temple curls and
something promising about the blankness of her
smile, maybe she wouldn't quite notice what you were
doing to her. They were not in Ramona's league, of
course, that zipping and buttoning apparition. But

then neither was I. And you had to start working your way up somewhere.

I disengaged my gears from Prudie.

"It's just I have to check something," I said.

Quickly into the prop house. Quickly grabbed the feather, slipped it into—which pocket? Not the inside where it tickled, not the back where it would get crushed. Finally I settled for twiddling it non-chalantly in my fingers as though it were a baton. It was ridiculous, of course, and for just a moment my heart quavered at the silliness of it. Never mind; at least it was something. I folded my cuffs. I tucked in my shirt, then flipped the collar of my crew coat so that it stood up at the back. Loose, that was me. Jaunty. Bold. Boldness the order of the day. Ginger was the favorite but the singers were closer, and I marched to Dolores's dressing room first. Squirrelly, I scratched at the door.

Nothing.

Again, louder.

"Speak, O noble one."

"Excuse me," I said, hoping it sounded noble enough. "Say, Dolores there?"

"Who?"

"You know, Erka." (How the hell did you say it?)

"Who?"

"You know—*Dolores*."

"Oh. Hey, Ruckka. It's a man for you."

"Oh, for heaven's sake. Just when I'm—"

The door opened. Two inches. Shirley Temple minus the curls, her head a briar patch of crossed hairpins. Pox-dabs of makeup sprinkled her face, about to be spread. "Yeah, what is it," she said shortly.

"Listen, I'm sorry to bother you, but I thought I oughta check this—"

"Does it have to be now? Because I'm not even combed out yet, and it's—"

"Yeah, I know, I'm sorry, but I hadda check," I said quickly. "I just wondered—you didn't by any chance lose something, did you? From your costume?"

"What is that, a feather?"

"Yeah, you wanta watch that shedding now," I said gaily. She looked at me with a blank expression. "I'm Artie Shoemaker—"

"We don't wear feathers."

"You don't?"

"Look, I'm not combed out yet—" She started to close the door.

"Maybe I'd better check with you later on it."

"I told you, we don't wear feathers," she said impatiently. "I just have that one little marabou fringe in the tavern."

"Yeah, well, I'll check with you later." I smiled airily, nodded my head briskly, very businesslike. And ran.

"What was all that?" I heard behind me.

"I don't know. Some character with a feather." And the door slammed.

I made my way along the corridor, pausing to regroup my forces at the bulletin board, cheered by the way everyone wandered around in a state of undress and no one minded. Life in the raw. And finally got myself to the dancers' dressing room, Pilgrim's Progress.

I knuckled the right hand, waved it vaguely at the door. It happened to knock.

"Yeah?" A throaty voice from within.

"Treat there?"

Then off, "Ginger, for you." An indistinguishable mumble in reply. (I could make out the word, ". . . Jesus.")

"Who wants her?"

"Shoemaker."

"Who?"

I swallowed my saliva. "Artie Shoemaker. From the crew." And heard the female bass say, again off, "Shoemaker-Something, I don't know." Again the mumble, then, "Well, how long you gonna be *in* there?" And finally to me, "She's tied up right now," followed by a laugh.

"I just have to check with her on something," I said, and heard the echo repeat within, "Says he has to check on something, I don't know." Another pause. Then to me, "Check on what?"

"Oh, look," I said, pretending that my patience was at an end because what were we being so formal about, and opened the door. Screams, consternation. A hasty scraping of chairs, a scramble for robes and towels, a jangle of combs and curlers clattering to the floor, bare backs and bra straps, Ginger half out of the john with a newspaper clutched to her chest.

"Listen, do you MIND?"

"What's all the panic?" I said casually but with eyes like porcelain saucers, pale, white, translucent. I backed out, fumbling behind me for the doorknob. "Now you happy?" I said from the other side again. "It's just I found a feather, and I thought I'd better check with you on it."

"A what?" The door opened a slit. I was presented with a bullet-head, hair pulled back to let her get at her makeup, a bony chest.

"A feather." I twirled it, smiling, smiling, till my face ached.

"What about it?"

"Maybe it dropped from your costume. Maybe, you know?"

She craned a corded neck back toward the dressing room behind her. (Dancers could be very cordy when you were up close.) "Anybody here lose a feather?"

"A *what?*" from the girls. Boy, they thought that was excruciating. "Hey, lose your feather lately?" and so on.

"Yeah, Popeyes here says he found a feather."

"Shoemaker," I muttered. "Artie. From the crew." My cuff had fallen again.

"Well, sorry, Shoemaker-Artie-from-the-crew, no feathers lost here," she said good-naturedly. "Us chickens here are all plucked." There was a howl of laughter in the room behind her. People in the corridor stopped to look. Even Harry stuck his head out of his dressing room to see what was going on.

That did it. I figured to make my move, but not with an audience of eight guffawing women and in Grand Central Station, to boot. I backed away. "That's all right," I said. "Maybe I ought to check with you later on it." (Mercifully the stage manager was calling, "Five minutes, five minutes, please.")

"You do that, Popeyes."

"Yeah. I'll definitely check with you later."

Her tongue tickling my back every step of the way, I hastily strode with great purpose out of the dressing room building right down into the middle of the backstage area; until with my head swollen and light, some great red balloon tethered at the end of my foolish neck, I looked down and saw my striding body and knew it had nowhere to go. And gratefully lost myself in the general shuffle of curtain time.

As the show went on I kept careful watch. At the prop table, up behind the scenery, down in both wings. I covered a lot of ground, but still no Ginger—that is, not by herself, not without a lot of goons leaning over her shoulder. Yet around me others managed. There came tiny Brenda-Something-the-dancer, pubey but nubey, heading for the dressing room to change; as she passed, Bob Westervelt lounged off a tree and followed her, twitching with purpose. Shenker was standing nearby with the other elder, Roy Bliss, who winked and said Be careful, Roberto. Beware the ass-p, lest you learn its sting. Oh my assp said Shenker. He and Bliss laughed, the senior chuckle, but Westervelt growled Awright you guys, and kept right on walking. I watched him and tiny Brenda disappear into the light of the dressing room corridor. All right, you guys; around on the other side I, too, station myself against a tree. It is a zoo, but I am a night animal, I will strike in the dark.

Wait a minute. Wasn't this the scene when the dancers had to wait behind the upstage harem wall? Right. Right. Now I had my own purpose. Not to be deflected when Joanne appeared suddenly with a prop pince-nez in one hand and its chain in another. "It *broke*," she said urgently. "How," I said, poised to leave. "Well, he was waving it," she said; "I told him not to wave it, but Fibby waves everything." "Right, we'll fix it tomorrow." "But he needs it in the next *scene*." An emergency. Joanne loved emergencies. Emergencies and my body were the reason she was in the theatre. "Okay, paste it," I said. "Paste it? Will it dry in time?" "All right, then use friction tape," I said, still on one foot. (Guess whose pinched parenthesis I was thinking of. Of my assp.) "Friction tape?" "Sure, a little friction tape." "On the pince-nez?" "Listen, if you don't know how to use a little simple friction tape," I said—and escaped at last. But by the time I got over to the harem, Ginger was gone again.

And so it went. When she came off after the harem number I passed her going the other way loaded under with the campfire for the second desert scene (I nodded; she didn't see me) ; when I came off with the campfire again she was going on in her duster and goggles for the entrance of the motor girls. Either the girls were always off changing, or the scenery was. Finally, about halfway through the last act, my big chance; a spot when she had no change and neither did I, except to return some Moorish tambourines. I hurtled back toward the prop table with the tambourines, ready to drop them and dash after her, when a movement caught my eye. Someone poking around the table, bent over. Filmy harem tights. Little pussy-willow feet rounded in black ballet shoes. Softly bowed legs. Pleasure-bent. About to unbend. I hesitated. She straightened up. My heart took a funny jump. It was Ramona.

"Something I can do for you?" Cool, that's me.

"Listen," she said distractedly (which made two of us) , "I'm going crazy. Did you by any chance come across a feather?"

"A what?" I said, blinking.

"I know it sounds ridiculous, but it came off this thing somewhere." She was looking dubiously at her costume. I was looking, too. "Don't ask me how feathers come to a harem, but if I don't find it they'll kill me." She picked up a quill pen from the table and was idly pulling it through her fingers. "—Oh, I'm sorry," she said suddenly. "Am I doing something I shouldn't?"

"Not that I can see," I said with simple admiration. "Why, what're you doing?"

"I don't know, but you were—" She hesitated.

"Were what?"

"Looking at me. Funny."

"I was? No, I wasn't. Why should I?"

"I don't know. I thought maybe I was doing something."

"Well, am I looking at you funny now?" I started rearranging the wine glasses into three rows of four instead of four rows of three.

"No. Well, I guess you're busy, huh."

I pulled my hand back from the glasses so fast I almost knocked one off the prop table. "No, no, not really," I said, catching the glass. "I'm just trying to see how many glasses I can break." She laughed. I pulled the feather from my pocket and held it up. "This what you're looking for?"

"Oh, thank God," she said. "You saved my life. Spratt just *loves* people from New York as it is." I could smell her makeup as she stepped in close to take the feather from my hand. Out of the corner of my eye I saw Ginger and the other girls lining up behind the desert fort for their entrance. Don't ask me what I was waiting for.

"You're from New York?" I said.

"Are you kidding, can't you tell?"

"Am I supposed to? Anyway, what's Spratt got against New York?"

"It's there, and he isn't, I guess." She shrugged.

"He's not the only one. There's a certain dislike of New Yorkers around here, a certain, I don't know, resentment. People resent it."

"Who resents it? No, they don't. I don't," I said stoutly.

"You're sweet." (That's what you think, Ramona, ol' kid, secretly I'm an animal. Or would be, if I could get the chance.) "Believe me, all I had to do was open my mouth and I was cooked."

"Why? You don't sound like you're from New York."

"Sure, I do." She smiled. "You just haven't been there. Actually, it's Brooklyn, right in the heart of Flatbush. You ever been to Brooklyn?"

"No. I haven't been to New York. I haven't even been east of Ashtabula." But should I tell her where I am beginning to see myself in the years ahead, should I tell her that in my mind New York is a city always in twilight, twilight just at the moment the streetlights come on, always in that instant of incandescence, and O should I tell her? "That is, not yet, anyway."

"See? There."

"One of these days, maybe. But you still don't sound like it to me."

"Yeh?" she said in a thick Brooklyn accent. "Dun't beleeve ev'rything yuh heah." And winked. Then waving the feather as she turned to go, "Anyway, thanks for the lifesaver."

"Any time, Ramona kid, any time."

She stopped. "Hey. You know my name."

"Well, I've seen you with Cooky," I said, and she looked right at me. I dropped my eyes. "You know, around."

"Yes?" she said. Then with an oddly veiled expression, "Don't believe everything you see either." She waved again and stuck the feather in the back of her waistband where it quivered as she walked away like an arrow pointing to the spot, sunk deep where it counted. O prophetic movement!

However. It was time to leave off dreaming and get back to business, for suddenly there was Ginger again and my God alone at last, heading upstage. "Hey, Treat," I called hoarsely. But as she stepped into the dressing room corridor Shenker and Bliss stepped out of it going the other way. With their crew coats tightly closed and their arms folded across their chests they stared serenely upward like a pair of antic mandarins.

"Observe the trees," Shenker was saying to Bliss as they came toward me. "Observe these crummy crumbs of Ohio nature, it's the crotch of the world."

"Yes, the crotch indeed," said Bliss. "Yes."

As they shouldered past on either side of me, one of them reached from under his crew coat and crammed a clump of damp cloth into my hands. "All right, you comedians," I started to say but they went right on by, muttering something about Get rid of it, get rid of it, and over their shoulders then I saw Sherman Spratt peering out of the dressing room corridor. He was wearing only his shorts.

"D'Angeli?" he called plaintively. "D'Angeli?"

I stuffed the pants under my crew coat. They were clammy and smelled faintly of public drains. Up at the dressing room doorway D'Angeli had appeared and was listening to Spratt, who was waving his arms wildly toward the dressing rooms, then out to the stage, his face a puckered fury. Members of the com-

pany walked by with quick, nervous glances at the
two of them, then hurried on without looking at each
other. Cutting around the worktables I passed Westervelt; he nonchalantly looked the other way. So he
knew, too. Nearby, Hlavacek cleared his throat conspicuously; they all knew. Spratt would be going home
in his bathrobe tonight.

Walking briskly I slipped through the door to the
auditorium at the light tower and onto the far aisle,
then into the bushes along the side of the auditorium,
out of sight and running because I didn't want to be
missed, my heart pounding, drunk with the madness
of reality—the reality that only we at the theatre were
permitted to know. Because it was one thing to
dream, to plan revenges. It was one thing to talk of
Spratt's pants and urinals, everyone could do that,
and did; but *actually* to sneak them away while he
thought they were being pressed and *actually* to
throw them in, *actually* to stand there and pee on
them, that was something else. That was stepping
over the line into some wilder level of reality, some
other dimension in which the truth of life was its
dreams, and its dreams, the truth. And *that* was the
theatre. Go explain that to my mother.

In the parking lot at the top of the hill I pitched
the pants into the back seat of the Pontiac, shook my
crew coat once or twice to air it out, then tore back
down the hill through the bushes. The finale was just
winding up as I slipped backstage again through the
light tower door. I drifted around, nodding at Shenker, winking at Bliss, raising my eyebrows at Westervelt. Coolness in the trenches, bravery under fire,
Daring was my middle name. I was ready to be deco-

rated and started to look for Ginger—but that wasn't who called my name.

"So, Arthur. Arthur!"

I turned around. Who should be chugging after me but Dr. Fuldauer, vest and all. "That's right," he said. "It is me, it is me, after all."

"Doctor Fuldauer, hi," I said distractedly, afraid I would miss the dancers again and trying to keep one eye out for the redhead. "What're you doing here?"

"You see, our paths cross again. I also am summoned by the mysteries of art." He seemed terribly excited about something.

"Well, that's . . , terrific," I said, still craning my head around. "So you enjoyed the show, huh."

"No, no, not enjoyed. I am *employed* now—just as you."

That stopped me. I looked at him. "Here?"

"Definitely, here. And I have you to thank."

"Who, me?" What was he talking about?

"I hear you say a theatre, so I call on the telephone. It seems they have an unexpected opening." He puffed out his chest and laughed. "You are gazing at the new watchman." Great, Mr. Henry's ghost, just what I needed. First half the chorus, then my kid brother's Latin tutor looking over my shoulder while I try to make out. "So," Dr. Fuldauer finished happily, "now we are colleagues, *hein*?"

"No kidding," I said, with as much enthusiasm as I could pump into a flat tire. "Terrific."

He was fairly bubbling. "Oh, it is a marvelous job, *wunderbar*. Later when everyone leaves, I sit with Virgil, with Cicero." He held up a paper bag, his voice suddenly confidential. "My wife gives me sandwiches. She worries a little. But I tell her the world is full of watchmen, why not me?"

The dancers were beginning to come off stage after the curtain call. I started to edge away. "Doctor Fuldauer, I—"

"You know, we also had in Düsseldorf a marvelous theatre," he said, rushing right on, "marvelous. In fact, I have some pictures. Here, look—" He was taking a frayed old envelope out of his pocket.

"Doctor Fuldauer, I wish I could, I really do," I said, cutting him off as gently as possible. "But actually I'm supposed to meet someone."

Instantly his expression changed. "Ah. Of course," he said, full of buddy-understanding. "A fellow artist. Go, go ahead. Virgil and Düsseldorf, we will all be here tomorrow."

That's what I'm afraid of, I thought as I fled up-stage. At the main backstage entrance I could see the usual after-the-show crowd starting to gather, waiting with congratulations and gushes. The actors were heading for their dressing rooms, giddy and loud, the gears already shifting into the bright and floating hour that follows the performance. I just had time to fall in step with Ginger. At last.

"Hey, just the girl I'm looking for."

"Well, if it isn't Popeyes."

"Yeah, beep-beep," I said. "Listen, do you happen to be doing anything after the show? I mean, why don't we chug a couple?"

"Awww, what's the matter, nobody wanted your feather? Poor boy, nobody wanted his feather."

"Actually, I tried to check with you before, but we had a slight emergency back here." I wasn't sure whether to say anything about Spratt's pants or not.

Crew was crew and actors were actors, but you never knew where dancers stood.

"Boy, you've really got your problems, haven't you, Popeyes?" She was teasing, but there was something nice about her all the same.

"Yeah, so I thought you could console me over a slight libation at Caruso's."

"A slight what?" We had reached the dressing rooms now, and some chorus guy in a Legionnaire's uniform called from down the corridor, "Hey, Ginge, ten minutes, right?" and she called back, "Yeah, yeah."

"—So I thought maybe a slight beer," I finished lamely.

"Gee, Popeyes, why didn't you open your mouth earlier?"

"I was going to open my mouth, but there was this slight emergency, see, and I was—"

"Come on, Treat," the chorus guy yelled again, "move it or milk it."

"Okay, don't get your bowels in an uproar," she called back, her hand on the doorknob. "Sorry," she said cheerfully to me. "The next time you've got a spare feather, look me up." And the door closed behind her. Shit-shit-shit. Well, there was always Shirley Temple Ruckka. Without missing a beat I hurried down to the room of the girl singers, rapped boldly on the door. Bull by the horns.

"Speak," said a voice.

"Yeah, is Ruckka there?"

"I haven't seen her."

"Well, tell her I'll be back, willya? It's Artie Shoemaker."

"Who?"

"From the crew. The character with the feather."

"*Who?*"

"Never mind. I'll be back."

I took a turn around the stage. It was empty. I unplugged the prop table and trundled it into the prop house like a madman. Joanne was rupturing herself under the last of the cafe tables and chairs. "What's the work sheet for tomorrow?" she asked, ready for a cozy conference. Dear Joanne: Nothing doing. "Check with me on it in the morning," I said, pulling down the folding door. In the orchestra pit the tarp was already on the piano, and around the scenery the lash lines were being thrown. "Coming over," called a voice. "So come already," muttered Cooky, tucking his shirt while he waited to grab the rope on the other side. "I ain't got all night."

In the crew room Westervelt was combing his hair as Bliss and Shenker watched. "Hey, Bob," I said, "wanna hack around, maybe chug a couple?" With his comb Westervelt gave a final loving flip to a widow's peak as blond and creamy as frozen custard. "Sorry, Shoemaker. Me and Hlavacek got girls, we're gonna hit the beach. Cooky might hook up with us later." Shenker laughed owlishly. "Yeah, Roberto is gonna toast her marshmallow, aren't you Roberto?" "Not to mention," said Bliss primly, "what she will do to his." "Awright, you guys," said Westervelt, slipping the comb in a pocket next to his heart. I hung up my crew coat, folded my cuffs, and went back to the girl singers' door. I knocked again. "Ruckka there yet?"

"Who?" Another voice.

"Ruckka."

"I think she's gone."

"What? Are you sure?"

"Hey, anybody see Ruckka?" Then to me, "Yeah, she came in and left, I think."

"Well, if you see her, tell her Shoemaker will be waiting at the box-office gate, okay?"

"Who?"

"Shoemaker, from the crew."

"Okay. But I think she's gone."

"Yeah, well, if you see her."

I walked through the backstage gate and leaned against the box office wall. The couples wandered past. Ramona came out with Cooky, smiled vacantly at me, then stared carefully at the ground before her. Cooky turned to walk backward, calling, "Hey, in about an hour out at Mentor, right?" From somewhere backstage Westervelt's voice hollered, "Right," and Cooky turned to walk on. He took Ramona's arm. His hair was freshly combed and gleamed wetly in the lamplight. I glanced at her, then away again. When they're out of your league, they're out of your league. I walked restlessly in a small circle, then leaned against the building again.

A few minutes later, Westervelt and a girl came out. It was tiny Brenda-Something, and she laughed as he walked by flexing his muscles. Then Harry and Fibby sauntered by, Harry with his brunette and Fibby with the chubby comedienne. Harry had drawn the girl's arm around his own waist, something I had never seen anyone else do. Except maybe Melvyn Douglas. "Hey, Shoemaker," called Harry. "Got a date? We gonna see you there?"

"You never know," I answered brightly. Cool, that

was me. Bravery under fire. Harry and Fibby disappeared up the path.

After a while a policeman shuffled to the gate. "Closing up," he said. "Everybody gone. You better get home, fella." The padlock snapped shut. He shuffled away. In a moment the lights in the dressing room building went off. Only the work light gleamed blotchily through the trees from the prop house. In its faint glow I could see Dr. Fuldauer sitting at the door, reading Cicero. Or Virgil. I turned and went up the hill to the parking lot. The Pontiac was the only car there.

I drove up to Taylor, slowing down to see who was going into Caruso's. Then for no reason I turned left and headed the other way, driving here and there through the night streets; once up past Marlene Goldhammer's house (where there was a light on in the living room and a darkened car like a squat toad in the driveway), smiling because I pitied her. When I came around the block again an hour later the car was still there. I cranked down the window and tossed Spratt's pants on her lawn, a salute from Artie Shoemaker. Then finally headed over to our driveway, where I coasted into the dark garage. For a time I just sat in the silent car. Oh, well, at least it was late.

When I came into the house Sanford was at the kitchen counter having some brownies and milk.

I glanced upward. "They in bed?" He nodded. Without another word I took my anatomy textbook from the counter, plopped it open on the kitchen table, and sat down. Sanford regarded me a moment.

"Well," he said, "I see you made your move, Tiger."

"Don't worry about me," I said, carefully avoiding his eye. "I . . . I may get a call."

"Oh, sure, sure. I mean, it's a known fact they all boff."

I glared at him. Thirteen-year-olds can be infuriating. "Boy, would you laugh if that phone rang right now."

"Yeah," he said. "I'd be hysterical."

The phone rang.

For a startled second we both just looked at it. Then I grabbed the receiver before it could ring again. "Yeah, hello," I said.

"Remember me? I play the drum," came Crystal's voice over the line.

"Oh, Harry—hi," I said casually, as though I got chatty phone calls at twelve thirty every night. I was watching Sanford's astonished expression with relish.

"What the hell happened to you, Shoemaker?" said Harry. "I'm lucky I found your number. Get your ass over here."

I caught my breath; I couldn't help it. "What, you mean now? Where are you?"

"Where the hell do you think I am?" he said, and hung up.

I was left with the phone in my hand. Slowly I hung up, then gave a the-general-died-at-dawn shrug and headed for the door. Sanford was watching bug-eyed, impressed in spite of himself.

"Artie, do you know how *late* it is? Where you going?"

"Caruso's."

"What's that?"

My answer was pure Melvyn Douglas. "Where everybody goes, baby. Where everybody goes."

When I cranked up the Pontiac and backed out of the driveway in the night, upstairs in my parents' darkened bedroom there was no movement. Only a heavy, wordless sigh, so loud that Sanford could hear it in the kitchen.

Halfway down the block, without hearing it, I heard it, too.

7

Love is a queer little elfin sprite
Blessed with the deadliest aim
Shooting his arrows from left to right
Bagging the rarest game . . .

—The Red Mill

For nine months a year Caruso's Coach House and Grill was nothing special, just a nondescript neighborhood bar in a neighborhood where nobody went to bars. From September to May the handful of customers mostly ran to tradespeople who worked nearby but didn't live there, the butcher and the mechanic from the Sohio station on the corner plus a few others, not so much truck drivers as deliverers, the guys who delivered for the dry cleaner, the bakery, the delicatessen. With only two undecorated rooms, bare wooden floor, a skee-ball game and a jukebox the place didn't exactly rate up there with the Stork Club.

But for three months starting each June another set of deliverers took over. For that was when the Theatre was underway; and during the summer season the bar was visited by the Magi, whose gift was to turn Caruso's shabby crib into a manger full of

messiahs, the members of the Kempton Hills company. Each night the little neighborhood place was
transformed into that hallowed summer theatre insti-
tution, the local bar which becomes theatre property
after the evening performance. The management of
Caruso's didn't know from tradition, but they were
glad to have the business.

When I got there the joint was loaded with Kempton Hills people, actors and crew. I spotted Harry
right away, sitting with Fibby, their women and two
or three others at a commanding table right in the
middle of the room, all of them waiting for Fibby to
reach the climax of another of his stories. Just inside
the door, I waited, too.

There was a double-shot boilermaker on the table
in front of Fibby, and while he talked his hand never
left the glass. In his late fifties now, he had jobbed in
from New York for the season. He possessed a deep,
throbbing stage voice and had been featured on
Broadway somewhere in the past, I knew that. But
sometimes it seemed he had not had a career, he had
merely had stories.

"So it's a long tour," Fibby was saying, "and we're
both going out of our tiny minds, right? So we keep
trying to break each other up on stage, naturally. So
finally we're playing this split-week in the Oddfellows
Hall or something in Scranton—which believe me is
the armpit of the *entire* world—and I had it all set up
with the stage manager, see. So that night I'm on
stage with her and she goes into her big second-act
monologue, and right in the middle—the phone on
stage starts to ring. So first she tries to ignore it, but it
keeps ringing. She looks at me but to *kill*—and I just
smile. Meanwhile, it's ringing, ringing, ringing, so fi-

THOSE LIPS, THOSE EYES

nally she picks it up and listens. Then she holds out
the receiver to me with this sweet smile, and says—"

" '—It's for you,' " said Harry, stealing the punch
line. "It was funnier the first time—when the Lunts
did it."

As the others laughed Fibby said good-naturedly,
"I'll get you for that, Harry." One thing about Fibby,
he never worried if you walked on his punch lines.
What did he care, he always had another story—probably about how somebody walked on his punch line
in the Elks Club in Altoona.

"Well, I finally made it," I said brightly as I walked
up to them.

"Sound the trumpets," said Fibby, and raised his
hand for another double boilermaker.

"You guys all know Shoemaker, the demon propman?" said Harry. There were nods and smiles
around the table.

"So what's up?" I asked. "You said to drop over."

Harry looked at me blankly and shrugged. "Don't
ask me." He paused, then glanced off to one side. "I
was calling for a friend."

I turned, following his eyes.

There across the room at a far table, Ramona was
sitting—alone. Her eyes were waiting for me. She
smiled just a little nervously and nodded her head
slightly, once. Jesus. Jesus H. Christ.

I started toward her. There is a special edge I have
felt with women two, maybe three times in my life.
Once was when I left a party in high school because
Mary Lou Busby had sent in a message that she was
waiting for me in a car outside. Another was when
Marlene Goldhammer ran across a crowded dance

floor to tell me she was sorry (it lasted a week) and I watched her pluperfect head come all the way through the other couples. I don't remember the third time but I threw it in because even in my life there must have been more than two. It is a feeling of pleasure that is so keen, so full of expanding anticipation you almost pray that time will stop, and it damn near does.

That stroll across the room at Caruso's was the longest, lightest walk I had ever taken. Somewhere along the way I was dimly aware of Cooky sitting half-pissed and ugly at the bar, aware they must have had a fight, aware of him glowering first at Ramona, then me, and especially at Harry for arranging it all, but who cared? On I went, across the room toward that face, the waiting attitude of the shoulders—not just expectant but receptive, promising there was nothing behind us, only what was ahead. Boy, did I enjoy that walk. After a month or so, I got to her table.

"Madam," I said. "Is this seat taken?"

With just a trace of a smile, still looking at me she said, "I . . . hope so."

I slid into the chair. Amazing how you can sit and float at the same time.

Across the room Harry looked impatiently at a nearby phone booth in which an actor had just hung up. In the same motion the actor picked up the receiver again, about to dial another number. Harry frowned. "Come on, willya?" he called. "Let it breathe a minute."

At the bar Cooky slowly looked up. He focused woozily on Harry, his eyes glittering dangerously.

The actor in the phone booth hesitated. "Give the rest of us a break," Harry went on. "I'm expecting a call—"

At that Cooky exploded off the bar stool. He lurched across to the phone booth, pulled the startled actor out, then flung himself melodramatically across the folding door.

"Oh, yeah," he declaimed loudly to the room, "stay off the phone, to be sure! To be *sure*. Nobody touch the phone, gotta keep the line clear. Because this is Harry Crystal's personal phone in person, the great Harry Crystal is expecting his nightly call—*which never comes*."

"It happens to be long distance—" Harry began mildly.

"Oh, long distance, did you all hear that?" Cooky shouted. A nervous, muttery silence had fallen across the room as the crowd watched him wave his arms, smelling something ugly ahead. "Long distance, long distance for Mister Hotshit Crystal. And I'll bet it's New York, right?" Harry said nothing, merely took a poker-faced swallow of his beer. "Oh, yes," shouted Cooky, with another reeling wave of his arms, "the famous call from the famous agent, the famous Mickey Bellinger. Oh, yes, he's coming to see Mister Hotshit Crystal, a special trip just to catch his performance in *The Red Mill*—I mean, *Desert Song*. I'm sorry, I get confused," he said with elaborate apology. "When *was* it he was supposed to come? Do tell us, Mister Crystal. Was it last week or the week before that or this week or next week—*or no week*?"

Harry smiled tightly at Fibby. "Catch this. At least a Tony Award performance."

"Oh, but never mind, gotta keep that line open,"

Cooky said loudly, and took a step toward Harry's table. "I mean, no telling who might call. It could be some of Mister Crystal's famous friends." Harry's smile turned cold, but he controlled himself. Cooky's sarcasm was whiskeythick. "Maybe Kit Cornell or Josh Logan." He paused. "Maybe the Lunts—whoever they are."

That did it.

Harry's head snapped up. His voice was tight. "Oh, they're nobody. Nobody at all." Suddenly he burst out in a blaze of incredulity. "Jesus, *what business are you in?* What are you, some kind of mongoloid? Who do you dream of at night, what names are in your head? Gene Autry? Hoot Gibson? Howdy Doody? I'm not talking about a box in your living room or pieces of film three minutes long and pasted together—I'm talking about the *theatre.*" The room rang with his voice. "An actor daring people to look at him for two hours. I'm talking about Pauline Lord, Walter Hampden, Laurette Taylor, giants that haunt you for life." Then the very blood in his veins seemed to surge. "Putzo, *I saw Barrymore!*"

Suddenly with his arm reaching for heaven he froze, gasped for breath, his chest convulsed. And he slumped to the table.

There was an instant's stunned silence.

"Hey," said Cooky, all at once sober. "Hey, is he all right?"

Then a dozen voices broke out. "What happened?" "Somebody get a doctor—"

Fibby leaned urgently over the crumpled form. "Harry-boy, you hurt?"

A breathless pause; no one moved. Then slowly, with difficulty Harry raised his head. "Ay," he said hoarsely. "Ay . . . a scratch, a scratch, marry, 'tis enough. Where is my page. Go, villain, fetch a surgeon."

It was not Harry but Mercutio dying, with Barrymore's rumbling, magical voice, that historic moment from *Romeo and Juliet*. For a split second nobody quite knew what was happening; there was not a sound in the bar except for Harry's labored breathing. He was in absolute command. Without hesitation Fibby picked up the lines.

"Courage, man, the hurt cannot be much."

"No, 'tis not so deep as a well, nor so wide as a church door, but 'tis enough, 'twill serve—ask for me tomorrow, and you shall find me a grave man." A sudden spasm lifted Harry upright in pain, anguish, and glory. "A plague o' both your houses!" he cried. A long pause. His head was sinking back to the table. With a last magnificent effort, in a voice already in the grave the words came. "They have made . . . worms' meat of me." The head was down.

Utter silence. Every face was riveted on Harry. Suddenly he popped his eyes open at Cooky—who was spellbound along with the rest—and impishly gave him the finger. Then with a wicked grin glanced across the room to Ramona's table. Like a cocked blunderbuss, like a bull that has been fixed by the empty cape, Cooky swiveled hastily to follow his gaze.

By then, of course, the table was empty. Ramona and I were gone. Long gone.

I headed the Pontiac down to the Western Reserve campus, all but holding my breath while Ramona sat silently by my side. I was thinking so hard I almost gave myself a fever. Where? Where? Finally I took a right on Magnolia Drive, then turned into the drive of a large old-fashioned house and pulled right into the back. A number of other cars were parked around the dark yard.

As Ramona looked uncertainly at the shadowy couples in the other cars I laughed self-consciously. "Ladies and Gentlemen. If you're wondering why I brought you all together . . ."

"Yoicks. Where are we?" she said.

"Behind my fraternity house." I shrugged helplessly. "I didn't know where else to go."

"Well. At least it's dark."

There was an awkward pause while we just sat there.

"All right," I said finally. "Why me?"

"Why not?"

"Are you kidding? Things like this don't happen to me, God doesn't allow it. Here's Cooky, this big jock operator—"

"A little too jock, maybe. Could be I need something else once in a while," she said softly.

"Such as?"

All at once she put her finger on my lips. Her voice was music in the dark. "Hey, hey—Mr. Shoemaker. Do yourself a favor, don't ask so many questions. You'll only be disappointed. There's nothing special to say about me. I'm just trying to get through the summer, that's all." She paused. The air in the car was electric, still. Then with a faint smile she said, "So if you're wondering why I brought you all together . . ." Her voice trailed off. She looked at me, waiting.

I didn't do anything spectacular, just turned to her. And she came into my arms, paused, and lifted her

mouth to mine. I tasted all the flavors; the firmness at
the edges, the softness in the middle, a hint of cold
cream, a lingering lick of pancake base, New York,
Brooklyn, and the white line down Broadway. Then
her lips parted naturally like a sigh and like a sigh
I drifted inside, exploring the Amazon, a trip up the
blue Nile. Ramona. Ramona the Queen of the Nile
At last we broke for a moment.

"God," I said huskily, "I'd love to think of something clever—"

She silenced me with another kiss. My hands went
under her blouse, wsich had somehow magically
come loose in one corner, slipped up and over that
rounded angle where her side became her back, along
the snowy field of skin, then snagged on the strap of
her brassiere stretched like a high tension line across
her back, begging to be released. As my fingers
groped, searching for something to loosen, she pulled
back gently. I froze, afraid I had been too clumsy,
gone too far. But all she said was, "Wait. It's a
French bra, it unhooks in front." I started to reach,
but she restrained my hand. "No, let me," she said
with the sweetest smile of all. "I know the way."

Pulling up her blouse one side at a time, she raised
it above the bra, undid the clasp, let the two sides fall
free. And two alabaster breasts swam up out of the
darkness toward my dazzled eyes. They went to my
hands like pigeons to the nest. We settled against
each other and began to sink slowly down in the
seat—when the glare of headlights abruptly swept past
us. Ramona blinked, then instantly turned her chest
against the seat, vanishing into her shell.

"It's okay," I said, looking hastily around, "just
some character pulling out." But when I turned back

she was quickly refastening the bra. Gone. Good-bye, Pigeons.

"Look, don't hate me," she said, rattled, "But I can't, not this way. I'm just getting too old to play Fumble-Johnny in parked cars. Maybe some other time when things feel right—"

I would never have to be guillotined; I now knew what it felt like. "Oh," I said. "Sure."

"We've got the whole season—"

"Sure, I understand."

She looked earnestly at the expression on my face. "Say you don't hate me."

I sighed. What the hell. "No, that's okay," I said. "I'm probably dreaming this whole thing, anyway. I'll probably wake up tomorrow, and you'll turn out to be my kid brother in the next bed."

She glanced playfully at my crotch, where the jeans were stretched tightly over my erection. "I doubt it." Then with a look that was part apology, part affection, and part plain common sense she gave the bulge a rueful little pat. "Poor fella. I hate to send him home in that condition."

Be a man, Shoemaker. If it kills you.

"Oh . . . I said. "He'll survive."

"This," said Professor Clement Brown the next morning, "is a spermatazoon." He was standing in front of a large drawing of a sperm cell on the blackboard. "I'm sure you've all seen them in large quantities," he drawled laconically; "we are going to study them one by one." He paused to look admiringly at the drawing. "Cute little tyke . . . don't you think, Shoemaker?" Pause. *Shoemaker.*

I sat up, startled, still half asleep. "Sir?"

"Are you with us, Shoemaker?"

"Yes, sir."

"I hope so. Trace the urogenital system for us, please."

"Uh, the testes," I started, "mesonephric duct, vas deferens, seminal vesicle . . . uh, seminal vesicle—"

"—Seminal vesicle, vestigial oviduct, cloaca," snapped Brown. Then he sighed. "Shoemaker, if you don't know the way," he said sadly, tapping the blackboard drawing with his pointer, "how will our hero ever get out?"

8

In old New York
In old New York
The peach crop's always fine
They're sweet and fair
And on the Square
The maids of Man-hat-tan for mine . . .

—The Red Mill

I did eventually get out, of course. The question was, what I got into.

I came to New York seventeen years ago fresh from graduate work (at a prestigious but generally useless drama school) and set myself up with all the stan- in the Village, and two roommates from the same dard beginer's equipment. No job, a shitty apartment drama school who didn't think much of my writing. But that was all right, because in those days I wasn't doing much of it, anyway.

What I did instead was make the usual apprentice circuit; Jim Atkins on Sheridan Square for donuts in the (overslept) morning, Rienzi's coffeehouse on Macdougal in the afternoons, and from there to the Figaro for another cup, drinking cappuccino I didn't want and couldn't afford, watching the other people and trying to figure out why they weren't obsessed with the sense of wasted time the way I was, wondering when they actually did any work. That, plus second-acting all the shows, going without an overcoat in December so you could pretend you had just come out of the theatre for intermission and your coat was inside, picking up a program in the lobby and walking in for the second act as though you had a seat; and the Bring-Your-Own parties in brownstone walkups and the midnight phone calls to anyone, it didn't matter who, just so you could keep yourself moving and put off that hour when the light would be out and you would be in bed with no one but yourself to talk to and have to listen to the dull throb of self-reproach. Also, the borrowing of money and the arguing over why Kazan had directed this moment that way and what Tennessee Williams *really* meant in *Camino Real* and whether Logan was gifted or merely commercial; and occasionally throwing yourself on the mercy of your married friends outside the theatre for a decent meal and the rage you felt when they had the nerve to start families of their own because that made you notice the time going by and above all what you never did was look at the calendar, because you were in the theatre and it was all going to happen. Tomorrow. In short, after two or three years I was a perfect candidate for oblivion. And then I got what I guess was my first break.

Two actress friends of mine tried out for the Actors Studio and used a scene from a one-act play I had written in drama school. One of the girls was an old-time buddy of mine, and the next morning I called to find out how it went.

"Don't ask me," she said in a peevish tone. "I should ask you. When we finished the scene they didn't say a word about either of us, they didn't ask us back for the next audition, nothing. All they wanted to know was who wrote the damned play."

So I got into the Playwrights' Unit at the Studio, which meant mostly that I could watch the acting sessions on Tuesdays and Fridays and listen to Lee Strasberg conduct the discussion afterward. There has been a lot of carping about Strasberg, but as far as I was concerned he made my drama school seem like kindergarten, he spoke with the true fire, and my days and nights after that were illuminated with the dream of art and theatre that had brought me barefoot and stumble-tongued to New York in the first place. As it turned out the Studio also became the crucial hinge on which my future turned, though not quite in the way I expected.

There was a cluster of young satellite would-be geniuses in orbit around Strasberg, naturally, dancing for attention at the feet of the Master. One of them was a whizbang named—will I ever forget it—Quentin Auerbach. He always sat at Strasberg's table in the local greasy spoon after class, and I heard he was looking for a project, something he could direct and present at the acting sessions. I hadn't written a word since I had been in New York, of course; but I rummaged through my old plays from drama school, dug out the one that seemed the least dewy and naive, and gave it to him.

"I am attracted to your piece," said Quentin at the acting session the following week. He always called plays pieces. It gave them the quality of an exercise at the piano, something that could be endlessly fingered and fiddled with, and never completed. Quentin taught some beginning sensory classes of his own somewhere and had all the jargon down cold. Actors didn't play roles, they performed tasks; they didn't have characterizations, they exhibited behavior. He was also fond of cryptic mottoes like Acting Is Not Acting and Trust The Work. "This project could make an important statement," he finished in holy tones. "I think the writing reveals a profound drive for spiritual health."

Since the play was about a young doctor who was a monumental fuck-up, that made me a little uneasy right from the start. Everything I wrote in those early days seemed to be about people who failed, I suppose in some perverse attempt to purge the rage I felt about myself. It was my subject, just as repressed sensuality was for Tennessee Williams. He was liberating sex, I was liberating failure—no matter what Quentin Auerbach called it. But when, after the first two weeks of rehearsal I tactfully suggested that everything in the play was being given the exact opposite meaning of what had been intended, Quentin took it as a compliment. "Any hack can direct a play the way it was written," he said. "Playing it against the lines makes it more interesting."

I tried to see it his way, but the awful truth became clearer with every passing day. The play made no sense like that, and I was about to fall on my ass in front of the most important theatrical talents in New York. Strasberg, Kazan and company watching Artie Shoemaker played against the lines. Finally after the dress rehearsal I could keep silent no longer.

"Quentin," I said, "this is going to be a disaster."

"Trust the work," he said.

So I did, and it was. Strasberg sat through the performance, listened patiently to all the perfunctory congratulations from the audience, then dispassionately proceeded to disembowel everyone in sight. The characters in the play were distasteful, he said; the antagonist was a boob, the protagonist was a boob, who could sympathize with such a love of failure? But futhermore who could really tell anything about the writing in the first place when the director was the boobiest of all and did the script in a way that made no sense? Amen. I had the satisfaction of seeing Quentin get his, but I watched from the confines of my own cozy grave. Poor Strasberg. A genius can't help what his disciples do in his name, and I never held him responsible for Quentin Auerbach. That would be like blaming Jesus for Oral Roberts.

I took the whole thing rather well, I give myself credit; except that the morning after the debacle I woke up with a raging stiff neck.

And an idea for a movie.

Incredibly enough, only a year and a half later it was actually sold to Warner Brothers. I was almost delirious. I had visions of sixty or seventy thousand dollars, I saw houses in Easthampton for the season, charge accounts at Meledandri, E-type Jaguars, my first real money in show business, the beginning of fame and fortune. Warner Brothers, however, saw it differently. They paid me a cool forty-five hundred bucks and then didn't make the movie. But they did ask me to write another. They didn't make that one, either, but an agent read it and got me fifteen weeks with Otto Preminger, who scared me to death and taught me how to live through it. Also, how to wean myself away from failure. And the Preminger thing led to another script, and that did get made. Badly, but made. Before I knew what had happened it was seven screenplays and eight development deals and fourteen disappointments later, and I was worried about where the next one was coming from because by then I had met Bertie and she had been crazy enough to marry me and quit her job in a fit of invincible optimism and I had both of us to support and was already muttering in my sleep when she said she wasn't really ready but she doubted she ever really would be so what the hell why didn't we try to have a baby anyway and then she was pregnant and suddenly eight years had passed before I even thought to look back.

All I did was get an idea for a movie. I never meant to renounce the theatre forever. (In fact somewhere I have the beginnings of another play, an outline and most of the first act, that I had to put aside when an important screen assignment—and the second baby—came along.) But the years roll on, and suddenly some Sunday morning you're a sitting duck for the mention of Harry Crystal. Just another mile marker to measure how far I had come. From something. And as it turned out, that item in the *Times* wasn't the end of it. Harry was reaching for me in other ways, too, though I didn't know it. About a week later I had a phone call out of the blue from someone who called himself Professor Murray Shenker.

"I'm sorry," I said into the phone. "I don't think I know any Murray Shenker. What number did you want?"

"The number I've got, because I've got *your* number, Artie Shoemaker, demon propman," cackled the Bronx accent at the other end of the line. "I remember you when you didn't know your ass from a ripsaw. Of course, now that you're a glamorous

Hollywood pap-peddler, I guess you don't bother with us peasants."

"Who *is* this?"

"Moe Shenker, you cretin."

"Moe Shenker. I don't believe it."

"So I hear you're this famous and wealthy screen-writer, pandering to the masses, filling their nights with sighs of mindless pleasure."

"No matter what I say to that, I'm dead," I broke in quickly. I've heard that tone before. "Listen, where are you? What are you doing now?"

"I'm in the department up at the State University in Buffalo—I took a doctorate, you know. We're small, but we do try to do one or two of the more significant things. I get to the city once a year or so, to take a look at Broadway and the piffle they try to pass off as theatre these days." He paused to let the superiority and scorn register. "Anyhow, why I called, some demented soul has offered me the use of his apartment while he's in Europe studying mime, and I'm having a few people over. Be a little wine and zucchini quiche, if you're interested."

Zucchini quiche. Jesus. I could taste the whole party already. "Sounds great. When is it?"

"Next Saturday. Of course I realize you Hollywood creative types spend all your spare time with your accountants, but if you can tear yourself away, feel free."

"Moe, I'm sorry to disappoint you, but I'll be there," I said, without the slightest intention of going.

"You will?" He sounded surprised.

"Sure."

"About nine o'clock, then. And you'd better show

up," said Shenker, "or I'll sic Danny D'Angeli on you."

"My God, there's a name," I breathed.

"The past is always with us," said Shenker sententiously, and hung up.

Is it? Oh, I was out, our hero had definitely gotten out. But as I hung up I stood there, a moderately successful screenwriter with a wife, two kids, a cramped apartment, and a mortgage on a modest weekend house in Connecticut, trying for a second to remember what I had wanted to escape so badly.

9

So we'll leave this
    Cold dreary old world, Dear
Where there's nothing
    That's quite what it seems
And we'll sail o'er the sea
Where for just you and meeee
There's a home
    In the Isle of our Dreams . . .

                    —*The Red Mill*

I knew what I wanted to escape that summer back in 1960, all right. Any number of Ohio persons, places, and things, and maybe chief among them was the concrete blockhouse down on Union Avenue with the sign on the roof that read *Barney Shoemaker Non-ferrous Metals.* My father's scrapyard, what a vista. A mountain of junker automobiles, rusted and stripped in the morning sun. Then other hills, a range of stockpiles of used metal—copper casings, rolled brass tidbits, what have you. Needless to say, it was not the horizon I had in mind for myself.

There wasn't any claim my father could make on me during the week because I had that anatomy course Monday through Friday, but on weekends I was fair game. Saturdays he would occasionally drag me down there on some pretext or other and bury me in the office on general principles, just to stiffen me up. And it didn't take him long after the night he heard me sneaking out to Caruso's. The following Saturday he had me down at the yard at eight in the morning, where I sat inside the little office building for two hours thumbing through grimy old records. At last I was finished with the ditsy make-work he had given me, and went outside to the yard carrying a bound sheaf of old delivery tickets. My father was standing near a giant heap of scrap plumbing, tubes, toilets, washbasins, bellowing at the driver who was backing his truck under the last of the pieces dribbling down from the conveyor.

"Give 'er a little more . . . more . . ." he bellowed. "More . . . hold it, whoa!" My father normally conducted business at the top of his lungs. It was the way real men did things. Finally as the roar of the diesel subsided he yelled up to the driver. "Okay, that's two ton for Bessemer, then the pickup at Chase Brass. And no holidays, I want to see you back here by lunch." The driver waved good-naturedly. He knew Barney Shoemaker.

My father turned to find me waiting. I held out the sheaf of tickets. "Anything else?" I said. My expression was tight. All I wanted to do was get out of there without the conversation I knew was coming.

He made no move to take the tickets. "You sure they're all consecutive? They're supposed to be consecutive."

"They're consecutive. So are the order cards," I said shortly. "Can I take off now?"

"Wait, talk to me a minute. I feel like I haven't seen you for a month." My father, trying to be offhand in front of a mountain of used toilets. Two gentlemen taking their ease in front of their club. "So," he said, casually (Ho-ho, you bet). "How's school?"

"No problem, a breeze." I turned to go. "Dad, I'm really gonna be late for work—"

"You have to go on Saturdays, too?"

"Yes, Saturdays, too. And when there's a change of shows, also Sundays, too," I said patiently. "You know that, Dad." I turned again. This time I had actually taken a couple of steps when his voice caught me.

"Arthur," he said. I stopped. There was a pause. Finally he said it. "I want you to quit that job."

"Well. I've been waiting for that shoe to drop all morning."

"I . . . I need you down here at the yard." At least he had the decency not to look me in the eye.

"To do what?" I said, more sharply than I meant to, waving the sheaf of paper at him. "Count tickets that have already been counted, to file cards that have already been filed?"

"I don't care. You can't do your schoolwork and that job at the same time. I haven't seen you open a book. How can you breeze if you don't open a book?"

"It's all labs—I do it in school."

"You got to study to pass anatomy," he said doggedly.

"Dad, you don't even know what comparative anatomy *is*."

Now it was his turn to be sharp. "I know it's the pre-med course that if you flunk it *twice* you'd better look for another way to make a living." He gave me a narrow look. I had no comeback to that one. "Your mother is so upset, I have to get you down here so we can talk in peace. . . . And all for what? At least if it was a real job—"

"Sure," I retorted hotly. "As long as it's delivering for a florist that I hate or washing spinach in the

basement of the A & P on Saturdays or selling haber-
dashery over Christmas or sorting delivery tickets, as
long as I have to miss football games or the Christmas
dance—*then* it's a job. But if it's something I enjoy—"

"Enjoy?" He pounced on the word. "What does enjoy have to do with it?" He gestured to include the
scrapyard. "You think I enjoy *this*?"

"Then why do you do it?"

He looked at me in absolute astonishment. "I don't
know what to say to you sometimes. I'm talking about
making a living." He was boring in. "You enjoy the
theatre? Wonderful. And what part of it are you
planning on for your future? You played around with
acting in high school, that was no good. Now you
gonna make the scenery, take the tickets? What?"

Yes, answer that one, Shoemaker. We're all ears.
But I couldn't. I was caught and I knew it. I couldn't
answer because the only answer I knew was no answer at all, really, was simply that moment each night
at the theatre when I sneaked into the nook at the
base of the stage-right light tower. The audience
couldn't see me but from there I could see the orchestra pit, the stage, everything. And each night at deep
twilight when the lights were just beginning to stand
out against the sky I would watch Harry do his number. It didn't matter what the show was, there was always that moment. That moment when it all came
together, when the lights and Harry and the audience
and the music combined in some chemistry that
reached out from the stage with a big hand to grasp
my face and squeeze it, that reached right into my insides and turned them, freed something that expanded under the heart and made me ache to be part of
it. But what kind of an answer was that?

"I didn't say I was going into the theatre," I said in a low voice.

He didn't look angry now, just worried. Very. "Artie, what's gonna happen to you? You're gonna get distracted by all this song and dance, you're gonna end up with a lotta holes and no donut. I'm afraid you'll get out of college, you won't be prepared for anything."

I winked jauntily and handed him the delivery tickets. "What're you worried about? I can always go into the scrap business."

His face closed. He said quietly, not looking at me "One of these days you're gonna wake up and discover you had scorn for the wrong people."

Nice going, Shoemaker. I felt like two cents. What did I want from him, anyway? I stepped over to him and put my arm around his shoulder in apology. "Dad, I promise. As soon as I see I can't manage the job and the course at the same time, as soon as I see I can't handle both, I'll quit. Okay?" He was still silent. "Okay?"

Finally he nodded. "If that's your best offer," he said with a sigh, "I guess I'm stuck with it." As I headed for the car he called after me. "Remember—keep your eye on the donut, Buddy-Boy."

About three hours later the donut herself—at least the one I was keeping my eye on—was up at the rehearsal area behind the auditorium, about to make her entrance in the run-through of a number. I was down on the stage lost among the general hammering, ratcheting, and sawing of a routine day for the crew. But I lifted my head at the faint siren sound of the rehearsal piano thumping away up on the hill, and smiled. We were already into the next show, *Rose-Marie,* which meant they were rehearsing the one after that, *The Vagabond King,* about the beggar-poet François Villon (to be played by Harry, of course) among the bewitching tavern girls of Paris, featuring my own Queen of the Nile.

Ramona and I had reached a certain precarious plateau since that night behind the fraternity house. Everybody thought we had become a thing, and only the two of us knew what the thing was—and wasn't. We caught each other for a moment here and there backstage during the performance, I usually walked her to Caruso's and then back to her rooming house afterward, even kissed her good night—but that was about it. We couldn't seem to get past that hitch, that moment when she pulled back there in the car, couldn't find a way to get over that hump of self-consciousness and into the wild blue yonder. I wasn't sure we ever would. She was still something of a mystery to me—and I wasn't the only one. Cooky sulked around us, pretending not to care but glowering with a sour-grapes contempt that did my heart good.

I might not have felt so chipper about it, though, if I could have seen him up the hill at that very moment standing to one side of the rehearsal with Ramona, trying to get a few answers of his own.

"What's wrong with tonight?" he was saying.

"I just don't want to," she said, trying to keep her eye on the rehearsal.

"Why not?"

"I told you, I'm busy."

"That never stopped you before."

"That was before," she said, trying to step around him. "Look, I've got a cue coming up—"

He blocked her path. "Busy with who? Not that kid Shoemaker again." He took her arm. "I can do a lot more for you than he can," he said with a leer and a suggestive jut of his crotch.

"Cooky, I really do have a cue—"

"*Can't I,*" he said insistently.

"How do you know what he does for me?"

"Boy, you are the original round-heeled wonder," he sneered. "You'll flop for anybody."

She flushed, then said, "Can I go now, please?"

"I spoiled you, that's my problem."

She looked right at him. "We all make mistakes," she said.

"What's that supposed to mean?" he said belligerently.

"Oh, go suck a tomato," she said, shrugging free, trying to catch up with the step as she moved on with the other girls.

Back down the hill Loomis looked up from his hammering at the young gimpy staggering in through the backstage gate under a load of Sealtest. Loomis glanced at his watch, then stuck the hammer through his belt. "Okay, you guys," he called. "Munjah."

I took one of the quarts of ice cream from the pile and sauntered over to the saw. Watch this, Folks. With one smooth gesture after another I deftly adjusted the chuck above the blade, casually flicked on the switch and zipped through the carton, then tossed one half to Hlavacek and picked up a plywood chip. Ace Shoemaker at the keyboard, quite a switch from his early days of terror. Still a dummy, maybe, but a dummy with style. After all, wasn't I a college man? I took my first plywood lick of fudge swirl. Then to a silent drumroll of triumph I cut around the canvas backdrop mountain in the *Rose-Marie* set, and headed for the rehearsal area up the hill.

Still spooning in the ice cream I moved through the auditorium, cutting across the seats. As I stepped into the far aisle and was just about to climb the last few steps to the rehearsal itself—a bicycle flashed by along the aisle, almost running me down. I jumped back, then went right on eating my fudge swirl. A moment later the bicycle came back the other way and coasted to a stop beside me. The rider was Sanford, of course.

"Ooga-ooga," he said.

"Bug off, Sanford."

He craned his neck to look at the rehearsal. "All right, which one is she?" Peering over the edge of the rehearsal area, he pretended to call, "Yoo-hoo, Ramona. Ra-moan-uh—"

"Very funny."

"Hey, Ra-moan-uh," called Sanford, "I hear you boff—"

"Sanford, willya *scram*?" I looked around hastily to make sure no one had heard.

"Can't I just see which one she is? I won't say anything, I swear." He looked so earnest, I hesitated. "Double swear," he said.

I sighed. "Wait here." I started up the steps. "The things I go through for the young . . ."

As I came into the rehearsal area the dance line was into the number, with Ramona in the lead position. While the rehearsal piano banged away the girls were trying a series of steps, all of them counting carefully under their breath as they went. Spratt was frowning as usual; the choreographer, a not-bad guy named Larry, watched critically. Harry was standing to one side busily oiling up his next target for the summer, another blonde with boobs like a compass, one pointing to Lake Erie and the other to New York. Harry was definitely a chest man. Sitting sullenly over in the other direction Cooky was staring insolently at Ramona. I didn't know if it was getting to her, but suddenly the choreographer broke in.

"No, no, honey—no, hold it," he called to Ramona. The music stopped. He walked over to her. "You're fudging that combination," he said. "Look, like so." And he did it for her, counting, "One two three four five SIX and SEVEN . . . and EIGHT. Got it?"

Concentrating, she repeated the end of the step. ". . . Five SIX and SEVEN . . . and EIGHT." She nodded. "I think so. Sorry."

Larry nodded to the pianist; the music resumed. Cooky just stared. When she reached the combination-step Ramona faltered briefly, then went right on.

This time it was Spratt who broke in and stopped the piano. "All right," he said wearily. "That's the fourth time. The fourth time is the charm."

"Sorry," said Ramona.

Spratt ignored her and turned to the choreographer. "Larry, I'm afraid you'd better simplify that bit."

"He doesn't have to simplify anything," said Ramona. "I can do the step."

Spratt bowed with elaborate sarcasm. "Yes, I forgot. You're Miss New York Twinkle-Toes, Miss Tops-in-Taps." Then he deliberately turned again to the choreographer. "Larry," he said in a superbored tone, "Could you make a note to simplify it for the child, please?" Then back to the other girls, "All right, let's pick it up again at the end of the number. We can't fart around with this all day."

Ramona did not move. "If you'll let me try it again ..." Her voice trailed off.

The rehearsal had grown deathly silent. There was a pause. Then Spratt turned to face Ramona like the messenger of death making a special delivery.

"My *dear* Miss R.," he began with relish. "I realize that a great *artiste* like yourself—a great *New York* artiste, I should say—has only come out here to give us poor provincial clods a break." For the first time Harry stirred uncomfortably. Spratt went on. "But this happens to be a rehearsal. If you want to brush up your technique—which, I might add, is not a bad idea—then go back to class."

Harry said quietly, "All right, Sherman, we know you're tough. Why don't you put away the knives?"

Spratt wheeled on him, one eyebrow raised in mock amazement. "Sherman?" he said. "*Sherman*? My, aren't we gracious all of a sudden, aren't we conciliatory. What's the matter, Harry-Boy? Forget your sword? I said we'll jump to the end of the number. *And we will jump to the end of the number.*" He bowed again to Ramona. "That is, if Miss Twinkle-Toes has no further objection."

Whatever Ramona was feeling, her face was like stone. She shrugged. "I could care less," she said.

The piano resumed, but I had seen enough. I turned on my heel and left. As I came down the steps Sanford was still waiting expectantly. I handed him what was left of my ice cream—I had lost my appetite for fudge swirl, anyway—and headed right past him, back toward the stage. I knew what I had to do.

"What about Ramona?" said Sanford in surprise.

"She's not here," I said shortly, and kept right on going, like a man who has suddenly had a vision of the Holy Grail. "Tell Mother I may not be home for supper."

"She'll have a bird—"

"I can't help it," I called back. "I just got a rush order."

Straight from heaven.

10

<hr>

When he asked me to name the day
Name the day
Name the day
I would say right away
Don't delay
If you love but me . . .

—The Red Mill

I marched straight down through the auditorium. Around me there was nothing but the desultory quiet of an Ohio summer afternoon, birds napping, leaves dropping under the heavy sun. But inside my head there were martial airs, chorus and orchestra in "Stouthearted Men," "Tramp Tramp Tramp," and "Captain Dick's Own Infantree" all rolled into one, building, swelling with determination. As I went my head was making a prop list of my own, marshaling the items I would need. I stalked across the orchestra pit, stormed through the paint frame grabbing brushes and buckets of color along the way, yellow for sun, green for fertility, red for the heart and the divine fire. Then without pause on to the pile of scrap lumber, choosing one splintery pole for the rod of my anger; next the tool rack for instruments of execution, staple guns, razor knives, tape to bind the enemy; and finally the scene dock for a piece of old muslin. No, not that one, too small; something bigger, that's better. Margin for error, room for my rage. And so into the prop house, still on the warpath, dumped the whole business on the workbench, rolled up my sleeves. I looked at my watch. Four hours until curtain that evening. And fell to with a will. Cunning. Cleverness. Craft. Santa's elf, Artie Shoemaker.

The fever of inspiration was on me. To my amazement everything came to my fingers, inventiveness I didn't know I had, skills my hands had never possessed, deftness, improvisation, brilliance. (Sort of. Most of the paint got on me, I clobbered my left knee, and partly stapled a finger. Onward and upward.) For the rest of the afternoon I worked, and straight through supper. I didn't so much as look up while I labored away, didn't notice the sun sliding lower in the sky, didn't hear the lapping murmurs of the audience beginning to arrive. Finally, just as the stage manager was calling Five Minutes I put down the last of the brushes, picked the remainder of the staples out of my finger, and slumped back. The masterpiece stood beside the workbench, something tall and thin and fat at the top, all of it completely covered by a sheet tied on with a drawstring, which then ran up to the ceiling and across toward the rear stairs through a series of screw eyes set in the rafters. I tucked the loose end of the string into a crack near the stairs. There. Ready for the unveiling. Finished at last. Made it before curtain time, too.

Curtain time. Jesus. Listening to the mounting stir of the audience and the orchestra tuning up in the pit I hastily slipped into my crew coat, ready for an evening of glory and reward.

But the whole thing started as a night of interruptions and disasters. The first one came as I heaved against the prop table to get it rolling, then instantly had to skid to a stop. There right in my path outside the prop house was an uncomfortable tableau. Ful-dauer ringed by the women from his tired frame house on Altamont Road. The blond Wagnerian wife, the mousy daughter Naomi, the distracted grandmother, three frowning furies. Nobody looked very happy. They did not see me back in the shadows.

Naomi handed him a brown paper bag while the grandmother simply wrung her hands to the accom-paniment of a low, steady moan. Then the wife held out a wool bundle.

"Take the sweater, Julius," she said.

"I don't need the sweater," said Dr. Fuldauer. Then to Naomi he said, "Tell your mother it iss July."

"July, July," said the wife wearily. "Julius, how many more nights do Naomi and I make sandwiches and drag them down here? For the few pennies you make we don't need this, *wir brauchen die paar Pfen-nige nicht.* Are you such a young man, to prowl around at night? *Bist du verrückt,* are you crazy?"

"I am fine here, I told you," said Fuldauer. The old lady moaned a little louder. "Oh, Ma, be still."

"Poppa," Naomi said unhappily, "*Höre mich an,* listen to me—"

"Yes, at least think of Naomi," the wife broke in re-morselessly. "*Was wird mit ihr passieren?* She is ashamed for her friends—"

"Please, Poppa," said Naomi.

"Let me be," said Fuldauer. "*Lass mich in Frieden.*"

"Yes," the wife said, "in this nursery school, *ein Kindergarten—*"

They were pressing in on him. "Please, Poppa, please," Naomi said again, and the old lady's moan went up another notch. Suddenly Fuldauer wheeled on her.

"Oh, Ma, *schweig still—!*"

That was when he saw me. Instantly the whole family fell stiffly silent. They stood just as they were, a frozen quartet while I pushed the prop table on by.

"Uh, excuse me . . ." I said.

They nodded formally to me, and I got out of there as fast as I could, mushing on toward the backstage area. When I was a safe distance beyond I could not resist a glance back over my shoulder. They were at it again, the same picture as before. The Wife accusing, the Daughter pleading, the Grandmother moaning. Spare me. I turned quickly back again. Glory was waiting.

I skidded the prop table to a stop at its appointed station behind the canvas Rockies, then quickly plugged in the lights and checked the props, my eyes all the while roaming the backstage area for Guess Who. Those pussy-willow feet. Those legs pleasure-bent. Those lips, those eyes. There she was across the stage, about to make her entrance with the other dancers right after the curtain. Wait a minute. Wasn't there a moment in the opening number when the girls paused near the wings on the other side? I put the last touches on the prop table and took off.

The number was a sweet little waltz called "Pretty Things" in Friml's old chestnut about the Northwest Mounties. Some of the girls were in crinolines (left over from a production of *The Chocolate Soldier*) and some were supposed to be Indian maidens, Ramona among them. I came pounding around the scenery after her, a lustful paleface, and crept into the wings. There she was dancing with the others, all braids and moccasins and a dime-store headband, radiant under her chocolaty Max Factor base. I couldn't understand how she kept her pride intact, why she wasn't hangdog and crushed. But to look at her you'd never know Spratt had zapped her in front of the entire company four hours earlier. Just that unblinking smiling face, that arched back, those perfect breasts rising and falling to the smooth beat of her heart. She was something. And as I stood just back out of the sight lines in the wings gesturing to get her attention I barely noticed the silent figure behind me.

Harry, much further back in the shadows off stage.

If I had looked more closely I might have seen a suspicious bulge up his sleeve—but why should I? He seemed to be innocence itself. Wearing an unbuttoned Mountie tunic, lounging carelessly against a unit of scenery due to move on in the first scene change, he looked for all the world like an actor in a casual moment, nothing more. So nobody noticed his eyes checking carefully from side to side. And all at once when he was sure no one was watching he slipped quickly around the edge of the unit and disappeared, melting into the darkness among the offstage scenery before anyone knew he was gone—least of all me.

I was still focused on Ramona, who had reached the pause in the dance number and finally noticed me windmilling at her. She sneaked a puzzled glance at the wings. I gestured again, overmouthing the words in a throaty whisper.

"I'll see you. After the scene shift. I've. Got something. For you." She frowned, not quite getting it. I pointed to her. I pointed to me. I pointed to the scenery. White Man Use Basic English. "Something for you. After the shift—"

I jumped a mile at the unexpected tug on my arm and wheeled around.

It was Dr. Fuldauer, vest and all, edging into the wings beside me. He was carrying the brown paper bag.

"Arthur," he whispered. "Iss that you?"

No, it's Pocahontas. "Doctor Fuldauer," I started to whisper back, annoyed, trying to keep one eye on Ramona, "you're not supposed to be—" He pressed a wax-paper packet into my hand. "—What's this?" I said.

"My wife brings them each evening, sandwiches. It's real German bread, you can't buy it."

Honestly, I thought. Honestly. "Doctor Fuldauer, I can't—"

"You talk to some people about art, they bring you sandwiches," he said ruefully, with a cracked smile.

I motioned him back. "I'm sorry, but there's a scene shift coming up—"

He did not move. Almost to himself he added, "You see, you see, that's how it is. In the end they take everything away from you. First your enemies do it, then your friends, then your own family." The smile had faded.

For a second I almost felt sorry for him. What fun was it to be Julius Fuldauer? But another time. The music was building to the end of the number, any second now everything would start to roll. As tactfully as I could I whispered, "Doctor Fuldauer, I really do have a shift."

He snapped out of it. "Yes, of course. I am in the way." As he turned to go I held out the wax-paper packet. "Keep the sandwich," he said flatly. "I don't want the damned sandwich." And he shuffled off in his blue suit.

From the stage now there was a crash of music as the number headed for the windup. Backstage the members of the crew hurried to take their positions for the shift. They bent to hook their towropes to the rings at the base of each unit, then straightened, standing at the ready, looking at the stage manager— who in turn was staring at the stage, his arm raised, ready to give the signal as soon as the lights dimmed.

And in that moment, with the crew like horses at the post, straining to run—who should stroll innocently out from behind one of the units but Harry, looking at no one, whistling under his breath. No one noticed the screwdriver in his hand.

"Hey, Crystal," Cooky yelled hoarsely, his towrope hooked to a unit, all set to go, "get your ass outta the road. You wanna get killed?"

"Not tonight," said Harry with a mysterious smile, "not tonight," and he sidestepped neatly out of the way. He paused next to me a short distance upstage where I was waiting with the props for the next scene. I should have known from the creamy expression on his face that something was up.

Then it happened.

The chorus on stage hit the final note. The applause started, the lights faded, the stage manager dropped his arm.

"Go!" he called hoarsely to the crew.

They went, all right. Westervelt, Loomis, and Bliss yanked stoutly on their ropes at the first dolly—and immediately fell on their collective asses as the towrings pulled right out of the unit. Shenker and Hlavacek heaved smartly on theirs, then lurched drunkenly free when the rings gave way on that unit, too, clattering to the cement with a loose jangle of hardware. Shenker stumbled against another flat which teetered dangerously in the wind; Hlavacek tripped over Westervelt and sprawled flat. All across the backstage area the helpless crew was reeling into each other, toppling like tenpins in the darkness as more rings pulled out. The disaster was so complete that even Joanne the prop gimpy could only gape in awe. People kept getting up and falling again, it was like watching a clown ballet, a scene from Laurel and Hardy or the Three Stooges. Climaxed when Cooky gave a tremendous he-man yank on his rope, which promptly pulled free like the others and sent him stumbling spread-eagled, arms flailing for balance toward another unit. With a lurching rip he disappeared right through the canvas.

Next to me Harry sighed happily, like a man who has just swallowed the last tasty bite of a gourmet dinner. "Go, team, go," he breathed happily.

Out in the orchestra pit the musicians were sawing away at the entr'acte music while the perplexed conductor stared at the scenery, which was supposed to be changing but had not yet budged an inch. As the orhestra reached the end he shrugged, signaled the players, and they attacked the whole thing again from the beginning.

Backstage there was bedlam, consternation as the crew tried to pull itself together.

"What happened to the rings—?" Westervelt was saying dazedly.

Cooky's head reappeared through the torn flat. "Who the fuck loosened those rings?" he cried in outrage.

Loomis scrambled to his feet, taking command. "Come on, we got a show to get through," he called hoarsely to the others. "We'll have to beef each unit by hand, let's have some beef here!" There was a pelting of running feet in the shadows as we all tore over to the unit. "Low, hit her low, where she sits," barked Loomis, "or you'll put your hand right through it." And we all bent double, lining our weight up against the dolly at the bottom. "Heave!" whispered Loomis. We heaved, but nothing happened. Cooky swore. "Let's move this bastard," he said. *"Shove!"* Straining for all I was worth I muttered to the man bent over in the crew coat on the other side of me, "Shove, you mother— shove!"

And a familiar voice answered, "So what—am I—doing?" The man looked sideways. It was Dr. Fuldauer inside the crew coat pushing with the rest of us. He grinned impishly then called, very gung-ho, to Hlavacek on the other side of him. "Shove it, mother!"

Hlavacek shot him an incredulous look—but the unit was rolling at last. We got it into place, then took off after the next one, then the one after that, heaving along with our rumps humped in the air and our chins near the ground like a herd of theatrical dromedaries. Fuldauer was right there in his crew coat huffing and puffing with everyone else, having a whale of a time. At last everything was in place for the next scene (the orchestra was plowing through the entr'acte stuff for the third time), and we all straightened our stiff backs with a groan.

"Okay" said Cooky, "soon as we hit the intermission, we'll have to get some new hardware on those units—" He broke off as Harry sauntered by, heading for his entrance.

"Here," said Harry, deftly tucking the screwdriver into Cooky's breast pocket as he passed. "You'll be needing this." Cooky just stared after him, a look of growing understanding—and rage—on his face.

And in that strangled silence Dr. Fauldauer sidled over to me, still wearing that crew coat which was miles too large for him. But he dusted his hands briskly and said with an odd look, "So, Arthur. Once again we serve each other, *hein?*"

Before I could answer, Westervelt barged up in his shirt-sleeves. Come to think of it, he had been dressed that way during the whole disaster, too, I just hadn't noticed. "All right," he said, "who's the guy, who's the smart-ass? Somebody copped my crew coat." He glared at me belligerently. "Hey, Shoemaker—you seen my crew coat?"

I was looking right at Fuldauer. He flashed me a look of mute appeal. I paused, then turned my back on the little man so at least I wouldn't literally be lying. "Not lately," I said to Westervelt, then started down toward the wings and left Fuldauer radiating gratitude in the shadows behind me. Because I had no time to dally with Latin tutors in stolen crew coats. I was ready at last to resume my search for

Ramona, ready to reap a little glory after the upheavals of the evening.

But God, it seemed, was not through with us yet. At first everything looked smooth enough when I peered out from the wings. There was Harry in the scarlet full-dress splendor of the Royal Canadian Mounted Police, stiff hat and all, every inch the baritone hero, his very teeth sparkling like the stars. The whole cast was lined up behind him, more Mounties, trappers, girls in their crinolines, Indian maidens, all part of the big ballad number, the title song. Harry was laying it out to that soprano in his best Nelson Eddy style. *You're gentle and kind,* he sang, *Divinely designed, as graceful as the pines above you.* His eyes went upward, and as if on cue—there was a faint rumble of thunder.

Though the other actors did not change their expressions you could see the sound register on every plastic smile. Even Harry flickered for a second. Everyone did, except for that glassy-eyed soprano, who was drinking in Harry's every word. *There's an angel's breath beneath your sigh,* warbled Harry. Then, slowing as he held that suspended moment before beginning the chorus, *There's a little devil in your eye—*

In the pause there was the first distinct . . . plop . . . of a raindrop on the brim of his hat. Then another. And another. Harry was launching into the chorus.

> *Oh Rose-Marie, I love you*
> *I'm always dreaming of you*

The drops had turned into a solid drizzle. Now a murmur could be heard out front. I peeked through a hole in the wings at the auditorium. There was a stir among the crowd. People were looking up in dismay, reaching for newspapers and programs to cover their heads. Beside me I felt something brush past as Spratt hurried into the wings. From the stage, still singing, Harry glanced questioningly at him.

"Just a sprinkle, keep going," said Spratt in a stage whisper, motioning him to continue. "It'll blow right over."

The words were barely out of his mouth when the patter on the scenery turned into a steady drumming, and it really began to rain—but *pour*. A wicked wind had started to come up as well. Led by Harry, the actors on stage were now in a mincing lockstep clog, gamely plowing ahead through the drenching downpour. Every tap of their feet on the concrete stage went *splot-splot* and raised a spray of wetness. The wind blew a notch harder, the muslin Rockies bellied ominously, and Bliss appeared urgently behind me. "Come on, Shoemaker, man the lifeboats, abandon ship," he hissed. "We gotta batten down or there won't be anything left. This place is gonna look like the Billy Rose Aquacade any second now."

Backstage, the crew was dashing around in a frenzy, throwing tarps over all the stage furniture that couldn't be carted inside, fighting to lash down the scenery, which was beginning to thrash around in the wind. "Grab this," barked Shenker, and tossed me a line that was tied to the backdrop. I reached for it and the wind snatched the rope right out of my hand like a wisp of smoke. I scrambled after the loose end as it snaked away across the cement, got one hand on it and fought to my feet, grabbing a tree to lash it to before the whole backdrop fell on the actors, the

Canadian Rockies billowing like a sail on a clipper ship. I fought the rope around the tree; *Two Years Before the Mast* with Artie Shoemaker. Then from the corner of my eye I saw Westervelt and Cooky picking up the old harem chaise from *The Desert Song* (now reprofiled into a Yukon trapper's cot). I started to yell, "Not that way, lift it from the bottom—" Too late. Each of them now had a piece of his own to carry. Cackling like madmen they dashed off toward the prop house. My poor chaise, orphan of the storm.

"The whole stage-right return's about to go next," Loomis yelled into my ear, and together with Bliss we ran back down to the wings. While we struggled to lash down the return I looked at the stage and had to stifle an impulse to laugh, it was all so crazy. The actors were still sloshing doggedly through the number. The crinolines had wilted in the rain and now clung to the girls like dishrags, their careful curls were all in straggles. Even the stiff brims (cardboard, naturally) of the Mounties' hats were sagging around the men's faces, beginning to look like so many soggy Bogart fedoras. One of the girls dropped her bonnet; it promptly floated away on a little rivulet and went over the falls into the orchestra pit.

Harry was near the wings, still singing, fighting an insane desire to giggle himself. He cast a demented look at Spratt—who was now standing behind the return under a huge golf umbrella.

"Keep going, I tell you," whispered Spratt. "It'll blow right over."

"Thank God," whispered Harry right back between choruses with the water dripping off his collapsing hat. "For a minute there I was afraid it was going to rain."

The bedraggled company got into their pose for the smash finish. Wringing wet, helpless with strangled laughter, Harry somehow got the last words out.

> *Of all the queens that ever lived*
> *I choose you*
> *To rule me*
> *My Rose-Ma-ree-yee-yee!*

He bowed low. The auditorium was completely deserted, save for two lonely souls sitting under the same soaking newspaper. Clap. Clap. Clap.

Five minutes later the soaked and bedraggled actors burst gleefully into the dressing room corridor from the stage. Spratt had finally bowed to nature and cancelled the rest of the performance. Bubbling and giggling like schoolchildren unexpectedly let out of school the actors headed for their dressing rooms shouting boisterously in a jumble of excited voices. "Hoo-eee." "All right, where's the party?" "Somebody say party?" "My place. My place, everybody. Hoo—eee!" Instant anticipation, high spirits charged the air. The show may have to go on, but look not for remorse from an actor with a sudden night off.

I was right there with the rest. Still wearing my crew coat, I elbowed my way along the crowded, jubilant corridor to the dancers' dressing room and knocked once. Then without waiting for an answer I opened the door. No protocol. A man no longer to be denied. There was the usual confusion, cries of indignation, girls reaching for clothes to cover up. Sorry, girls, no big eyes, no porcelain saucers, not this time. Shoemaker on the march. I made a beeline for Ramona, who was already down to her damp tights and bra at the makeup table.

"I've been waiting for this all night," I said. "Come on." Without another word I grabbed her hand and dragged her just as she was, bare bra and all, out the door.

She just had time to throw a towel around her shoulders as I pulled her along the corridor toward the outside door. "Waiting for what?" she said, clutching the towel and trying to keep up. "Where're we going, what is all this?"

"Nothing. Just a little surprise to cheer you up."

"I don't need cheering up, I'm fine."

"Okay," I said. "Laugh."

"What?"

"Laugh, I said."

"Ha-ha-ha," she said mechanically. "Why? I don't want to laugh."

"There," I said in triumph. "See what I mean?" We had reached the exit door from the building. I started out.

"It's pouring," she protested.

"So what? You just did half of *Rose-Marie* in the rain, pretend it's a dance."

Then she *did* laugh, and I dragged her the fifty feet through the open to the prop house.

We dashed in the front door, shaking the water off like ducks. My mystery creation, still covered with its sheet, was standing conspicuously right where I left it. I took Ramona by the hand, steered her the length of the room to the rear, then positioned her about halfway up the stairs to the second floor so she would be elevated, sort of like on the launching platform for a ship or the unveiling of a statue. Historic moments deserve respect. Also staging.

"Stand right there," I said.

"What for?" In answer I reached into the crevice, took out the end of the drawstring, and put it in her hand. "What's this?" she said.

"Go ahead. Pull it."

She looked at me suspiciously. "If this is some kind of gag—"

"Pull it and find out."

She did. The string moved jerkily up the wall, through the screw eyes in the ceiling, then back down again to the mystery, where it undid the knot (that had almost been the hardest part of the whole business). And the sheet fell off to reveal a gigantic cockeyed prop flower about five feet high, more or less a daisy, with huge floppy muslin petals. It had been almost an hour since I had seen it, and I was a little surprised myself at how overblown it was. Silly, really. But secretly I still thought it was terrific.

Ramona just looked at it. Then some angle in her face let go, softened into a curve. For a second she couldn't find the words. What can you say about a five-foot daisy? "Artie. You nut."

I cleared my throat auspiciously. "Ahem. Ahem again. Silence, please. I am honored to bestow upon you the Order of the Golden Whoops-a-Daisy, which is awarded only to those who have been publicly dumped on by Mr. Sherman Spratt. As one of those who has been previously so honored—"

Ramona suddenly glanced to one side and above, her finger to her lips. "Shhh," she said.

I broke off in surprise. Still looking, still with the finger warning for silence, she motioned me to her. I crept up the steps. From where she stood, her head stuck up just high enough in the stairwell to see into the floor above. And as I tiptoed up beside her and peeked over the edge, I saw, too.

A shoe-level view of the second floor. The jumble of sofas and settees and love seats, the shelf of tacky mandolins without strings, the tin shields and comic-strip battle flags. Homemade heraldry. And there before a plywood throne with peeling gilt stood Dr. Fuldauer.

He was still wearing the oversized crew coat, but across his shoulders now he had thrown a moth-eaten old fake ermine. A prop sword was buckled at his waist. "If 'twere done, 'twere best it were done quickly, *schnell*," he muttered and drew the sword. Pulling himself erect in the baggy coat he said dramatically, "Every inch a king." Then he saluted an imaginary court and sat, a butterball Macbeth, King Lear, with dandruff.

I wasn't going to get my ass reamed for this one. "He's not supposed to be there," I whispered low, about to move.

"No," said Ramona softly, her hand on my arm. "Leave him alone."

I looked at her. Eyes still riveted on the old man, she drew the towel more tightly around her like her own robe of state. I felt a flicker of shame. She had been to that court. She recognized the blood royal, she knew the cry of the annointed. *Give me my robe, put on my crown; I have/Immortal longings in me.* In front of us Fuldauer sat on the plywood throne, muttering. After a moment, bowing, we backed on silent feet away from the King.

And while I was thus lost in the prop house there was another faded member of the royal family I could not see; Fibby Geyer, the boozy old character actor, who was at that moment working his way along the corridor toward Harry's dressing room.

Inside the room Harry was seated in front of the mirror, taking off his makeup in high spirits. The night stretched invitingly ahead of him; the blonde with the two compass boobs was waiting, and both were pointing to a snug harbor. *Show me the way to go home*, he sang happily under his breath as he slapped on the cold cream, *I'm tired and I wanna go to bed—*

There was a knock at the door, and Fibby stuck his whiskey nose in. "Harry, you busy? Can I talk to you here for half a sec? I'm not sure I'm gonna make that party."

"Tsk tsk tsk," said Harry, motioning him in, "Fibby, you're slipping."

"So what else is new," said Fibby with a wry smile. He seemed slightly embarrassed. "Mind if I close the door?"

Harry shrugged. "Feel free."

The older actor shut the door, then fussed with the knob another second to make sure it would stay that way. There was obviously something on his mind. He seemed agitated, ercited, worried, all together.

Harry nodded toward the makeup table. "It's in the drawer."

"No," said Fibby, shaking his head, "that's not what I meant, not this time. For a change I don't want a drink." He smiled ruefully again. Then he sat heavily on the cruddy cot against the wall. "With a smile of self-mockery, he sat," said Fibby. There was a nervous pause. He seemed not to know how to start. "Oh, boy, I hate hardluck stories," he said.

"Come on, what hardluck story?" said Harry, to buck him up. "You've had a solid career—"

"*Had* is right." All at once Fibby leaned forward excitedly with what was on his mind. "But, hey, Harry, this time I think I got a shot at getting back. A real shot—something that will establish me again." He paused, wet his lips. "Maybe I will have that drink." He got up, opened the drawer of the makeup table, took out a bottle of Four Roses, and poured himself a stiff one.

"Shit, that's great," said Harry warmly. "What is it, Broadway?"

"Well, not quite," said Fibby. "It's a soap. Out of Chicago." Then he added quickly, "But a continuing part, at least two segments a week."

There was just a flicker of hesitation before Harry forced himself to smile. "Fabulous."

"Yeah, and none of this television bullshit, either," Fibby went on enthusiastically. "Radio—the real thing." He grinned weakly. "My nose may have turned into a sponge, but I still got the voice that charmed thousands, hey? What's more, this time they came looking for me. Got the call today."

"Nothing like a call," said Harry, still hanging on to the smile.

"Amen. Actually I haven't quite nailed the part yet, but my agent says it's practically a lock." Pointed pause. "All I gotta do is get to Chicago for the audition."

Without hesitation Harry said, "How much do you need?"

Fibby pulled a scrap of paper out of his pocket, waved it. "I'm gonna insist on giving you an IOU, you understand—" Harry was reaching for his checkbook. "Sixty-five dollars ought to do it," Fibby said apologetically. He watched Harry write. "I can't tell you how much I appreciate—"

"Forget it. A soap, that's money in the bank." He handed the other actor the check.

Fibby looked at it, stunned, "Harry. This is for two hundred bucks."

"What do you care," said Harry. "You're giving me an IOU aren't you? Fuck it, take the sleeper, go to Chicago in style." Then with a puckish wink toward the check he added, "Just pray it doesn't bounce."

They both laughed. Pain has many faces.

By the time I got back to the dressing room building with Ramona most of the company had already changed into their street clothes. Several of them were standing just inside the door of the building, holding their hands outside.

"Hey," said one of the chorus boys, "it's letting up."

Fibby, fully dressed now, banged out of his dressing room and came up behind them. "Okay!" he cried, hugely jovial. "We all ready for my farewell party?" He grabbed one of the girls and did a little clog, singing, *"Chi-kah-go, Chi-kah-go, that todd-uh-ling town."* And they swept out into the night, celebrating already, Fibby leading the way.

It was a few minutes later, while I waited for Ramona to finish changing, that I saw the compass blonde trip lightly down the corridor and tap at Harry's door.

"Harry, we're waiting," she cooed. No answer. "Harry?"

From inside the dressing room came Harry's voice, oddly muffled. "Not now."

"Oh, get this, it's Mister Star," said the blonde teasingly, and rattled the doorknob. Then she stopped in surprise. "Harry—is this locked?"

"Do you mind?" came Harry's voice. "I'm not alone."

That did it.

"Ex-cuse me," the blonde said huffily, and stalked off down the corridor.

Inside the dressing room, where neither she—nor I—could see, the lights were out. Harry wasn't lying, exactly. He was sprawled on the cruddy cot, his arm around the bottle of Four Roses. He stared reflectively and took a long, pensive slug. It wasn't the first. *Show me the way to go home,* he sang softly. *I'm tired and I wanna go to bed. . .* His voice trailed off. Then without looking he reached over the table, took Fibby's IOU, and carefully tore it up. As the pieces dribbled from his hand into a wastebasket full of cold-cream Kleenexes he muttered to no one in particular, "You're excused." There was a long pause. He took another long swallow, then spoke again to the darkness. "We're all excused . . ."

The party was jammed into some tenor's summer apartment about three blocks away. It was the converted second floor of an old house, but you couldn't see much of it that night because the place was wall-to-wall chorus people and stage crew, shrieking and jabbering. Someone had produced two gallon jugs of Gallo which were actually wine and not cherry soda, and the party was afloat on it.

Balancing two full Dixie cups I worked my way through the crowd over to the old upright piano. Someone was banging out a waltz from the first show of the season, *The Red Mill,* which by now of course had gone to join that great pantheon of past productions in the sky and thus qualified as a sentimental memory.

> *If he'd say that he loved but me*
> *None but me*
> *Only me . . .*

I set one of the cups down before Ramona, who was leaning on the piano. Her expression seemed distracted, had been all evening, in fact. It was as though some faint oppression were weighing on the back of her brain, the kind of look that goes with the question *What am I doing here with all these people?* I just hoped it didn't include me.

"You okay?" I asked under the singing.

In answer she merely nodded and joined in with the others. Whatever the thought had been it stayed behind her eyes, reserved for Ramona. *What a paradise life would be*, we sang together.

> *Life would bee-yee . . .*

Only, I meant it.

The two of us were still singing as I walked her home along the surburban street an hour or so later. The rain had ended. The wet sidewalk was glistening in the glow from the lampposts like a silvery strip of footlights ahead of us. Ramona was carrying her giant daisy, swaying a little from side to side as we finished the song.

> *I would say right away*
> > *Don't delay*
> *If you love me* . . .

Our voices fell away. We ambled a few steps further in silence.

"Well, here we are again," I said finally. "All dressed up and no place to go."

"Just as well. You've got that course tomorrow."

I shuddered. "Don't remind me."

"Well, that's how it is," she said with an odd smile. "Into each life a little summer must fall." And all at once—she whirled away from me down the sidewalk in that same combination-step she had fudged at rehearsal that afternoon, the daisy spinning with her as she went, feet skimming, arms pinwheeling, a gossamer queen in the night, no fudge now, doing it perfectly again and again and again, SEVEN and EIGHT and EIGHT and EIGHT.

At last she paused for breath, shoulders heaving.

I burst into applause. "Bravo, bravo—!" then broke off in amazement. Her shoulders weren't heaving for breath. She was sobbing.

I rushed down the sidewalk to her.

"Hey. . . ." I touched her arm solicitously. She pulled away, keeping her back to me, fighting for control. "Come on," I said softly, "don't let that creep Spratt get you down."

She raised her teary face defiantly and tried to shrug. "Me? I could care less."

"Listen," I went on in a rush of enthusiasm, "you're too good for this place, anyhow—"

"Sure, sure," she said, drying her eyes.

"I'll bet you could work anywhere, New York, Hollywood . . ." She gestured derisively. "Why not?" I said. "You're good enough."

She shook her head impatiently. "*Good* enough isn't good enough—you've gotta *care* enough. And I don't. It just never seemed worth it to me. What, knock your brains out to be in the fourth road company of *My Fair Lady*? Who needs it."

"I don't believe you."

"I told you," she said, "Don't expect too much of me, you're gonna let yourself in for a big disappointment. I have no big plans, no special neon dreams. I'm just a gypsy."

Just a gypsy. God, how wonderful that sounded. And how far away. The other side of the moon. "Boy, I envy you," I said moodily, head down, scuffing at the sidewalk. "At least you're *in* the business, *in* the theatre. Me, I've never really been *in* anything—not the crowd I hung around with in high school, not college, not even really in pre-med. I have to pound every single equation, every stupid cranial nerve into my head. And I'm in the theatre least of all. I don't really know what I'm doing down there," I snorted. "And probably never will."

"You'll learn." She cocked a speculative eye at me. "You'll probably end up a sensitive playwright, or something."

"No," I persisted, "I mean what it must feel like to be *inside* the business, to be part of the *life*. I mean, you look at the life some people lead—my father, Doctor Fuldauer—you wonder how they can stand it." I sighed. "Boy, I tell you, sometimes the idea of making a living is a mystery to me."

"Yep," said Ramona with a grin. "Definitely a playwright." Then teasingly, "Hey. I thought we were talking about me."

"We are, we are," I said earnestly. "You're really part of it all. You could be great if you wanted to—"

"What do you know," she scoffed.

I spoke quietly, but I meant every word. "I could spend my life," I said, "watching you dance."

She stopped and stared at me, then shook her head with a helpless little laugh. "Artie Shoemaker," she said, and paused. Then softly, "Listen. How soon can you find us a place?"

I just looked at her, not sure I had heard right. Was this how it happened? Just like that on a suburban street after the rain, no fanfare of trumpets, no ruffle of drums? Could she mean it? Could she actually, achingly, unbelievably, conceivably mean it?

"Come on," she said. "I'll make you a man of the theatre."

Bring your own trumpet, Shoemaker.

I kissed her good night dazedly at her rooming house door ten minutes later, my thoughts rising wistfully to the widow's forbidden bedrooms above. A place, a place, where could I find us a place? I was so dazzled by the thought that I almost forgot one other minor disaster that still had to be faced.

When I got into my bedroom at home still later that night I shook the thirteen-year-old wizard in the next bed.

"Sanf." Again, more urgently. "Sanf, I gotta talk to you, you gotta help me."

Finally he came awake, shaking sleep from his beetle brows, precocious and intent. "What happened?"

"Disaster."

"The chaise?"

"They walked away with the top." He laughed. "Come on, cut it out," I said.

"Well, why did you build it that Farmer Brown way? I told you how to build it."

"I know, I know. I just thought this way would be quicker than cutting all that wood for glue wedges."

"You mean you were afraid of the table saw, is what you mean."

I ignored that one. "D'Angeli's talked to me about making it stronger a thousand times. I'm afraid they'll can me."

"Great. Mother'll give a party."

"Come on, Sanf. I'm desperate."

"Okay, okay," he mumbled. "I'll drop down tomorrow and see what I can do." He pulled the covers up and rolled over again.

That kid. I'll bet he's laid before he's fifteen.

11

Ah! sweet mystery of life
At last I've found thee
Ah, I know at last
The secret of it all
All the longing, seeking
Striving, waiting, yearning
For 'tis love and love alone
And idle tears that fall

The burning hopes, the joys
The world is seek-ing . . .

—*Naughty Marietta*

"Forget it, Goldman," I said loftily into the pay phone at the back of the prop house the next morning. "I wouldn't dream of borrowing your room, I wouldn't dream of defiling your sacred goddamn sheets." I hung up. "Some fraternity," I muttered. Then I turned to Sanford, who was at the workbench rebuilding the chaise, and stuck out my hand. "Gimme," I said.

He put down the hammer, took out his coin purse, and looked inside. "That was the last dime."

I racked my brain for a second. There had to be somebody. I had already tried two out-of-town guys from my anatomy class who usually went home for the weekend, but they had foresworn the pleasures of Youngstown until after the lab practical exam next week. Then a graduate student in psychology but he was working with his rats at home that weekend and besides he had a roommate. Another buddy from high school whose parents were away for the month but he was afraid the neighbors might think it was him and anyway he was nervous about his mother's porcelain collection in the living room (I swore we wouldn't shake the living room, but from the pounding of my heart at the thought I wasn't so sure). Also two guys with a cottage out at Mentor but that was a bust, the next-door neighbor was a minister from Willoughby who kept bringing out neutered Methodists for weekends of Christian fellowship. Plus someone else with a trailer but he was going to Cedar Point, a cousin in Painesville who wanted to know if Uncle Barney was coming, too, even the juvenile delinquent mechanic at the gas station who was supposed to be living with a woman in a rooming house somewhere and he was, but it turned out to be his mother. Finally I had worked my way through everyone at the fraternity house. Brother Goldman was at the end of the list. I glanced at Sanford now and shrugged. "That's okay. I don't know anyone else to call, anyway."

Sanford was still looking inside the purse. "Boy, that's over a dollar's worth of dimes we went through," he said glumly. "What's the big deal?"

I said nothing, just turned to the workbench and began to load up my arms with a tinsel crown, a scroll, two droopy crepe paper roses, a handful of tankards, and some other Frenchified odds and ends that they had asked for up at the *Vagabond King* rehearsal. Suddenly I stopped and whirled back to Sanford, the words literally torn out of me in frustration and despair. "Don't you understand?" I cried. "A dream is waiting to come true—and I can't find a bed to put it on!"

"You can have mine," said Sanford cheerfully. "If I can watch."

I glared at him and stormed out.

Without knowing it, of course, I was headed right for another storm that was brewing on top of the hill. Absorbed in my troubles I trudged through the auditorium feeling good and sorry for myself, not looking to left or right. And marched into the rehearsal area without noticing that the rest of the company was just standing around. I waved a small hello to Ramona—but she averted her head and motioned me to say nothing. Only then did I realize that the whole rehearsal was in one of those deathly crisis silences. And suddenly it hit me. Harry was nowhere in sight.

As my hand died at the end of its wave Spratt looked at me with his sweet viper smile. "Would you like a semaphore?"

Dummy up, Shoemaker. I set my armload down on the rehearsal table as quietly as I could.

"What's this?" said Spratt, looking disdainfully at the props. "Ah, yes. I'd recognize the masterly Shoemaker touch anywhere. Earnest but inept."

I just swallowed and said nothing. You'll never make me talk, Herr Goebbels.

"Well," Spratt went on sardonically, "at least we have the props, such as they are. Now all we need is the actor. The famous Mr. Crystal—who may be going back to the Great White Way sooner than he expects. A *lot* sooner."

"Do you want me to look for him?" volunteered Fibby.

Spratt held up a lordly hand. "No, no. We'll wait."

I flashed a silent question to Ramona. Where is he? Her eyebrows went up with the baffled answer. Who

knows? I sidled unobtrusively toward the steps leading from the rehearsal area. Spratt looked elaborately
at his watch, then spoke with the voice of death.
"We'll all just sit here and wait like good little boys
and girls. How can you expect someone to hang himself—if you don't give him enough rope?"

I sauntered casually down the first few steps. Then
took off.

I tore back down through the auditorium, running
as though my life depended on it. Or *someone's* life,
anyway. Across the orchestra pit in three steps,
through the scenery and into the dressing room building, then pell-mell to Harry's door, where I rapped
smartly.

"Harry?"

I flung the door open; empty.

Back down along the corridor like a madman to
the Green Room. "Harry?"

Strike Two.

Next stop, the costume shop. Two girls were being
fitted as I burst in. News, especially bad news, travels
like a cold sore from lip to lip around a theatre, but
for some reason it always seems to hit the costume
shop first. The designer, his mouth full of pins, knew
who I was looking for before I opened my mouth.
"Sorry, darling," he said. *"Pas ici."*

Out the door into the backstage area again I
stopped cold, stymied. Where the hell could he be?
Then bingo, a brainwave hit me, an instinctive
hunch, and I set off again.

Past the Administration Building, past the box
office I went, running as fast as I could through the
park, on by the jocks at the baseball diamond and the
goody girls combing their hair while they pretended

not to watch; pounding up the hill to Taylor, past the dry cleaner, the shoe repair, the butcher, finally lunged for the door to Caruso's, yanked it gaspingly open, and plunged inside.

I stood in the doorway, chest heaving, eyes blinking at the sudden dimness after the sunlit street, and ran my eyes down the bar. No one. Deserted except for the usual handful of regulars nursing their midmorning beer. Strike Three. So much for instinctive hunches. I was turning to leave when the bartender saw me—and jerked his head toward the corner of the room.

There inside the phone booth was Harry, his face pressed urgently against the mouthpiece. I walked over. Through the closed glass door I could hear the note of anxiety in his voice.

"But he *promised* me next week, he would come next week," said Harry into the phone. Then quickly, "No, don't put me on hold, I'm trying to tell you it's long distance, I'm running out of change. Jesus, don't put me on hold in Ohio. I've *been* on hold all summer. Okay, okay, don't get sore," he said, then, placatingly. "Just tell him to get back to me as soon as he can, willya? Tell him it's urgent, I'm on a rehearsal break, I haven't got long. Tell him . . . it's urgent. Okay?"

He hung up, slumped frustratedly in the booth a moment. Then he banged the door open and stalked across the room to the bar, barely noticing me.

"They're . . . they're waiting rehearsal," I called uncertainly after him.

"Yeah, yeah, in a minute," said Harry brusquely, as though he had hardly heard. "He's gonna call right back." To the bartender he barked, "Lemme have a beer. Cold, for a change." He drummed his fingers on the bar, lit a cigarette, wrenched a drag out of it.

I was getting anxious myself. "Harry," I tried again, "Spratt's really getting sore—"

He whirled on me, flaring. "Listen, I got Bellinger nailed in his office, I know he's there! I'm not moving until that phone rings." His voice was low, a rod dragged across gravel. "Fucking agents . . ."

The violence of his answer startled me. This was Harry as I had never seen him before, as though some bright mask had dropped to reveal the smoldering cinders beneath. There was a pause. I was almost afraid to ask the question.

"Isn't he coming?"

"Oh, he'll show up. He's gotta show up." He took another nervous drag.

"But if it's only a question of when—"

He laughed harshly. "That's a short word for a long wait—and I'm in a hurry. Time's winged chariot is breathing up my ass, baby. Meaning, I can touch up my hair but not my life. I lost ten big ones—five in the army and five catching up." He was looking in my direction but his eyes went right through me, unseeing, focused on some irretrievable distance beyond. Suddenly his voice was big with bitterness. "I mean, who's Robert Preston, who the hell is Theodore Bikel? why didn't *I* get a short at *The Sound of Music* or *Music Man*? All right, so Drake can sing—but I can move, too, don't forget that. How many of them can move?" He glared ferociously at the phone. "Come on, you bastard, *ring*."

I was trying to understand. "Why does it *have* to be New York?"

"I'll tell you why. What's it cost to buy an orchestra

seat here, four bucks? Well, in New York it's eight.
How much the public will pay to see you—that's what
you're worth. And I'm an eight-dollar actor. Tell that
to Sherman Shitface."

He paused. A wintry look came into his eyes, his
voice grew hard. "Let me warn you about this
business. If you're not a winner, it's shit. You spend
your life on hold while they offer the part to the
other guy. And I'm not gonna piss away my best years
scratching through stock at the Pittsburgh Playhouse,
I'm not gonna end up an old watchman falling down
the prop house stairs with a coronary. Or like Fibby
Geyer, farting around with Shakespeare in a bar.
Christ, fifteen years ago I saw him *play* Romeo with
Le Gallienne. And *now* what's he doing?"

The question was rhetorical, so my blithe answer
caught him by surprise. "Oh, don't worry about
Fibby," I said. "I heard he was going to Chicago for a
terrific job."

Harry's expression changed. "Yes—of course," he
said quickly. "I forgot."

"Got it locked up, I hear."

"Yeah." Harry's voice was vacant. "He'll be great."

I took advantage of the lull to try one last time.
"Harry, come on. Please. If you get canned, how am I
gonna handle my love life?"

There was a moment that hung in the balance
while Harry looked again at the phone. Suddenly he
grinned and shrugged his shoulders. "What the hell. I
guess Bellinger knows where to find me."

The smile seemed so natural, so effortless and air-
borne I couldn't tell which Harry was which, whether
he had taken the mask off or put it back on. He slid

off the bar stool, took a step toward the door, then
stopped, and turned back.

"Oh—while I think of it," he said matter-of-factly.
"Tomorrow's strike-night, the end of *Rose-Marie.* You
might get home late. In fact, you might not be able
to get home at all. Here, in case you need a place to
flop—" He took a small object out of his pocket and
slid it along the bar. It stopped neatly in front of me.

His apartment key.

Hallelujah. Artie found us a place. I picked up the
key gingerly. The metal was cool and factual, but it
felt hot to my touch. And strange.

"I'm sorry I won't be there myself," said Harry
with a meaningful look. "I hope you'll excuse me. I
always was a rotten host."

For those who don't know, strike-night was the hallowed summer theatre ritual that happened after the
final performance of each show in the season, always
on a Saturday night. It was theatre at its most heroic,
an insane spasm of wild chaos—especially at a monster open-air place like Kempton Hills—in which the
monster set for the show that had been running was
taken down, pulled apart, and stored, and the monster set for the next show dragged on stage and
muscled up in its place. Every aspect of the production was involved—lights rehung and refocused, old
costumes collected and packed away, new costumes
unpacked and hung out. The whole frantic thing was
done in one shot, everyone on the crew worked like a
fiend and no one left until the spasm was spent, because the entire new production had to be ready for
the dress rehearsal the next day. Which meant it was
a night of violence and abandon, a time when the

theatre became a contained zoo where the animals
flung themselves around in a frenzy of do-or-die energy.

Backstage that next night at the last performance
of *Rose-Marie* you could sense the coming mayhem
almost an hour before it actually started. As soon as
the curtain went up on the second act members of
the crew started to drift into the shop, where Loomis
was handing out wreckers' tools as though they were
Winchesters before an Apache raid. Crowbars were
pulled off the rack, hammers, ratchets, razor knives
handed out like forty-fives. It was *High Noon,* the
Gunfight at the OK Corral, over-the-top-at-dawn,
Remember the Alamo.

By the time the cast hit the last sweet note of the
finale the crew was lined up in the wings, tools at the
ready. I had a crowbar and a hammer. Two-gun
Shoemaker. But I was thinking only of that sweet
hour when it would all be over, the key to Harry's
apartment burning a hole in my pocket under the
crew coat. I had caught up with Ramona and slipped
her the word earlier, when she came off stage after
"Indian Love Call."

" I lined up a place." I had said casually.

She glanced at me quickly. "For tonight?" I
nodded. "Where?" she said.

"Nothing special," I answered. "A penthouse on
Fifth Avenue."

"In that case I'll wear my mink nightie," she
grinned. "I'll be waiting in the car." Then she suddenly squeezed my hand. "I'm glad," she said softly,
and ran off.

She was glad? I didn't think I'd live until I put the
key in that lock and opened it.

So there I was, chafing at the bit, waiting off stage with the other horsemen of the apocalypse. As the cast finished their final bow and the houselights came on, the crew burst out onto the stage at a dead run, the bulls let out of the chute.

The first moments, of course, were simply an orgy of destruction. Westervelt and I were in the lead. In one reckless superhuman jump I leaped up, grabbed a dutchman—the strip of canvas used to cover the seam between two flats—and tore it right down to the ground. My first scalp. The Kempton Hills production of *Rose-Marie* was on its way to history. From there I dashed over to join Bliss and Shenker who were wrenching the nails out of the backdrop. The nails were double-headed resins and each one came out of the wood with a screech of protest, *yeep yeep yeep*, until the Canadian Rockies folded like a stack of giant cards, and we jumped back as it dropped off the front of its supporting scaffolding in a cloud of grit and dust. I strong-armed one huge piece all by myself and headed across the stage with it to where a team of people with ratchets were unscrewing hardware from the flats, zapping away furiously with long mechanical screwdrivers. Fuldauer was there, swimming in his crew coat as usual. He wore it all the time now, and went around calling everybody mother. I staggered up with the flat and dropped it beside him. He bent over it with his ratchet immediately, calling briskly to Joanne and another gimpy working with him.

"All right, mothers, let's go here!" He flashed me a grin.

I charged back into the fray, ripping the canvas from the fake logs that made up the frontier inn. The work was, if possible, picking up in tempo, building to a kind of general, continuous frenzy. There was a constant din of hammers, thudding platforms, the screech of nails, the zapping of ratchets. From the corner of my eye I could see through the open door into the corridor of the dressing room building, where things were almost as hectic as they were on the stage. I had a glimpse of Harry peeling off the last of his Mountie uniform and tossing it to a costume gimpy who was bustling along collecting costumes from the principals, swapping crinolines and uniforms and fake frontier homespunerie for the rented Parisian rags of *The Vagabond King,* which opened next.

What I couldn't see, and a good thing, too, was Ramona in her dressing room, the last of her makeup off, changing her clothes. About to put on her blouse she paused, smiled to herself. The reached for a vial of perfume, tipped it, and ran one scented finger down the cleft between her breasts. *In the valley of the shadow, thy rod and thy staff they comfort me.*

By one in the morning the flats were gone and the stage was a clutter of debris, nothing left of the old set but scaffolding and platforms. Harry's key was a hot coal in my pocket. In a sweat to finish up I attacked a huge platform top by myself and wobbled across the stage with it balanced on top of my head like a giant tray, then half-dropped, half-dumped it next to Loomis with a loud crash.

"Whoa, King Kong, take it easy," said Loomis, raising one midwestern eyebrow mildly. "You trying to do the whole strike by yourself?"

"I want to get out of here," I panted.

"What's your hurry? So you get to bed an hour later. What's the difference?"

The difference was Paradise an hour sooner, that was the difference. I looked up just in time to see Ramona emerging from the dressing room building. Our eyes met; she motioned up the hill with a look that said she would be waiting. I nodded. I'll be up to getcha in the pickup, honey. Soon. And I was just about to attack the platforms again when Westervelt yelled behind me.

"Hey—Shoemaker. Somebody looking for you."

I turned.

There were my mother and father approaching from the other side of the stage, big as life. Bigger. I just looked at them stunned.

"You're here," I said as they walked up to me, mainly because I couldn't think of what else to say. "Why didn't you warn me? Why didn't you tell me you were coming?"

"I just wanted to see with my own eyes," my mother said primly. "I just wanted to see what was going to take so long tonight."

"Well, uh, I'd love to show you around," I said, in a positive sweat to get rid of them, "but the thing is I'm kinda busy right now."

"That's all right," she said placidly. "We'll wait until you're finished."

"What?"

"We'll wait," she said again.

"I wish you could," I said, fighting a feeling of blind panic, "but you can't."

"Why not?" said my father.

"Well, see," I began calmly while a voice inside me was screaming *Don't you dare, God, don't you dare screw me up tonight, I'll get you for this, God.* "See, it might take hours, it might even take all night—"

"All *night?*" my mother broke in, shocked. "What can take all night?"

Nothing—if you don't leave. Absolutely nothing. I could see the whole glorious evening ahead sliding off the edge of a cliff, disappearing before my very eyes. They would hang around. We would all go home together and that would be it, so much for Paradise. The prophet Artie Shoemaker, permitted to borrow the key to the Promised Land but not to open the door. The Twelve Tribes had arrived to chaperone. While I racked my brain for something to say, my father suddenly bent down and picked up a piece of scrap lumber.

"My God, look at this," he clucked.

"—That's right," said a familiar voice. "Number one pine, clear. Fifty-three cents a running foot."

It was Harry watching from a few feet away. I flashed him a stay-away glance, but if he caught it he made no sign. Just ambled over with his hand out and his creamiest smile. Come on, Harry, I've got enough trouble as it is.

"How do you do, my name's Crystal. I'm afraid I work with these demented people," he said, shaking my father's hand. "It's a pleasure to meet the parents of a boy like Arthur." The face and body were Harry, all right, but I almost didn't recognize the voice. It had the measured cadence of reassurance and stability, two cooked vegetables and sensible hours; he could have been the neighborhood minister or a college dean.

My father was still examining the piece of scrap wood. "This is prime lumber." His tone was faintly offended. "You could really *do* something with this stuff, build real houses—"

"That's right," nodded Harry affably. "And we chew it up for nothing. Just so people can look at a phony fairyland for a couple of hours. Kid stuff." Behind him some of the crew were staggering in with the first of the units for *The Vagabond King*, a Parisian tavern in the fifteenth century, overblown, romantic, right out of a storybook. "Silly thing for grown people to do, isn't it?" continued Harry. "Hard to believe."

"Well, I didn't want to say it," agreed my father, somewhat mollified, a little surprised that he had found someone down at this crazy place who actually talked sense.

"Sure," said Harry softly. "Sometimes I think we're the last of the world's children down here. Just arrested development, I guess." He paused. "But for those two hours—when the sun goes down and the lights come up—we do make people believe . . . a little." His voice was very soft now. "In a way, you know, the whole thing is no more impossible . . . than God."

His words fell on them like a gentle breath over a troubled stream, blowing with it but damping the rough spots over the rocks. My mother was still a little sniffy, though.

"That doesn't explain why Arthur has to stay out all night," she said.

The Dean had an answer for that one, too. "Gotta have the new set ready for the dress rehearsal by noon tomorrow. Even a fairyland takes work," Harry admonished gently, then basted her with another creamy smile.

"Well. . ." she said weakening.

Then Harry laid in the clincher. "Mrs. Shoemaker, if it'll make you feel any better," he said with the simplicity that only the truth can inspire, "I'm not going home tonight, either."

They left five minutes later.

Harry's apartment didn't exactly have a view of Fifth Avenue. In fact it didn't have a view of anything except the back of a delicatessen on another part of Taylor Road. It was on a side street of older, shabbier houses, dark and silent at four in the morning, and at first I couldn't even find the address. Then I spotted the number nailed to a tree, pulled the pickup over to the curb, and Ramona and I got out.

The walk went up the front then around to the side. There was a door with several bells; obviously the house had been broken up into more-or-less apartments. The hall beyond the entrance was dark, and I hesitated for a second. Ramona raised an eyebrow. I smiled bravely in return and pulled open the sagging screen door. After you, kid.

The stairs inside were dark, too, but I took her hand and we groped our way up. There were three or four doors on the second floor, most of them with things like empty beer bottles and Heinz macaroni-and-cheese cans outside. I found the right one and tried the key. What do you know, it worked.

Inside, it was like the backstage of an actor's life. There was a sitting room of sorts with some weary furniture, a sink full of dishes, a skillet with the grease dried at an angle, a bathroom with a pull-chain light, a rumpled bed. On the table beside the bed was a wad of mail addressed to someone I had never heard of and sevearl dog-eared copies of *Variety*, all of them open to the page with The *Legit Bits* column. Plus two battered scrapbooks and a stack of glossy résumé photos of Harry. An open suitcase stood beside a nearly empty closet. Harry traveled light, I guess. Just took his scrapbooks, his heart, and the phone number of his agent. The past, the present, and the future. For a few moments I wandered from one thing to another, touching this and that. I don't know what I had expected. But this wasn't it.

"Not exactly the bridal suite, is it?" I said apologetically.

"So what? At least it's ours," she Ramona. She was standing near the table.

"Yeah. You've got a point." I realized she was waiting. I walked over, put my arms around her, and we kissed. But some shadow at the back of my mind was fluttering its wings, distracting me. As we parted I looked around uncertainly. "I just wish I knew where this Harold Krebs guy was, that's all."

"Who?"

I picked up an envelope from the stack of mail. "There's all this stuff here addressed to someone named Harold Krebs. Harry didn't say anything about a roommate." I looked around again, as though I half-expected him to come in at any second.

Ramona laughed. "You're too much," she said, and held up one of Harry's résumé photos. "Meet Harold Krebs." I must have looked flabbergasted, because she smiled again and said, "You look like someone who just stumbled into Superman's phone booth and found out he is Clark Kent."

I could feel my face go red. "Who said anything

about Superman? So he had to change his name for the marquee, that's all. Big deal." While I cursed myself inwardly for being Simple Simon my eye skittered across the table and fell on one of the tattered scrapbooks. I began to turn the pages, reading the dateline of the reviews pasted inside. "Westport, Cohasset, Lambertville—"

Ramona stood beside me, reading some of the headlines. I could feel the reminder of her hip against mine. "'Crystal Shines as Count Danilo,'" she read from a clipping marked Denver. "'Crystal Glitters as Gaylord Ravenal.'" That was Grand Rapids. "'Harry Crystal Stars in *Chocolate Soldier*.'" Louisville. As I continued to turn the pages she said, "Come on, it's all more of the same."

"Where's the stuff from New York?" I said, still looking.

"Harry? The closest he ever got to New York was a Shubert tour of *Blossom Time* that folded in Baltimore." I guess I looked a little crestfallen in spite of myself, because she added uncomfortably, "Look, don't make me the giant killer. What's the difference, anyhow." She turned away.

I suddenly remembered the business at hand. God, if I wasn't careful I was going to blow it. "Right, what's the difference," I said, closing the book. I smiled and took her hand. "Listen, you really are Ramona, aren't you? I'm not gonna get to New York this fall and discover you're someone else, am I?"

There was just the briefest second as it registered. "You're not coming to New York." She thought I was kidding.

"Wanna bet?"

Something flickered in her eyes. "How can you come to New York? You'll be in school."

"Maybe—and maybe not. I've been thinking about that playwright thing you said—"

"*I* said? Look, I was just talking. I didn't mean you should—"

"I know, I know. But even if I am in school I get a long weekend at Thanksgiving. I've got it all figured out. I know just the corner I'm going to meet you on. In the West Fifties, about six o'clock, when everyone is hurrying home from work—"

She had turned back and was looking at me. "What do you know about the West Fifties? Artie, you scare me a little," she said earnestly. "You're like someone floating inside a soap bubble, and any edge it touches will make it pop."

"You mean you won't be there at Thanksgiving?"

"How do I know where I'll be Thanksgiving?" she said helplessly. "I'm having enough trouble trying to be where I am now." She looked uncertainly around at the shabby apartment in the middle of the night, then at me.

She seemed so lost for a second that something welled up and turned inside me. And I kissed her, but really kissed her this time, deep and sweet. I felt her concentrate against me, focus, then yield. Her arm went around me, her hand sliding up to spread against the back of my neck. It was hard to tell who was clinging to who. Softly, almost breathlessly, our lips parted. But not our bodies.

"I know one thing we can both do on Thanksgiving. Think about tonight," said Ramona softly. She turned and led me to the bed. "Come on. We'll make a memory."

I sat on the bed, riveted by the picture, by the details that would stick in my head forever. The way she reached down, undid the thongs, and slipped out of her sandals. The way she hooked a thumb of each hand into the waistband of her jeans and pushed easily down, collecting her panties on the way, the sound the cloth made as it slid down over her hips. The small, precise shrug to make the blouse drop down her arm. The very moment, the hair-second of eternity—when the bra was unhooked and fell from her shoulders. Until she was sitting naked beside me on the bed. And started to unbutton my shirt.

I groped for something appropriate. "Ramona? I love you." I may even have meant it.

"Oh. . ." she answered gently, "you don't have to say that. Here. Do to me the way I do to you." We were both sinking backward, a bed fit for the Queen of the Nile and her Consort.

"I just want you to know," I said, "that I don't believe any of this is really happening."

At which point the phone on the bedside table rang. The sound was deafening. I looked at it stupidly for a moment, then fumbled for the receiver.

"Uh, yeah—hello," I said into the phone, trying to collect myself. A breezy man's voice at the other end was asking for Harry. "No, no one's here. I mean, he's not in." Which netted me a wisecrack from the other end. "Well, no wonder I sound confused," I said belligerently. "You always call people at five o'clock in the morning? Who is this, anyway?" At the sound of the name I stopped fooling around and snapped to attention. "Right. Right," I nodded, trying to remember what he was saying. "Right. Right. I'll tell him. No, no, that's okay," I said as the voice

at the other end finished, "I happened to be up, anyway."

I hung up. There was a pause. Then at Ramona's
quizzical expression I said slowly, "That was a
message—for Superman. Mickey Bellinger will be
here Thursday." And I dropped back on the pillow,
laughing.

Smiling herself, Ramona asked, "You okay?"

"Fantastic." A moment later as her mouth slid
down toward my waist, heading south for the tropical
zones, I murmured again, "Fantastic. Absolutely
. . . fantastic."

And all the while, Harry's glossy photo looked
down on us from the bedside table in smiling bene-
diction.

I hear you calling me
Lovely Vienna, so gay so free
City of love and sparkling wine
You're such a part-of
This heart-of mine . . .

—*"Vienna, My City of Dreams"*

The party Ramona and I had that night was in all
ways superior to the one Moe Shenker gave in New
York twenty years later. When I accepted his invitation I never figured actually to show up, of course,
but I reckoned without Bertie. I caught her huddled
over the phone the day before with that familiar
battle-fatigue look.

"What are you doing?"

"Getting a sitter for that party tomorrow night, of
course. It *would* be on a Saturday."

"I didn't know you wanted to go."

"I don't. But you *told* him we were going," she said
firmly. "So we have to go." Bertie can be like that.
Honor is not a meaningless word to her.

Shenker's borrowed apartment was actually a loft
down in the depths of SoHo, one of those remodeled
barns in which space was defined by different built-in
levels. The kitchen was up a level, the bedrooms were
down, the library was up a half, the living room was

down two; which meant you spent the evening going up and down stairs playing King-of-the-Hill.

The funny thing was, I couldn't really figure out why I had been invited. Except for one or two people whom I dimly remembered as being in the chorus of *The Desert Song* the others all seemed to be academic theatre types from colleges out of town, come down to the city to sniff and scorn, interested only in Off- and Off-Off Broadway where they cultivated theatre as they would mushrooms, in caves and basements. The neon palaces of Broadway, of course, were both above ground and beneath contempt. The loft was a sea of corduroy, naturally, but the really big thing was hair. Moustaches, goatees, beards, the whole out- fit looked like a gallery of nineteenth-century Ameri- can presidents. There was a Ulysses S. Grant, a Grover Cleveland, and at least two Martin Van Bu- rens with muttonchops draped lavishly down from their ears. Shenker's own Fu Manchu moustache had spread like crabgrass across his face, but to me he was still the same Bronx mongoose. Only with a more limited vocabulary.

"Artaud is *the* seminal figure, of course," he was saying while he took Bach's Third Brandenburg off the stereo and put on the Fourth. As he dropped the needle he added, "Next to Brecht, that is." Shenker's dissertation was on *The Uber-Marionette and Its Relationship to the Verfremsdung Effekt in the Plays of Bertolt Brecht.* (Honest. It really was.) "Aliena- tion and the Theatre of Cruelty, they both have the same thrust, really," he went on. "Keep the audience threatened, off-balance. That's the only hope for the future." He was talking to another professor with a fringe of beard right along the ridgeline of his cheeks, which made his face look like a talking prayer shawl.

The shawl nodded sagely. "Artaud is simply a restatement of surrealism," he said. "Simply surrealism restated."

"What do you think?" said Shenker suddenly to me. I was standing next to them sparring with a plate of Greek salad, having already fought and lost with the zucchini quiche.

"I don't know," I said foggily. "I never really read Artaud."

"You haven't?" Shenker seemed amused. "You can't understand Grotowski without it."

"Who's Grotowski?" I said.

"You're putting me on," said Shenker. "I thought you were interested in the theatre."

"I am—or I was. But that's beginning to be a while ago, Moe. It's a long way from Kempton Hills."

"Murray," said Moe.

I didn't know how far it was, in fact, until we got into what had happened to some of the other people from that summer. The most astonishing thing was the casualty list. Beginning with Danny D'Angeli himself.

"Coronary," said Shenker. "Left a wife and four kids with cereal-bowl haircuts in a house full of do-it-yourself furniture."

"Seventy-five drachmas," I breathed. "You hear about anybody else? Hlavacek, Westervelt, maybe Bliss?"

"Hlavacek went to art school, dirty feet and all. And Bliss is chairman of the department at some Bible school in South Carolina where they don't believe in fags." This last for the benefit of Professor

Prayer Shawl, who smirked on cue. "And I suppose you know about Cooky."

"No, what? After that summer I never heard of him again."

"And never will. He had a stroke."

"A *stroke?*"

Shenker nodded. "Aged twenty-nine. Keeled over while he was out bowling somewhere. Can you believe it? *Bowling.*" He shook his head. "Could be right out of Camus." Then he looked at me slyly. "But the best of all is Sherman Spratt. He's still there in Cleveland Heights, running an after-school drama program for the board of education. Does prepubescent Shakespeare in the junior high."

I shuddered.

"Each man writes his own epitaph," said Professor Moe Murry Shenker.

"The past is always with us," I countered. If he wanted to play the game of pithy statements I was willing to out-pith him.

"Everybody at that place ended up about the way he deserved," announced Shenker. Then added, quickly, "No offense meant."

"Glad to hear it. You had me worried there for a minute."

"No, no," said Shenker from a great height. "After all, there's a place for popular entertainment in the arts, too." He paused, then said casually, "Film, for instance, has great possibilities. The reason so many of those people turn into whores is that they never think of stretching the medium."

"I suppose." Somewhere inside my head a Distant Early Warning signal started to flash faintly.

He was warming up. "In fact, it's a wonder to me

that no one has ever considered some of the major seminal works that cry out, simply cry out to be translated to the screen. Works that would really stretch the medium." He leaned confidentially toward me. "Have you ever thought of *Waiting for Godot?*"

"As what?"

"A film, of course."

So that's what I was doing there. I looked at him. "*Waiting for Godot?*" I said.

"Actually, I've already worked out a little outline, thirty pages or so. If you're looking for something worthwhile you might like to run your eye over it. The potential symbolic resonance is enormous. I've even used certain applications of the Alienation Effect as Brecht sets it forth in the *Organon*—you do know Brecht's *Organon?*"

"Whoa, Murray," I said, holding up my hands. "You got me hopelessly outclassed here, you're way beyond me. I'm just a hired gun, I try to write parts and pictures that stars will want to play and be in, so some poor producer can convince a studio to put up six or seven or God-knows-how-many million and make the damned thing. That's all I do. And all I'm looking for right now is some more of this terrific salad." With that I turned and fled toward the food table while Moe cried after me, "Don't be a whore, stretch yourself."

As I threaded my way through the sea of corduroy and facial hair I suddenly noticed something familiar about the older man standing with his back to me at the salad bowl. There was a vaguely remembered slope to the shoulders, dropping but not quite down, sort of what you could call a declining jauntiness, and an indefinable theatrical cut to his jib. Then he swung around with a plateful of salad. There it was, the same jut to the chin, the same crest to the eyebrows.

"Remember me?" said Harry Crystal softly. "I play the drum."

"My God—Harry." He was dressed like a Hollywood set; all facade but not much of a building behind. The sports coat was dapper but the cut was old; the shoes were buffed but the leather had seen better nights. And he was wearing, of all ungodly things, an ascot. In this crowd. Jesus, he had taken a chance.

"What are you doing now? No, wait a minute, I remember," I said. "You're playing in that Off-Broadway thing. The O'Neill play."

"Guilty as charged."

"What part?"

"The old man. You are looking at James Tyrone himself, himself," said Harry, striking a pose. Then with the old grin, "I hadda do something. The Shuberts stopped sending out *The Student Prince*." We both laughed. Good old Harry. "The miracle is," he said, "it might even turn out to be a halfway-decent production. They're talking about moving it uptown in time for the Tony Awards."

"Terrific." My eyes were searching across the room for Bertie.

"Listen, I got a coupla tickets for a preview, if you're interested in using them."

It would have been great to say yes. It would have been great to say Chill the bubbly, we'll raise a cracked glass to Sherman Spratt and old times. But the truth was I was beset by age, I was afflicted with a half-forgotten dream of my own, I was earning a living. And the last thing I wanted to do was sit through an evening of Harry Crystal in *Long Day's Journey into Night*. "No kidding. When are they for?"

"Next Wednesday's the only night left. We open Thursday."

"Well, I'd love to see it."

"Say no more. They'll be at the window in your name." He was obviously pleased. "Glad you can make it."

"Couldn't keep me away. The only thing is," I said, nodding in Bertie's direction, "I ought to check with my wife. Just to see if she has anything in her book."

His smile never wavered. He didn't even blink. "Sure, you'd better check," he said.

"But if we can possibly be there—"

"Sure. Don't make a problem for yourself." He made a face and put down his salad. "I don't know how the Greeks can stand all this feta cheese. Even an actor can't eat it."

I waved casually and made my way across the room to Bertie. She was standing against the wall, nodding politely at some Rutherford B. Hayes who was trying to put the make on her by talking about castration images in early English mystery plays. I leaned over to her ear.

"Tell me we're busy on Wednesday," I said.

"What?"

"This Wednesday, we're busy, right?"

"We'd better be," she said. "I stood in line for an hour to get those tickets to *Elephant Man*."

"Saved by *Elephant Man*," I breathed.

"A solid hour. Everybody else has contacts so they don't have to wait in line. Why don't you have contacts?"

"I do. Only they're for flops. I can get us into any flop in town."

"So I've noticed," she said, then paused. "Saved from what?" she asked. But I never got to answer because Shenker was booming at Harry from across the room.

"It was all the most *unbelievable* shit—right, Harry? Those creaking old operettas, those hokey one-lung productions. God, that was a summer out of time and memory. The Kempton Hills Theatre, what a farce. We all should have been indicted for fraud."

For some obscure reason I felt a pang.

"Why?" said Harry quietly. "They paid for a show, we gave them a show."

"Sure. *The Red Mill* and *The Desert Song*." He rolled his eyes comically to the accompaniment of knowing professorial smiles around the room.

"None of them asked for their money back, as I remember. In fact, the people loved it."

"Oh, the people," said Shenker impatiently. "I'm talking about theatre."

"So am I," said Harry. "There was an audience. There were actors. They got an evening's entertainment."

"*Entertainment,*" exploded Shenker. "What does that have to do with it? God, if all we had to do was pander to audiences instead of challenging them, if all we're going to worry about is pleasing the people," he said scornfully, "if *that's* the test—"

Harry shrugged. "I always thought it was one of them," he said mildly. He reached for his coat. "Sorry to take off, but I'm late for rehearsal and I gotta run my lines first."

Shenker couldn't seem to drop it. "Why, Harry, you

surprise me. I thought you already knew the Red Shadow."

Harry glanced at him, then said, still mild, "Happens to be *Long Day's Journey.*"

"Not *O'Neill!*" cracked Shenker. "Most overrated dramatist in the American theatre. He writes with his elbows."

"Maybe," said Harry. "But it's a helluva part." He paused, then couldn't resist. "They're talking about moving it uptown."

"Perfect place for it," said Shenker promptly. "Certainly doesn't belong in a *real* theatre. An audience full of expense—account Babbits stuffed with steaks from Sardi's—"

"—And me." The words were out of my mouth before I could stop them. "Next Wednesday, right, Harry? Just leave them at the window."

Harry was looking at me in faint surprise. So, by the way, was my wife.

"You sure?" said Harry.

"Wouldn't miss it," I nodded cheerfully, feeling good for the first time all evening. "You know how it is," I said to Professor Murray Shenker. "Us whores gotta stick together."

When we left a few minutes later Shenker was still cooing "Stretch yourself!" seductively in my ear, and Professor Prayer Shawl was saying, "Simply surrealism. Surrealism restated."

13

—•—

When you're pret-tee and the world is fair
Why be bothered by a doubt or care
For to worry is to double
                    trouble
There'll be enough of that hereafter . . .

                    —The Red Mill

The past may or may not always be with us, but
when you are in the past it is with you, all right, up
to the neck. And if that past is a summer theatre you
are in it up over the eyeballs, you simply notice nothing else. Certainly it was all I could see that first summer at Kempton Hills back in 1960—and all that
Harry could see, too. Following the dawn phone call
from Bellinger he was a man driven by one thing and
one thing only. Even after the next show opened on
Monday he kept working on his lines every chance he
got, he conned the pianist into playing for him, he
ran his numbers, reran them, then ran them again.
He rehearsed by himself before the rest of the company arrived and again after they broke for supper,
he was altogether a man possessed, focused like a
beam of sun through the lens of Bellinger into a
single burning dot fixed on the performance that
coming Thursday. The few days before then were all
framed by the sight and sound of him singing and

dancing, and everything else that happened was tucked into that frame like good-luck snapshots stuck around the edges of a dressing room mirror.

These were some of the other little pictures:

The stage crew gathered in a knot backstage one afternoon, trying to incite D'Angeli to riot after Spratt had unloaded on him as usual. It seemed there was a problem with part of the set for *Vagabond King*, one of the dollies didn't quite fit through the slot in the backstage trees and couldn't be rolled on when the cue came. So it had to be taken apart on the spot and something else improvised, which in turn left some of the set unfinished, particularly the backdrop. We were still working on it through the first three nights of the show. And the morning after opening night Spratt had come backstage and exploded. "You are a clown," he had screamed at D'Angeli in front of the whole crew. "You are a fumbling Farmer Brown idiot, can't you even measure the space between two trees? The sets look like something that came out of a Cracker Jack box, anyway, and now you can't even get the mess on stage." D'Angeli said nothing, his face white. "Go back to high school, go back to your shop courses, you woodbutcher, you have all the talent of a wastebasket. The next time," fumed Spratt, "there won't *be* a next time." The truth was that D'Angeli was either a genius or a hopeless Rube Goldberg hack, I couldn't tell which. The crew of course was behind him to a man. The only problem was they may have been trying to push him off a cliff.

"All right," said D'Angeli faintly as Spratt stormed off, "let's get right onto that backdrop."

Shenker was glaring after Spratt. "Why do you take such shit from that chinless schmeckle?"

"There are," said D'Angeli softly, "economic considerations."

"I'd kick his economic nuts," said Cooky.

"Over his head," amended Westervelt.

"I'm not here to play cowboys and Indians," said D'Angeli, "and neither are you. Let's go. We want to beaver right on with that backdrop."

"I'd tell him to shove the mothering job," said Loomis sullenly.

"It's not your job, it's my job," said D'Angeli. "And I want to see a new brace on that stage-right return, too. Let's not have any more trouble." As he walked away he shook his porky head slightly. "Cowboys and Indians," he muttered, "do not appreciate economics."

Then another picture, this one in the shape of a heart: Ramona and me. After the night at Harry's the thing between us had become a fact of backstage life. Each of us was now the one the other turned to whenever there were a few slack moments. I waited for her at the rehearsal break, she shared my ice cream at Munjah, I sat in her dressing room and saw the slips from the fortune cookies she had saved and pasted on her mirror. *A night for love and adventure,* read one. *Make the most of your talents* was another. Though we had no bed to call our own I knew we would find one, and so did she.

The rest of the company seemed to know it. too. There was the moment when Ginger Treat, the perky redhead, fell in step beside me as she came off stage after "Huguette's Waltz" (*Never try to bind me*) on opening night. "Well, I see you found another feather, Popeyes. But I guess you didn't bring it to me." A mock sigh. "Too bad. We could've had fun."

"Next time," I promised.

"Oh ho, now I gotta get in line. Tell me, what is the secret of your success, what exactly is it about you, Popeyes?"

"I don't know. But if there is anything, I sure wish somebody would tell me." We both laughed, but I really wasn't paying much attention.

Because I was Ramona's guy, and everything about her fascinated me. The way she moved that was both woman and child at the same time, the starchy feel of her crinoline slip against the softness of her skin and all the little mysteries as well; the smell of her soap, the tips of her fingers, the very bones of her ankles. My head was full of plans, I couldn't stop making them. And while the sound of Harry endlessly rehearsing came from the stage I worked in the prop house with my hands heavy from the memory of her rear end, waiting for the next *night of love and adventure.*

And the last snapshot, a quickie: Bumping into Fuldauer in the wings where he was listening to Harry rehearse "Only a Rose." I kept tripping over the old man everywhere. He was always hanging out with the crew, a new and confidential look in his eye as befitted one of the boys. And just before dinnertime on the afternoon of the big performance there he was in his crew coat, humming along with Harry under his breath. He smiled when he saw me and lifted his eyebrows with the lilt of the song.

"Just like Düsseldorf, huh, Doctor F.?"

He waggled his hand. "Like it—and not like it," he said. "What is as good as it once was? But this is a nice score, this show. Not like Lehar, maybe, but not bad."

"I didn't know you were such a theatre person." I wasn't exactly kidding him, but I wasn't exactly not.

His laugh had an odd edge to it. "What did you think, I was only a person who taught Latin and tutored in the summer, a person who has always three women riding him like harpies?" I must have looked startled, because his expression softened. "Oh, in Germany before Hitler I was a person like other persons, I had a beautiful life. Not just the theatre, but also the cafes, the women. Could you believe? I had my academic robe, my wife was beautiful, it was a pleasure to go out on the street." He shrugged. "Well, who has not lost? I lost one thing, some another." He pointed upstage to D'Angeli who was watching worriedly as the backdrop was finally being beefed into place. "Look at him. He loses every day. So. What should I do—complain here in this wonderful country that has given me so much, that has given me, a professor at the *Universität,* an opportunity to teach high school Virgil?"

He looked at me, suddenly intent. "You understand? It is not that they chase you away from your home and make you earn your living like a chicken, pecking among the cinders. It is that they took from you what you were. What you *were,* that's what they took from you. Do you understand me, Arthur? And after that you are always looking over your shoulder to see who will take it from you next."

His face relaxed. "Still, sometimes you get a little of it back. My wife is still a handsome woman, and this is not such a bad robe, either." He snapped the cuffs on the crew coat with a grin. Out on the stage

Harry's voice hit a sweet phrase in the song. Fuldauer swayed with it a moment, listening. "He is not bad, Mr. Crystal, *hein?*"

"Harry?" I said. "He's terrific. Some of them can sing, but he can move, too, you know. How many of them can move? He could be a star. He's got everything."

"Well," said Dr. Fuldauer, "let us hope that is enough." I looked at him, but he gestured impatiently. "Go, listen to the rehearsal, not to me. I talk too much. Go."

So I went out on stage, then down into the auditorium, and sat in the box which Harry had reserved for Bellinger because he wanted me to check the sight lines on the number. He did the song twice and was not satisfied, then twice more trying to iron out the kinks and get the thing exactly the way he wanted it. Finally he started for the fifth time.

Only a rose to whi-ih-ih-sper, blushing as ro-ses do, he sang, then went a shade flat on the last word. The pianist struck the note sharply to bring him back on pitch. *Ro-ses do,* corrected Harry and slid on to the next, crooning, *Oh, I'll bring along a smile or a song—* Suddenly he broke off, waving to the pianist to stop. "No, no, kill it, no good, muddy. I know Mickey. He likes a clean attack, a big voice—"

I stood up wearily. "Harry, it's suppertime. I gotta get home."

He waved me to sit. "Wait, I just want to get this." Then he paused. "You *sure* he said Thursday?"

"I swear to you—for the eleventh time—Thursday."

He started to pace excitedly. "Somebody must be casting, I know Bellinger. This is Mister Dollars-and-Cents, a real meat peddler. He wouldn't come unless there was something he could sell me for." He looked up prayerfully. "Well, keep your fingers crossed."

"It all depends on the weather," I said, staring anxiously at the sky. There were a few fleecy clouds, nothing particularly threatening. "If this just holds, if we just get a break—"

"The weather is not what I was thinking of," he said archly.

"Harry, you do the number great. That's all that counts."

There was a derisive snort from Harry. "What counts is whether he got laid the night before and how's his heartburn." He sat on the stage right where he was, figuring feverishly. "He casts the Rodgers and Hammerstein stuff, maybe it's the new Rodgers and Hammerstein. Must be a decent part, he wouldn't schlepp all this way unless it was something decent. Could even be something featured."

"Harry, you're gonna miss supper—"

"Fuck supper. If I get this part I'll buy you six suppers. I'll take you to Sardi's, we'll suck up a little cannelloni, they have terrific cannelloni at Sardi's." He paused, dazzled at the splendor of his own thought. "Jesus, a featured part in a Rodgers and Hammerstein musical." He jumped briskly back to his feet. "Well, if he got laid I'm in business, if he has a hard-on I'm in the toilet." Then to the pianist, "Hit it."

> *I'll bring along*
> *A smile or a song for anyone*
> *Only a rose for youuuuuu!*

As I trudged up the hill away from the theatre I could still faintly hear the rehearsal piano thumping away in the orchestra pit. It had never occurred to me that Harry would be nervous about his performance. I figured he would just naturally sail right through it like Walter Hampden or Barrymore. But maybe they got nervous, too.

I had just started along the street—when suddenly there was the pickup truck rattling over to the curb beside me. The passenger door swung open. On the other side my father was behind the wheel.

"Get in," he said. I looked at him in surprise. "*Get in.*"

I got. He reached across me to close the door, then drove off again without a word. There was an uncomfortable silence while he stared straight ahead through the windshield. I settled myself for a rough ride.

After four grim blocks I finally said, "Well. To what do I owe the honor?"

"The dean," he said shortly. He pulled an envelope from his pocket and dropped it in my lap. "Isn't it wonderful? He's such a busy man, and he takes the time to write me letters." He tapped the envelope. "You want to explain this?"

I didn't even have to take the letter out of the envelope. "It's nothing," I said. "You were right, that's all."

"Is that so," he said impassively.

"I couldn't handle both things." I took a small breath. And dove over the precipice. "So I dropped the course. You get a refund."

"Wonderful." His voice was as dry as the Sahara. "Your mother can use it to buy a gun to kill herself. Or you. I'm afraid to take this home for her to see. That lousy job . . ."

"Dad," I said earnestly, "it's not just a job. It's—it's a whole different life."

"Ycah," said my father, unimpressed, "I saw what it is. I saw what was sitting in this truck." And then I realized that he and my mother must have seen Ramona waiting for me as they walked home from the theatre on strike-night. He knew why I had stayed out all night. Knew that it had nothing to do with building a fairyland, either. He reached into his wallet, took out ten dollars, and flipped it at me. "Here," he said, "here's ten dollars. Go down to that whorehouse on Prospect Avenue and buy yourself five more lives."

I flushed, but said nothing.

"Arthur, you gonna piss away your whole life because you want to get laid a coupla times?"

"If that's what you think it is," I said tightly, "forget it. I'm not going to say another word."

"Fine. Don't say anything, just tell me this. How do you expect to get through college if you keep dropping courses?"

I figured I might as well get it over with. "It doesn't matter. I've been thinking the whole thing over." Then with barely a pause, I dropped the bomb. "I'm going to New York in the fall, anyway."

What followed may have been the longest pause of my life.

"*You're going to quit school?*" he said, aghast. "With only one year left to go? What for? What can you do in New York?"

"Try to be a playwright." I felt a little mad, but it did have a noble ring.

"A *what?*"

"Dad, I don't expect you to understand—"

"A playwright? Have you ever written anything?"

"Not really. But I've got a feeling."

His voice was half-bewildered, half-pleading. "Look, you don't want to be a doctor, you want to commit financial suicide for a while—all right. But at least finish college first. Equip yourself for *something*."

"You don't *need* to go to college to become a writer," I said. And then added with the simple certainty of the angels, "What you need is to understand people."

A long silence fell between us.

Finally, a little scared, I said, "Dad . . . I wish you were on my side."

He never took his eyes from the windshield as he answered. "Oh, I am, Arthur, I am. I hope you get everything you want from this theatre business. I hope you win the Nobel Prize." He paused. "Because if you don't finish college, Sonny Boy, you're gonna need it."

We drove the rest of the way home without a word.

I never tried for the Nobel, fool that I was. Compared to the disasters which lay ahead of me that night, it would have been a cinch.

14

Oh give me that night divine
And let my arms in yours entwine
The Desert Song calling
Its voice enthralling
Will make
you
mine!

—*The Desert Song*

In the dressing room before the show that evening nothing seemed any different than before. There was the same silence, the same harsh light, the same trembling leaves through the window—though the angle of their shadow was somewhat closer to the autumnal equinox; with or without Mickey Bellinger the planets continued in their appointed round. Finally there was the same drawn and ravaged face heaving itself into view before the same mirror. The same pause to study the ruin.

Then as he did every evening Harry raised his fingers and left the first two orange blobs of makeup on his forehead. He looked at his hands. They were trembling. And if you were the same fly on the same wall that was there the first time you might have guessed. This was the night of nights. This was a man whose fate could be decided in the next two hours.

Harry picked up the liner-pencil. It slipped through his shaking fingers, clattering to the table.

He let it lie for a moment, turning a jittery face to the window. There was the murmur of the first cars pulling to the curb, doors clunking open and shut, the first Ohio pillars saying how-do to each other while they twitched the creases out of their summer flannel. On a desperate impulse Harry yanked open the drawer and took out the bottle of whiskey. About to unsrew the cap and tilt it to his lips he hesitated— then slammed it back in the drawer. Instead he rummaged through the litter on the tabletop, found the usual crushed cigarette, and got it lighted. Then using two hands he managed to get the pencil to his eyebrows again. The first stroke was wobbly. But not the second.

There. That was better.

He hunched himself toward the mirror.

Outside, the auditorium gates were opened, and the first people began to shuffle in. Prudie Rendlesham and her ushers bowed and scraped, reverently skirting the empty box that waited for Bellinger. In the dressing room Harry was coming back to life, as usual, under the restorative magic of the makeup. He pulled on François Villon's breeches. Next into the boots, stamping to settle them properly. Like the trunks of two trees they gave him support, firmness, line. Then the blouse, flowing and soft. As he buttoned the cuff his lip curled, his eyebrow arched, he was partly Villon already. Last, a shrug into the cape and he was all there, the beggar-poet of France and *To hell with Burgundee.* He reached automatically for the talcum to powder down—and there again was another slip of paper under the puff. Harry unfolded the paper.

Give 'em hell, it read. And was signed *Artie.*

* * *

Out in the corridor I had a pretty good case of nerves myself. After the conversation with my father I felt as though I had called my own bluff, had indeed crossed the Rubicon. The only thing was, I wasn't sure it was Rome that lay ahead of me. Still, I was on my way to being part of it all now, I was really on my way. I told myself, of course, that it was my hopes for Harry which had my teeth on edge and gave me a strange shortness of breath.

About the time he was reading my mash note I was just leaving Ramona at the entrance to the dancers' dressing room. "See you after," I said.

"You mean, the limousine awaits?"

"Sure. The big Caddy pickup with Shoemaker painted on the door." She laughed. "Still haven't found another penthouse, though," I added apologetically.

"That's all right," she said with a pixy look. "You never can tell, I might even try it in the limousine. See how the other half loves."

"At your service, madam." I tried to look excited, but my eye kept straying toward Harry's door. "So. It's his big night, I guess."

"Yeah. I hear his agent likes to call people at five in the morning." She looked at me, waiting for my smile.

But I wasn't listening for the joke. "Keep your fingers crossed," I said, with another nervous glance down the corridor.

"Hey. Relax."

"Me? I'm relaxed. I'm fine."

"Be thankful for one thing," she said lightly. "At least it's not *your* audition."

From the way I hurried out of the dressing room building a few seconds later you might have thought it was. Down past the set I went, around the stage manager's booth and right in behind the stage-left return where there was a peephole in the canvas through which I could look at the house. The audience was really beginning to fill up the seats now, chatting and fanning and buzzing. But that box seat was still empty. Shit. I pulled my head away again to find Cooky lounging insolently against the return beside me.

"Oh, my goodness," he said with a mocking smile, "don't tell me he's not here yet."

"Who's not here?" I said, trying to sound casual.

"Your friend Bellinger, of course."

"Don't be ridiculous," I said. "It's way too early." From the dressing room building I could hear the stage manager calling, "Five minutes, five minutes, please."

"Yeah?" said Cooky. "Tell me all about it, Mister Show-Biz."

But before I could tell him to go pee up a rope another Mr. Show-Biz came strolling around the edge of the wings. It was Dr. Fuldauer, the Düsseldorf impressario himself, proudly showing his daughter Naomi around the backstage area. He was still swimming in that crew coat which was oceans too large for him, with each of the cuffs turned back twice. Naomi, on the other hand, was wearing a skimpy, shapeless summer cotton dress which she had outgrown a year ago. Every now and then she would stoop quickly when she thought no one was looking and tug at her sagging bobby socks that kept disappearing into her shoes, which were as large as the dress was small.

Down for those socks and up again she would go, the
way a bird pecks at a worm, darting her head worriedly this way and that. But if she was a melancholy
little sparrow, Fuldauer was a pouter pigeon as he
showed her around, gesturing and lecturing impor-
tantly like an old pro.

"And this is where we operate the lights," he said,
waving toward the switchboard.

But Naomi was plucking distractedly at his arm,
still looking around uneasily. "Poppa, is this really all
right, me being here?"

"Why not? Why shouldn't it be all right?" said Fuldauer expansively, pointing to the scene dock. "And
over there, where we store the old scenery, so." Then
he steered her to a place just off in the wings. "Now,"
he said, "if you stand right here you can see the show.
The actors will come right by you." The stage manager was calling, "Places. Places, please." Beyond
them I could see Harry, resplendent in full makeup
and costume, emerging from the dressing room building and heading downstage.

"Poppa," Naomi was saying.

"You can watch the dancers, listen to the orchestra—"

"But, Poppa," said Naomi worriedly again, "what
if they ask me for a stub? I didn't pay, I just walked
in."

"Of course you walked in," said Fuldauer grandly,
as though he owned the place. "You are with me,
aren't you? They know me—" He broke off as Harry
walked by. "Good evening, Mr. Crystal," he said.

"Yeah, whaddya say, kid," answered Harry with a
preoccupied nod and kept on going toward the return.

"You see?" said the little man to the fretful girl,

"They *all* know me. Now you stand there and enjoy yourself." For the first time the corners of Naomi's mouth turned up in a small smile. "And don't make eyes at the actors." At that she laughed outright, and he smiled gaily. Papa the pigeon and his sparrow daughter. *Sometimes you get a little of it back,* I thought.

As Harry walked up to me at the return I stepped quickly back from the peephole. Out in the pit the musicians were tuning up. "They haven't even started the overture," I said to him quickly. "There's still plenty of time."

"Last call for places," said the stage manager.

"Oh, sure," said Cooky with a heavy laugh. "Two minutes at least."

In the pit the overture was starting. Taking his time, barely glancing at my strained face, Harry put his eye to the peephole. He stared impassively a moment. Unless Bellinger had magically materialized in the last three seconds I knew Harry was looking at an empty box seat. But when he pulled his head away again there was nothing on his face but a relaxed grin.

"Boy," he said, "you can count on Mickey. Never shows until the last split second." Then as he turned to pass Cooky he nodded amiably. "Whaddya say, Cook? Pulled out any towrings lately?" And sauntered off upstage.

Boy, that Harry. He was beautiful.

What I could not see was the moment after he turned the far corner of the wings. Alone, out of sight for a second in a hidden angle of the scenery, the smile fell from his mouth. Suddenly his face twisted. He pounded his fist savagely against a platform.

Once, Twice. Three times, the words wrenched out of him.

"*Shit-son of a bitch*. Just once just once just once. Couldn't somebody just fucking *once* be there? Just fucking *once!*"

He paused, panting with frustration and fury. Then he sagged, stumbled blindly, almost fell.

The stage manager stuck his head around the corner behind him. "Harry, you all set?"

There was just the flicker of a pause. Slowly Harry turned. He was wearing the same old grin and wink. "Loaded for bear," he said.

From the moment the show started it was clearly down. Not bad, not terrible, just flat. Cues were a hair late, the scene shifts were ragged, the songs half a beat behind the conductor. Everybody in the company was humping, trying to force it along, but the life and love just weren't there. It was as though that single empty box seat had a hypnotic effect. Everyone was waiting for Elijah, except that Elijah had decided not to make it this year, sorry. Harry seemed empty, strangely dull, forcing himself through the part. And when François Villon was just going through the motions they were just motions.

The first act came and went, and still no Bellinger.

Somehow things staggered into act two. The vapid soprano, now dressed as a noble member of King Louis's court, faced a mechanical Harry.

"Are your words brazen or true gold?" she recited.

"My words are my life," answered Harry listlessly.

God, it was awful. In despair down at the stage-left return I looked for maybe the three-hundredth time through the peephole at the box seat. Still empty. I turned away to find Cooky dogging me like the Ghost of Christmas Past. "Good old Mickey Bellinger," he said, with that crossbones grin. "You can count on Mickey."

I saw him first.

A natty figure working his way down the aisle toward the box. It had to be him. There was a telephone hunch to his shoulders and a suntan that went right up over the top of his bald head, but the clincher was the careful blankness of his face. Whatever expression it had was the kind you got with a manicure in a ten-dollar barber shop, colorless but glossy. His jacket was rumpled from travel, but the cut was nothing you would find hanging in the rack at Higbee's above two pair of pants, either. Mickey Goddam At-Last Bellinger. He took his seat in the box and sat there, bald head shining, arms folded across his chest, a Broadway Buddha in a double-breasted blazer.

I snapped my head back toward the stage.

Harry hadn't seen him yet. He was standing in a half-hearted cavalier pose against a plywood balustrade, staring into space while the soprano came down some stairs toward him, emoting heavily. "And you wrote me this?" she said. Then pretending to read from a piece of prop foolscap she intoned, "If I were King, ah, Love, if I were King/ What tributary nations I would bring/ To kneel before your sceptre—" She had reached Harry. That was his cue. He took her hand as though it were a prop, drew it to him, and kissed her mechanically. His eyes were open, roaming idly across the stage, the wings, out to lunch. Then his glance happened to drift across the audience.

And the box seat.

It was as though he had plugged his finger into an open wall socket. An electric current surged through him right up to the roots of his hair—and he released all the voltage on the unsuspecting girl. She twitched in astonishment, then wrapped both her arms around him and hung on for dear life. The perfunctory embrace suddenly became a torrid, mashing clinch. It was Gable grabbing Jean Harlow, John Gilbert attacking Garbo, Errol Flynn soul-kissing Maid Marian.

As they broke, with the poor girl trying to get her bearings, Harry trumpeted the rest of the lines, *"And to swear/ Allegiance to .your lips, your eyes, your hair;/ Beneath your feet what treasures I would fling/ If I were King."*

Still reeling, eyes a little glazed, the soprano gasped, "What manner of man are you to speak to me like—" She never got out the rest of the line because Harry seized her again, hung another torrid one on her (which was definitely *not* in the script), then flung her from him.

"I would dare that and more!" he cried in clarion tones and made a flying exit, leaving the dazed soprano looking as though she had been gang banged by the Cleveland Browns.

I ran back to the prop table just as Harry came tearing up, a galvanized bundle of demonic energy, and rummaged wildly through the props. "Gimme gimme gimme, where's that fucking rose—"

I whipped it out. He grabbed it, stuck it in his teeth, clasped his hands excitedly over his head in the sign of victory, and took off downstage again. I ran after him to watch. In the dimness of the wings he pelted to a stop, hastily checked his costume one last time. This was it. He settled himself, took one last deep breath, and stepped onto the stage. As the lights hit him he broke into the song, giving it everything he had.

Only a rose I gi-ih-ihve you
Only a rose dying away ...

The number went well enough at first. I was standing in the wings pulling for him the way you would a racehorse. Come on, Harry. Go, kid. Go. Only gradually did it begin to dawn on me that something was just a shade below par. Not wrong, exactly; just not quite right, not quite *there*. For whatever reason—whether trying too much or starting too late—a certain edge was missing. What's more, I could see that Harry was beginning to sense it, too. He sang louder, smiled more brightly as he went on.

Only a smile to keep in mem-ore-eee
Until we meet some other day-yay ...

Any actor will tell you. Sometimes the harder you push, the worse it gets. Harry tried everything, looking for that groove. Louder, softer, brighter, darker, nothing helped. Then as if things weren't rough enough, I heard the sound of loud voices coming from somewhere up behind the scenery. What were they trying to do to him, for God's sake? I ran toward the noise, looking for the loudmouth.

It was Spratt, of course. He was staring waspishly at the hapless D'Angeli, in the midst of a circle of dancers who were waiting to go on in the number, Ramona among them. They were all standing behind the large blank canvas of the backdrop that had just finally been hauled into place that afternoon. As I came barreling up, Spratt was looking at the backdrop in a rage. "All right, where is it, *where's the entrance?*" he said loudly. "Just show me where."

From off downstage I could hear the strains of Harry fighting his way through the song. "Hey, hold it down," I said. "Shhh—"

"For three nights," said Spratt, louder still, ignoring me, "we had an entrance here for the dancers." He waved his hand dramatically at the solid stretch of canvas. "And now you've got this thing up—"

"Shhh," I said again.

"I told you, Sherman," muttered D'Angeli unhappily, "the exigencies of production—"

"Exigencies, my sainted ass," cried Spratt. He was practically shouting now. "You promised me a hidden upstage entrance for the girls. Do you see an entrance?" He waved hysterically at the blank canvas again. "Their cue is coming up any second now. How are they supposed to get on stage for the number, flap their tutus and fly?"

"What's the matter with you guys?" I said, still trying to tone them down. "There's a show going on, you can hear all of this on stage—"

"Oh, yes, excuse me," Spratt snarled at me suddenly. "We might rattle the Master, the great star. Blow it, Shoemaker."

I stared at Spratt, and for the first time I felt something harden inside me. Suddenly, without another word I turned and grabbed a razor knife from a nearby workbench. The blade glinted briefly in the dressing room lights. Spratt's eyes bulged when he saw it; involuntarily he took a step back.

My voice was low. "You want an entrance, Sherm?"
I wheeled to the canvas. In one continuous movement, up, across, down, I slashed a huge square hole
right through the bottom of the backdrop. "There's
your entrance."

Spratt eyed me warily for a moment, then turned
hastily to the dancers. "All right, let's go, don't miss
your cue, let's go." As Ramona stepped up he
couldn't resist one last zap. "Even you ought to be
able to stumble through that, Miss Twinkle-Toes."

She gave him a level look. "That's right. Even me."
And she moved on through the hole after the other
girls.

I thought it over. "You know, Sherman," I said
quietly, "you really are a little prick." Then turned
my back on him to watch the rest of the number.

Ramona paused to give one last cool glance at
Spratt. Then she was on, the lead dancer, but dancing as even I had never seen her before. Dancing for
spite, for the hell of it, then dancing for herself, for
fun, gliding, spinning, barely grazing the ground,
each movement full out but controlled, not too much,
not too little, right in the groove, the groove, the
groove. Until she came to rest, hesitated, then joined
with the others. But some sort of special light seemed
to dwell on her.

That was all, really, just that one dazzling inter-
lude—which brought her past Harry as he picked up
the second chorus again, heading for the windup. He
struggled valiantly, trying to make up for the earlier
part with a smash finish. *I'll bring along/ A smile or
a song/ For anyone . . .* There. He had it now, finally.
Only a rose . . . for youuuu! he sang, arms wide to
the world. I applauded like crazy.

Backstage after the curtain he handed me his props. His face was a study.

"Nice show," I said tentatively.

He shot me the eyebrow. "Yeah. Unforgettable." He was just slipping out of his cape when Bellinger came in the side door from the auditorium.

"Hi, Kiddie," he said offhandedly to Harry's back, his eyes roaming around.

Throwing the cape on the prop table, Harry whirled around. Complete astonishment was written all over his face.

"Omigod—Mickey. Was it tonight, were you out there *tonight*? I forgot you were coming, it went right out of my head."

I tactfully busied myself at the prop table.

"You were sensaysh, Kiddie," said Bellinger. "Just dynamite."

"You should've caught the dress rehearsal, the dress would've put you away," chattered Harry brightly. "But, Jesus, tonight? A disaster area. The attacks were sloppy, I don't know *what* the conductor, the conductor was out to lunch—"

Bellinger turned to me—not because he wanted to talk to me specifically but only because I was the one who happened to be standing there. "Don't you love this guy? I love this guy." His eyes were still moving. He never quite looked at Harry. "Relax, Kiddie, you were dynamite. When you get back to town, give me a call. I've got something lined up for you." A tiny, neat pause. "The second lead."

Harry's face lit up. "You're kidding."

"Bellinger don't kid."

"Come on, you are, you're kidding."

"Bellinger don't say things twice, either."

"Mickey, you're incredible. The second lead—"

"That's right," said Bellinger. "The Shuberts are sending out a *Student Prince* package. You'll be a wipe-out."

Uhhh. Right in the balls. Harry's eyes glazed. "*The—Student Prince*?" he said.

The agent's eyes were still skipping here and there. "They booked the full circuit. Cohasset, Hyannis, Lambertville—"

Harry was trying to hang on to his smile. "Gee, that's . . . that's great. Great. But, see, Mickey," he paused, lowered his voice confidentially. "See, I was sort of looking for something, you know, back in town. Can't you find me something back in town?"

"Sorry, Kiddie. Nothing right for you this season."

"Couldn't you try—"

"—I said there's nothing this season." He was getting impatient.

"That's what you said last season. Mickey, would you look at me a minute, please?"

Mickey looked at him, all right. With a flick of his eyes like the end of a whip. For the first time there hey," he said, "we're getting a little hysterical here. was a hint of something unpleasant in his tone. "Hey, Don't you want the part? Work is work."

"No, no," said Harry hastily. "I didn't mean it that way, don't take it that way." He tugged at the other man's arm. "Look, why don't we go to my dressing room where we can talk—"

Bellinger deftly detached himself, smooth as silk again. "Gee, Kiddie, I'd love to, but I gotta catch a train."

"But if I'm gonna sign with you," said Harry, grasping for the last morsel, "shouldn't we—"

"Sign, what for? Why don't we just keep it on a basis of trust?" said the agent soothingly. "So you think about the job and let me know." He started off, then stopped. "Oh—one thing. Who handles the girl, do you know?"

"What girl?" said Harry dully.

"That lead dancer. I'd like to meet her."

Harry looked at him as though hearing the question for the first time. "The thing is, Mickey," he said low, glancing discreetly toward me, "she's kinda tied up—"

Bellinger laughed without mirth. "Oh, Kiddie, I positively love you. I'm not looking for action. I just want to talk to her. I got laid last night." He clapped Harry on the shoulder. "So you can stop worrying." He was already moving away. "Call me, now," he said. "You know the number."

Harry watched Bellinger walk away. I could hardly bring myself to look at him. The grin on his face had congealed into a mask; his respiration was shallow, like someone in shock. He turned woodenly to the prop table to pick up his cape—but it wasn't there. Harry looked dully around. Then his eyes focused.

Fuldauer was standing with Naomi a few feet away, and they were laughing. The cape was in his hands. He was holding it for her to see, swinging it boldly to show her how it fit.

"Oh, Poppa," giggled Naomi.

"Here," said Fuldauer, "you want to try it?"

"No, no, I couldn't—"

"Go ahead, it's all right." And he started to swirl the cloth around her shoulders.

"Hey!" yelled Harry sharply. "Get your hands off

that!" Fuldauer looked at him blankly. "Just what the hell do you think you're doing?"

Fuldauer was shocked, stammering, "I . . . I'm sorry, I meant no—"

"Who told you to mess with the costumes?" shouted Harry. He stormed over and snatched the cape from the girl's shoulders. She almost cowered. "Never touch an actor's costume!"

It was like watching a hit-and-run accident. All I could do was stand rigid, paralyzed.

"Excuse me." The old man's face was pale. "Excuse me, I was just showing my daughter how—"

"Your *what?*" exploded Harry. "What is this, a guided tour? Why don't you just invite the whole fucking audience backstage?" All his bitterness and frustration were spilling over. Gripped by the flow of that blind bile he wheeled suddenly and called to Spratt, who was walking by. "Sherman, can't you do something about this? Can't you keep these people the hell out of the way when we're trying to work?"

"What people?" said Spratt, stopping to look. Everyone within earshot was caught by the ragged edge in Harry's voice, staring in embarrassment, unable to move.

"Is that too much to ask?" raged Harry, his control gone. "How can anyone give a decent performance with all these clowns hanging around? *Some of us are trying to give a decent performance.*" All at once he was close to tears. But he refused to acknowledge it, blinking fiercely, his chest heaving. "I mean, some of us are trying, are trying to—" he started again, then broke off and walked unsteadily away toward the dressing rooms.

Spratt watched him go, then stalked like Fate up to Fuldauer and Naomi. "What is all this?"

"Please," appealed Fuldauer, "I am not in the way. I work, I help—"

"Wait a minute, who are you? Aren't you the night watchman? What are you doing in that coat?"

Naomi turned and bolted off.

"No, Naomi—come back," called Fuldauer after her, then turned back to Spratt. "Please, I . . . I only borrowed it, not to keep. I work, I help—"

Spratt snapped his fingers. "Let's have it." Fuldauer looked at him. "The coat," Spratt said stonily again. Slowly, one sleeve at a time, the old man pulled off the coat. He folded it carefully. Then he handed it to the director.

"All right," said Spratt. "I don't want to see you down here during the show again. The watchman has a chair at the gate. Go sit on the chair."

Fuldauer nodded mutely. Then he turned and started upstage. "Naomi," he called softly. "Naomi, wait. Don't go home. Naomi . . ."

I started walking myself. Fast. I had to move, someplace, anyplace, just get away from there. Without any real idea of what I was doing or where I was going I went into the dressing room building. But instead of heading for the dancer's room I turned the other way and marched down the corridor until I found myself outside Harry's door. Inside I heard his voice saying softly, "Bravo. Bravo there, Kiddie." There was the sound of a bottle clinking against a glass. "And now, for an encore—"

I wrenched the door open.

Harry was seated before the mirror, stripped down to his shorts and T-shirt. The painted mask of his

makeup stood out vividly above his pale neck. A glass
of whiskey was in his hand; the bottle was open on
the table. He glanced at the open door, then waved
me in with the hand holding the drink.

"Hey. Pull up a glass and sit down."

I said nothing, just stared at him.

There was a pause as he drank. "Just one of those
nights, huh?" He poured himself another.

"I forgot to give you something," I said then. I
held out my hand. In it was the key to his apartment.

Harry dusted it with his eyes, then glanced away
again. When he spoke, his voice was light. "No
hurry," he said. "You might need it."

I made no response, just put the key on the table
and turned to go. Then I stopped, unable to keep it
in any longer. "He's just an old man for crying out
loud. A harmless old man. You didn't have to dump
on him like that. There was no call for you to do
that." I couldn't seem to stop saying it. "Why did you
have to do that?"

"What do you mean," said Harry brightly, "that
was my best performance of the night." He slid the
key along the table toward me, just as he had that
day in Caruso's. There was something near a plea in
his voice. "Keep it, anyway—for luck."

With a vicious movement I swiped the key to the
floor. "I don't want your bed—or your luck, *Mr.
Krebs*," I said bitterly.

"I don't blame you," he answered softly. "I don't
either."

I left Harold sitting there.

Ramona was taking forever. The pickup truck was
parked on the street near the theatre, and I sat be-

hind the wheel waiting for her to come up the hill. What Harry had done was still thrashing around in my brain. Poor Dr. Fuldauer. Fuldauer and his miserable sandwiches, his pathetic gratitude, his three harpies. The innocent die young—and old. And so I sat fidgeting, looking at my watch.

A half hour went by; still no Queen of the Nile. Then another fifteen minutes. I saw the actors leave. I saw the crew leave. I even saw Mr. Buddha Bellinger get into a taxi and leave. What had happened to her? Finally I looked at my watch one more time. Then got out of the truck and started back down the hill.

At the bottom I went through the backstage gate, then stopped in surprise. The lights in the dressing room building were out. Where was she? I cut down past the tool shop toward the set. Then across the backstage area I saw her coming out of the far end of the dressing room building, dressed in her street clothes. She started dreamily across the rear of the set in my direction. I watched her, standing in the shadows around the tool shop. Every few steps she skipped happily. Then for no reason all at once she whirled in a graceful dance turn. I opened my mouth to call to her—when suddenly a man's voice from the other side of the stage started to hum "Only a Rose."

Ramona stopped in surprise, looking around. So did I.

The humming grew louder. She looked the other way.

And Dr. Fuldauer stepped out from the shadows around the prop house. He was wearing his three-piece suit again. Still humming, he applauded briskly, calling, "Encore! Encore!"

270   DAVID SHABER

Out of sheer good spirits she dropped a curtsey.

"I watched you dance tonight," he said. "It was wonderful. Wonderful."

"Thank you, kind sir." And for some reason she giggled. Their voices carried clearly on the still night air. Something made me wait there unseen, listening.

"You are laughing," said Fuldauer. "You think I just talk—"

"No, no," Ramona said to him. "I've just had some incredible news, that's all." She took a step closer, peering at him. "I'm sorry—you're the night watchman, aren't you?"

Fuldauer laughed ruefully. "Temporarily. For some of us it is a short season. I think . . . I am making my farewell appearance." He looked absently around the stage. "You know, we had also in Düsseldorf a marvelous theatre. Marvelous." His eyes came back to her. "In fact, here, I have some pictures—"

He reached into his pocket and took out the same old envelope. She stepped closer, curious, as he took off the rubberband and started to thumb through them.

"You see, that one," he said, pointing, "that one is *Die lustige Witwe,* what you call *The Merry Widow.*" She stood beside him, looking at the photo. "Lehar," he said happily. "I went three times. The costumes, the music—how it made you feel, I cannot tell you."

Ramona smiled. "Great, huh?"

"The dancing. . . . Of course it was all waltzes then." He paused. Then there was a subtle change of tone in his voice, as though forty years had fallen from him, leaving the air of a young German blade. "You waltz, fräulein?" he said.

"Not since dancing school."

"A lost art." Humming a few bars, he started to sway gently right where he was standing, looking at her.

She smiled again, then began to watch his movement, swaying with him. He extended his arms in invitation. She cocked her head gaily, then slipped into them. They took their first step together. Still humming he turned her once. And again. She laughed aloud. As their first tentative steps gathered confidence Fuldauer broke into the words. *Wien, Wien, nur du allein,* he sang. It was the haunting old waltz about Vienna, the city of dreams, sweet and soft and a little sad. They were really moving handsomely, turning, sweeping with the rhythm—when I accidentally knocked against the door to the shop and it banged, then banged again.

Ramona stopped in mid-step. I hastily pulled further back into the darkness. "Hey, that's spooky," she said, peering in the direction of the door. "What was that?"

Fuldauer was still holding her. "Nothing," the wind at night . . ." he said vaguely. They hesitated.

Then both his arms went around Ramona's back and he kissed her awkwardly. For a brief moment, half in surprise she did not resist. Fuldauer clutched her fiercely, his head against her hair. She just stood there. But as his hand started to slide onto her breast she gently, deftly extricated herself from his arms and began to back away, waving gaily as though nothing had happened.

"Thank you, kind sir," she called. "You waltz divinely."

Blowing him a last kiss, she turned and skipped off.

I slipped quickly back to the backstage gate and out again. Running hard, keeping to the darkness of the trees I managed to get up the hill ahead of her. And I was in the truck, waiting, as she came to the top of the walk. She moved dreamily to the truck, opened the door, and got in. There was a pause while she simply stared through the windshield.

"Do you mind if I just sit here in a quiet daze?" she said finally. "You won't believe what happened to me."

My heart was still pounding from the run up the hill, but I managed to keep my voice almost casual as I turned on the key and started the motor. "I might."

"I can hardly get the words out." She paused again, then spoke slowly. "Bellinger says I'm going to be in a Cole Porter show. A real *part*, too, with lines—and a song." She sounded as though she were in a dream. "*I'm gonna sing a Cole Porter song on Broadway.* Can you believe it? And Bellinger wants me to sign with him, too. Wild. Simply wild." She shook her head, trying to pull herself together. "Listen, would you mind terribly if we cut it short tonight? I've got a million letters to write—"

I leaned over abruptly and cut the motor off again. She broke off, looking at me in surprise.

"You're not going to say a word about it, are you?" I said incredulously.

"About what?"

"He made a pass at you, I saw him. Jesus."

Her look at me ran through it all; that I had been there watching, that I had said nothing, that she understood. Then in a different tone she said, "Not really."

"I saw him," I cried. "He had his hand on your tit, for chrissake!"

"So what?" she said mildly. "Just an old guy looking for a little life. It was kinda sweet, really."

It wasn't that I was jealous of Fuldauer, of an old man. But the matter-of-fact way she accepted it, thought nothing of it made me feel the ground was moving out from under me. I laughed wildly. "Oh, terrific. Terrific. I'm talking about coming to New York, and you let some dirty old man feel you up—"

"Artie, will you stop with New York?" she said earnestly. "You can't come to New York, it would never work."

"Why not? It fits right in with vacation—"

She gave a helpless little laugh. "Oh, baby," she said. "I'm married."

Full stop. I just looked at her. "You're what?"

She nodded.

I could feel my face turn to stone. Letting go of the wheel, I leaned back against the seat. There was a long silence. A car went by us, receding up the street until its taillights were two red dots in the distance. I watched it turn the corner and head off for happier scenes.

Well," said Ramona finally. "That cast a slight pall over the conversation."

"Why didn't you tell me before?"

She shrugged. "I thought you knew."

"How could I know? You let me make all these jerk-off plans . . ." I could go no further.

There was a pause, then real pain in her voice. "I'm sorry. I really thought you knew."

I started the motor again. "No," I said. "But I'm learning."

*　　*　　*

It was not too many minutes later when I pulled the truck into the garage at home. I got out, closed the door, and shuffled slowly toward the house, head down. Then I realized my father was sitting in the darkness of the back porch, waiting.

"Arthur? Is it you?"

"It's me." I sighed. "It's me."

"You feel like talking a little?"

I shook my head and started up the steps. Then I hesitated. "Uh, listen, about this fall," I said. "I guess . . . I'll be going back to school, after all."

I could feel his eyebrows go up in the dark. "No New York?"

I shook my head again. "Maybe I don't know as much about people . . . as I thought I did."

"I'm glad," he said. But he didn't altogether sound that way. God knows what he wanted to do when he was twenty. He put his arm around my shoulder and we walked through the door in mutual consolation.

I went down to the theatre the next night like Jack the Ripper returning to the scene of the crime. Except I didn't know if I was the victim or the killer, or a little of both. I didn't want to see anybody, I knew that. I hid in the prop house until just before curtain, then shoved the prop table out the door and across the backstage area at the last minute. There was the usual preshow bustle, bright and busy, around me, but I kept my head down, skidded the table to a stop at its station, plugged in the lights, checked the hand props. And all the while I had a sickening sense of apprehension in the pit of my stomach, the disasters of the night before weighing on me.

It wasn't so much Ramona. Oh, the thought of her was a gob of pain, a dull ache somewhere in my chest. But I had been there before. No, the problem was Harry. What was I supposed to do about Harry?

It didn't help any when Cooky waved loudly to me from across the stage. "Hey, Shoemaker," he called. "How's your friend, the great Harry Crystal?" And he laughed raucously.

I pretended not to hear. Goddam Harry Crystal. I was sorry for him and furious at him at the same time, but mostly furious. I was learning that when an idol goes smash it breaks into odd-shaped pieces with tricky edges. I was fed up with him, he was a fraud, he deserved what he got. But I was dreading the whipped face that was going to come out of that dressing room door.

I didn't have long to wait. The overture started, and as if on cue Harry appeared in the doorway of the dressing room building. But what a transformation from the night before. Head up, glorious, and sparkling in full costume and makeup he strode through the backstage area, sweeping along like a whirlwind, a typhoon, his cape billowing over his shoulder. He swept up to the prop table, all business, checking his cape, buckling his sword with a flourish. Then he cocked his head toward me.

"You ready for the magic word?" he said confidentially. "Bishkin." He paused dramatically. "It hit me like a flash."

"No kidding," I said, my voice flat. "Who's that?"

"You never heard of Lou Bishkin at the Morris Office? What business are you in?"

I didn't feel like playing the game, anymore. "Come on, Harry," I said in a low voice. "I'm not in this business yet—and you know it. What's more, after last night I'm not sure I want to be."

A short distance away Ramona was walking toward the wings and her place for the opening number. I couldn't help flicking my eye at her, then unhappily away again—but not before Harry caught it. Understanding flashed in his eyes.

"Sure, that's right," he said. "The girl's married, the actor's a bum. So when the season's over, forget the whole thing."

"Well, what is this," I said belligerently, "a lousy summer job, that's all."

"Sorry. This kind of hunger doesn't fade with the leaves, my friend."

"You don't just decide to be a playwright—" I protested, but he cut me off impatiently.

"Who said you did? Don't you understand? Playwright, no playwright, *none of that matters*." He looked at me intently. "I've been watching you. They play the first three notes of the overture each night, and you faint. Whether you know it or not, you're hooked. Take it from me—if you quit now you'll have an ache in your heart the rest of your life."

I could feel myself flush. "Boy, you're full of beans tonight," I said evasively.

"Me? I'm a busy man. I gotta play this turkey for two more weeks, then I got a tour of *The Student Prince*. Now give me my props and get out of the way."

There was a long moment while he was busy with his sword and I looked at him. Then the words came out in spite of me.

"This guy Bishkin," I said slowly. "He's really big, huh?"

Harry promptly put his arm around me and swept me right along with him down toward the wings.

"Are you kidding?" he said confidently. "He can walk me right into people Bellinger can't even get on the phone." We were passing Fuldauer, who was heading for his chair. "Hiya, kid," waved Harry, "whaddya say?" Then back to me, "I don't know why I wasted my time with that schmuck Bellinger, anyway. All he knows is this summer-stock shit. His *reflex* isn't Broadway, you know what I mean? Now, Bishkin—oh-ho-ho. *That's* Broadway. You sign with him, its Tiffany's all the way."

I couldn't help it. I felt this nutty surge of hope. "You still gonna try? I mean, I was afraid that after last night's show you'd be—" I waggled my hand, "— you know."

"What, that? Forget it," said Harry casually. "Even Barrymore wasn't Barrymore *every* night. I'm still worth eight bucks, baby. Once in a while you get a little change back, that's all." Then he said determinedly to himself, "I just gotta keep working—*and hang on.* Yessir . . . Lou Bishkin, that's the guy."

We reached the wings just as the overture was finishing. Ramona and the other dancers were in a line waiting for their entrance. I couldn't resist one more look at her, then turned back to find Harry watching. I forced myself to sound bright, trying to shake the memory of last night's pain.

"It's . . . it's great you can get to him. I mean, somebody bigger like that."

DAVID SHABER

Just about to make his entrance Harry paused to look me squarely in the eye.

"If it's not him, it'll be someone else." His voice had the ring of rock-bottom truth. "Shoemaker, in this business you learn one thing. There is *always* a bigger agent, a better job—and a prettier girl."

And he stepped on stage into the light.

I stayed in the wings to watch. Alone and shining and heroic, Harry filled the follow spot. *Some day,* he sang, *you will seek me and find me.* I became aware of someone standing beside me. I looked, it was Ginger. She glanced up at me, her eyes shining luminously under the makeup, and smiled. How is it I had never noticed her eyes?

We both watched Harry. As he started the last chorus of the song the spotlight began to iris down on him, narrowing in, swallowing his legs, moving up his body. *Surely/ You will come and remind me/ Of a dream that is calling/ For you and for me.* He was in the groove tonight. The son of a bitch was marvelous. I reached out and took Ginger's hand. She looked up at me with those eyes. Her red red lips moved.

"Found another feather?" she whispered.

"Shhh," I whispered back, squeezing her hand while I watched Harry. "I'm working on it."

On stage the spotlight had irised down on Harry until only his face was left floating in the dark. His voice rose in a final surge. *My soul will discover/ The soul born for her lover*— Oops. He was just a shade off on that last note. But he fought for it, struggled— and finally hit it square and true. *The man with the heart of a king!* sang Harry Crystal triumphantly.

As the note finished, the spotlight irised out and the face was gone. But not quite. For just a moment

more that voice seemed to echo, the ghost of that
smile to linger, before they gave up at last and dissolved into the darkness.

Then the applause began.

15

---◆▶───

Some day
When the winter is over
Some day
In the flush of the spring . . .

— *The Vagabond King*

I suppose it's inevitable. Your perceptions of yourself change, your perceptions of other people, too, even actors. That night at Kempton Hills I couldn't get enough of Harry Crystal, but as I sat on the IRT subway that Wednesday night twenty years later—with Bertie a model of ash-blond patience beside me—I wished we were going anywhere but to see him.

I knew now that Harry would never really make Broadway, that he was not a star and never would be, that he was just a competent, pleasant actor with a limited range, a so-so voice, and a certain flair for stock. The idea of going had been a great gesture at Moe Shenker's cannibal party when it looked as though we were going to be the entree. But there was no Moe Shenker to crow over now. There was just me and poor Bertie and Harry, with an evening of tragic Eugene O'Neill to grind our way through. I just hoped I deserved whatever I was going to get.

I guess over the years I had gone sour on actors.

Their self-importance, their self-indulgence, their self-admiration. Once, riding up Central Park West I had seen John Carradine get off the bus at night wearing his wide-brimmed actor's hat and cape-over-coat. As he stepped down onto the pavement he bowed gallantly to impress a waiting lady, then saun-tered off down Seventy-third Street as though every eye in the world were on him. Poor bastard, I thought, he still thinks everybody wants to be in show business. Oh, I kept in touch with the theatre, but it no longer seemed quite the same to me. It wasn't even really show business. And I rode on home that night to read a novel on gang rape, which some movie producer with his finger on the pulse of the public was sure would be a natural for Raquel Welch. Or Streisand. Or his mother, if he could get Warner Brothers to go play-or-pay with her. *That* was show business.

After we got off the subway on Wednesday night we ate at an Indonesian restaurant in the Village. The chef was from Ecuador and the meal was awful. But the final blow was the screw-up when we got to the theatre, which was down a flight of stairs off Sheri-dan Square. There were no complimentary tickets left in my name, but there were tickets. Plenty of tickets. At twelve bucks a pop. So I forked over the twenty-four dollars and we went down into this cramped basement with the scenery patched together at one end, and squeezed into our seats.

There was no escape. Inevitably, the play began.

From the very beginning there was something odd about Harry, and it took me a while to see what he was doing. It didn't break over you all at once, it wasn't like a flash of lightning or a clap of thunder.

Harry wove his performance about you one stitch at a time. At first, in fact, it seemed so easy, so natural, that I thought he was just walking through it, because after all they didn't officially open until tomorrow. Then I began to catch on. I didn't know how Harry was going to cope with O'Neill, but I had forgotten that he was playing the part of James Tyrone, that Tyrone was an actor—and so was he. He didn't use any of the Red Shadow's hokey bravura, there was no flinging of capes or François Villon's posturing. No beggar-poets here, no chieftains from the Sahara. Harry wasn't playing those parts, he was doing something else. And by the time he got to Tyrone's famous speech about himself there was no doubt about it. Harry was playing Harry. An aging, disappointed actor. I kept hearing echoes of him through the O'Neill.

Remember me? I play the drum.

He was using everything, showing it all. The light that used to be in his eyes, the longing for Shubert Alley, the Stage Deli, the life of art, the dream of talent that had started it all. "I could have been a great Shakespearean actor, if I'd kept on," cried Harry as Tyrone. *I'm an eight-dollar actor.* "The first night I played Othello, he said to our manager, 'That young man is playing Othello better than I ever did!' " He looked like the hero in the follow spot back at Kempton Hill. "That from Booth, the greatest actor of his day or any other!" Harry's head was back, his arm was up reaching for the ceiling and heaven beyond. The ceiling was cruddy but the arm was glorious. I had a flash of his pose at Caruso's a thousand years ago.

Giants that haunt you for life.

He didn't flinch from any of it. The whole summer-stock merry-go-round, the cruddy apartments in widows' attics, the same dingy bars after the same shows; what happened when the dream started to go sour, the humiliation when he realized his limits, the handwriting on the wall, the indifferent agents, everything. He drenched Tyrone's face with his own pain. "I'd lost the great talent I once had. They didn't want me . . ."

Let me warn you about this business. If you're not a winner, it's shit.

He absolutely terrified me. I didn't know what he was going to do next. It was a Harry I had never seen. Because it was Harry. Every move was true, filled with conviction, simplicity, and shivery excitement. We sat there, frightened for our lives. He built it, he dropped it, he paused, he rambled, he drank, he posed. Until by the time he reached the final moment of Tyrone's despair we saw beneath it the choice the actor had made. Or that had made him. "Well, no matter," he said as Tyrone. "It's a late day for regrets."

I gotta keep working. And hang on.

Finally the curtain fell. Bertie and I sat, unable to move. The audience in the little room roared, they cheered. Then slowly they got up and left. And still we sat. It didn't seem we could ever move. Finally we got to our feet, too, and walked up the aisle of the empty theatre. At the door I hesitated for just a second, with the last of it rolling over me.

Get yourself some glory, Shoemaker.

We left the theatre in silence. I felt light-headed, almost giddy, larger than life. We walked without a word all the way up Seventh Avenue to Twenty-third

Street. Then we walked some more. It was Twenty-sixth Street when Bertie finally spoke.

"You've still got that play you started and put away."

"Yeah. I guess. Somewhere."

"I know where it is," said Bertie. She paused. "And so do you."

I do, indeed. And if that play is running as you read this, you'll know I finished it. If it isn't, you can assume that I'm working on it, trying it, taking it from one producer to another—hanging on. For it wasn't so much that Harry was wonderful, which he was; or that the production moved uptown and he won a Tony Award, which he did, in fact two months later. After all those years. All those years. No, it was just that he had reached out with the hand of his performance and squeezed my face and turned my insides and sent me out into the night afterward, shaken and expanded, filled with what great theatre sometimes gives you. The wonderful delusion that there is hope for us all.

Class Reunion

RONA JAFFE

author of
The Best of Everything

"Reading Rona Jaffe is like being presented with a Cartier watch; you know exactly what you're getting and it's just what you want."—*Cosmopolitan*

Annabel, Chris, Emily and Daphne left Radcliffe in '57 wanting the best of everything. They meet again 20 years later and discover what they actually got. Their story is about love, friendship and secrets that span three decades. It will make you laugh and cry and remember all the things that shaped our lives.

"It will bring back those joyous and miserable memories."
—*The Philadelphia Bulletin*

"Keeps you up all night reading."—*Los Angeles Times*

"Rona Jaffe is in a class by herself."—*The Cleveland Press*

A Dell Book $2.75 (11408-X)

Bestsellers

- [ ] **COMES THE BLIND FURY** by John Saul $2.75 (11428-4)
- [ ] **CLASS REUNION** by Rona Jaffe $2.75 (11408-X)
- [ ] **THE EXILES** by William Stuart Long $2.75 (12369-0)
- [ ] **THE BRONX ZOO** by Sparky Lyle and
  Peter Golenbock $2.50 (10764-4)
- [ ] **THE PASSING BELLS** by Phillip Rock $2.75 (16837-6)
- [ ] **TO LOVE AGAIN** by Danielle Steel $2.50 (18631-5)
- [ ] **SECOND GENERATION** by Howard Fast $2.75 (17892-4)
- [ ] **EVERGREEN** by Belva Plain $2.75 (13294-0)
- [ ] **CALIFORNIA WOMAN** by Daniel Knapp $2.50 (11035-1)
- [ ] **DAWN WIND** by Christina Savage $2.50 (11792-5)
- [ ] **REGINA'S SONG**
  by Sharleen Cooper Cohen $2.50 (17414-7)
- [ ] **SABRINA** by Madeleine A. Polland $2.50 (17633-6)
- [ ] **THE ADMIRAL'S DAUGHTER**
  by Victoria Fyodorova and Haskel Frankel $2.50 (10366-5)
- [ ] **THE LAST DECATHLON** by John Redgate $2.50 (14643-7)
- [ ] **THE PETROGRAD CONSIGNMENT**
  by Owen Sela $2.50 (16885-6)
- [ ] **EXCALIBUR!** by Gil Kane and John Jakes $2.50 (12291-0)
- [ ] **SHOGUN** by James Clavell $2.95 (17800-2)
- [ ] **MY MOTHER, MY SELF** by Nancy Friday $2.50 (15663-7)
- [ ] **THE IMMIGRANTS** by Howard Fast $2.75 (14175-3)

At your local bookstore or use this handy coupon for ordering:

Comes the Blind Fury

John Saul

Bestselling author of
Cry for the Strangers
and *Suffer the Children*

More than a century ago, a gentle, blind child walked the paths of Paradise Point. Then other children came, teasing and taunting her until she lost her footing on the cliff and plunged into the drowning sea.

Now, 12-year-old Michelle and her family have come to live in that same house—to escape the city pressures, to have a better life.

But the sins of the past do not die. They reach out to embrace the living. Dreams will become nightmares.

Serenity will become terror. There will be no escape.

A Dell Book $2.75   (11428-4)